SCARWEATHER

SCARWEATHER

Anthony Rolls

With an Introduction by
MARTIN EDWARDS

This edition published 2017 by
The British Library
96 Euston Road
London NW1 2DB

Originally published in 1934 by Geoffrey Bles

Cataloguing in Publication Data
A catalogue record for this publication is
available from the British Library

ISBN 978 0 7123 5664 0

Typeset by Tetragon, London
Printed and bound by
TJ Books Limited, Padstow, Cornwall

CONTENTS

INTRODUCTION

Scarweather is an unusual crime novel written by an unortho-
dox novelist. C. E. Vulliamy was, among many other things, a
keen archaeologist, and he makes splendid use of his specialised
knowledge in this agreeably leisurely mystery. The action begins
shortly before the start of the First World War, and events unfold
gradually over the next decade and a half.

The narrator is John Farringdale, a young barrister who is
remarkably innocent, despite his professed interest in "the psychology of the criminal". He serves, in effect, as Dr Watson
to Frederick Ellingham, a gifted intellectual cast in the role of
brilliant amateur detective. The principal setting is the epony
mous Scarweather, a remote spot on the north coast of England.
Farringdale, his cousin Eric Tallard Foster, and Ellingham, become
acquainted with Professor Tolgen Reisby and his attractive,
younger wife Hilda, who live at Scarweather, but when Eric
becomes enchanted with Hilda, matters take a dangerous turn.
To say much more would be to risk a "spoiler", although it
must be said that Vulliamy's main focus as a crime novelist lay
in intriguing his readers with something out of the ordinary
rather than hoodwinking them with a classic whodunit puzzle.
Indeed, the dust jacket of the first edition earned the disapproval
of Dorothy L. Sayers, when she came to review it, so plainly did
it give the game away.

Colwyn Edward Vulliamy (1886–1971) was a Welshman who
was educated privately before studying art in Cornwall. He owed

his unusual surname to a Swiss ancestor, a clockmaker who settled in Britain during the eighteenth century; the family business
became clockmakers to the Crown, an appointment retained for
more than a century. Vulliamy served in France, Macedonia, and
Turkey during the First World War, and the time he spent in the
Near East kindled his interest in digging into the past. When peace
came, archaeology was, according to his obituary in *The Times*,
"his chief subject of study". He had published a Fabian Society
tract in 1914, but his next three books were *Prehistoric Forerunners*,
Unknown Cornwall, and *Immortal Man*, the last being a study of
burial customs through the years. In 1930, two years before his
first crime novel appeared, he brought out *The Archaeology of
Middlesex and London*.

The author of his obituary in *The Times* opined that: "Vulliamy
was a writer of individual and rewarding quality. Although he
was without academic training of any kind, he had the tastes
and capacities of a scholar, and it is possible that his early work
both as an archaeologist and a historian might have received
wider recognition if it had been supported by the conventional
authority of a university post." The obituary paints a picture
of a gifted man with varied skills and interests, but makes only
fleeting reference to his detective fiction. It was often the case
that authors who wrote detective novels during "the Golden Age
of Murder" between the two world wars did so as a sideline; the
long list of examples includes such luminaries as G.D.H. Cole,
the economist, and Cecil Day-Lewis, the poet who wrote crime
fiction as Nicholas Blake. Yet in many cases, they are more likely
to be remembered today for their detective stories than their more
serious and supposedly more "worthy" work.

Vulliamy wrote ten crime novels, in two distinct phases. *Scarweather* was one of four books published in a burst of activity lasting three years, from 1932. These books were published under the pen-name Anthony Rolls, presumably to differentiate them from his more academic work. Whilst the novels suggest the influence of Francis Iles, author of the best-selling psychological crime novel *Malice Aforethought*, which appeared in 1930, they are nevertheless distinctive.

After *Scarweather* appeared, Vulliamy seemed to give up on the genre. His main focus shifted to biographies of imaginary historical characters, which afforded him plenty of scope to indulge his taste for satire. It was also perhaps typical of his taste for the ironic that he wrote a biography of a famous biographer, James Boswell. Yet he returned to crime fiction in 1952 with *Don Among the Dead Men*, which was later filmed. Five more books followed, with the last (the very unusual *Floral Tribute*) appearing in 1963.

Dorothy L. Sayers admired Vulliamy's writing, and praised it during her time as a reviewer for the *Sunday Times*: "he handles his characters like a 'real' novelist and the English language like a 'real' writer — merits which are still, unhappily, rarer than they should be in the ranks of the murder specialists". However, the versatility that was one of his strengths perhaps also accounts for the fact that his crime fiction slipped out of sight for many years; this particular book has not, so far as I know, been reprinted in Britain for more than eighty years. He never created a series detective—although one wonders if in *Scarweather*, he was auditioning Ellingham for such a role—and it is usually more difficult to establish a following as a crime novelist if each book one writes is a "stand-alone". It is not, therefore, entirely surprising that his mysteries have long been overlooked. But it is high time that twenty-first century readers had a chance to enjoy Vulliamy's idiosyncratic plotting and sly wit. His work deserves its place in the British Library's series of Crime Classics.

MARTIN EDWARDS
www.martinedwardsbooks.com

PART I

We Go to Aberleven

CHAPTER I

I

M Y FRIEND ELLINGHAM HAS PERSUADED ME TO REVEAL TO the public the astounding features of the Reisby case. As a study in criminal aberration it is, he tells me, of particular interest, while in singularity of horror and in perversity of ingenious method it is probably unique.

Although I agree with Ellingham, I may as well say that I present the case with extraordinary reluctance. It would be far better if Ellingham, who actually unravelled the mystery, told the story in his own businesslike way. I have little skill as a narrator, and I particularly dislike the autobiographical form which I am obliged to adopt in telling my own version of this fantastic tragedy. I do not mean to say that I object to playing the traditional and honourable part of a Watson. That has nothing to do with it. My difficulties or diffidences are of a personal kind. In telling the story I shall have to speak with unflinching candour about people who are closely bound to me by ties of affection, and about events which it is now painful to recall. I must also refer continually to my own thoughts and actions in order to give the reader a steady and coherent narrative. To many, such an opportunity for self-display would be delightful; to me, it is an ordeal of the most hateful description. But there are circumstances in which personal reluctance ought to be overcome. There can be no doubt that the case of Tolgen Reisby is not merely an astounding adventure in the ordinary sense of the words, it is also a most valuable contribution to the study of the criminal mind—that is, to a definite aspect of mental disorder.

As a barrister, I am profoundly interested in the psychology of the criminal, though I am fully aware that a knowledge of psychology is not considered desirable by those who devise or administer the laws of England. It was against this particular weakness of mine that Ellingham chiefly directed his attack. It was my duty, he said, to place on record a case both exciting and instructive. He also pointed out (rather cruelly, I thought) that I had plenty of spare time which I could occupy both pleasantly and profitably in writing a book.

There were other people to be consulted—one especially—and they ultimately gave their consent, with the obvious proviso that I should carefully disguise the names of persons, towns and localities. All this led me in the direction of an autobiographical novel, and in this form the story is to be told.

I have given this brief explanation in order that my readers may see why it is that I have decided to publish the case, and why I am obliged to appear so prominently in the narrative. I can at least promise that I shall not forget my function as a mere narrator, and that I shall keep within the limits which are prescribed by the function.

2

My own name is John Farringdale. My father, who owned a considerable property in Dorset, died when I was a boy; and I had the good fortune to be his only son. After her husband's death, my mother bought a house in Richmond. She had never cared for the trifling amenities and the primitive amusements of provincial life, and she was anxious to be nearer the more intellectual society with which she was already acquainted in London.

At the time of this move I was being educated at a famous public school. My sister Vivian, three years older, lived at Richmond with my mother. In 1911 I went to Cambridge. I had already chosen the profession of the law.

But I am not writing the history of my life, and I need give no further immediate particulars concerning myself. It is enough to say that in 1913, when the action of this drama commences, I was twenty-one years old.

During the period of my University life I had two great friends. One of these was a man about fifteen years older than myself, a reader in chemistry who lived with his wife and young son at Cambridge. He was a man whose career had been extremely brilliant, and his exploits in colloidal chemistry were familiar to scientific men in every part of the world. But the charm and origi-nality of his character made him, in my eyes, far more remarkable than his exploits in science. I have never known any man with a wider range of interest and of real attainment. He had a faculty for acquiring rapidly, not the rudiments alone, but the most reliable and intimate knowledge of any science or study. He was a gifted musician, and his playing of the *klavierwerke* of Bach, though academic, placed him in the professional category. Yet with all his learning and accomplishment he was a jocular, simple fellow, not incapable of being sardonic, though totally incapable of being ill-natured, petulant or conceited. Unlike most intellectual men, he had been an oarsman and athlete of unusual promise, and his dedication to a life of study was a matter of deep regret and of great astonishment to the President of the C.U.B.C. It was, I think, this diffusion of interest and rapidity of acquirement which prevented him from rising at once to the highest eminence; but I can truly say that I know of no man who got more out of life or who was more generally attractive. I shall endeavour to display certain aspects of his intricate though delightful character in the course of my book. His name was Frederick Ellingham.

My other great friend at this time was a young cousin of mine—Eric Tallard Foster. He was two years older than I was, we had been at school together, and he left Oxford in 1912 in order to study medicine at the London Hospital. His parents had died in India, victims of the plague at Amminadar, and he had been brought up by an elderly spinster aunt, Miss Muriel Tallard Foster, at Highgate.

Eric spent a good deal of his time in our house at Richmond, where my kind mother was always glad to see him. We used to amuse ourselves in a variety of ways, some of them more commendable than others; our subjects of debate extended from neoplatonism to the tunes in the latest musical comedy. Eric was interested in archæological matters, particularly in the bones of ancient men, and he tried hard to work up my own enthusiasm.

On a Sunday afternoon we would go splashing about in the dreary gravel-pits of the Thames valley, looking for bits of chipped flint or the relics of a mammoth, and Eric always hoped that he would see the skull of a real Neanderthal man protruding from the side of the pit. This important skull, if we ever did find it, would go down to posterity under the label of *homo Fosteri*, or perhaps *homo Tallardensis*; for it is well known that every fossil cranium represents a new variety of the race.

I was perhaps fonder of Eric, at that time, than I was of anyone else. Our circumstances were not dissimilar. We were both of us the only sons of our parents; we had both lost our fathers, and both had been reared from boyhood by solitary women. We had a common interest in family affairs. Each of us had made up his mind to work zealously at his profession; and as these professions were different, there could be no question of rivalry.

No doubt Eric resembled me in many ways, but I cannot believe that I was ever so persistently romantic or so ready to fall in love. Perhaps I lacked his advantages in this respect, for I am of a bleak, saturnine appearance, while poor Eric was undeniably handsome. He was tall, fair, muscular, with a fine easy generosity in his manner and approach. Women of all ages found him attractive, and they might very well have made a mess of his life if he had not been fortified by a reflective mind and a chivalrous nature.

I think he had been falling in and out of love since he was about eleven years old. Serious affairs, too; no flighty flirtation or passing caprice. Fortunately he was too simple, too serious, and probably too poor, for the minx or the mere philandering female, and so he was preserved from real trouble. Moreover, besides being deeply and incurably romantic, he was easily shocked, he was a sentimental Puritan, a youth who kept in view the uncompromising lineaments of an ideal mistress.

From his childhood Eric had been extremely fond of my sister Vivian; but she, poor girl! had the ominous Farringdale countenance and was therefore disqualified in the competition of ideals.

His love of archæology was the means of introducing Eric to a very singular man, Professor Tolgen Reisby, who occupied with much honour the Pattervale Chair of Genetics in the

University of Northport. They were both members of the London Archæological Union, and Reisby had been greatly impressed by a paper which Eric had written on the Menite cemetery of Tarkhan.

Reisby was a man of prodigious intellect and of wide scientific knowledge. Although chiefly known for his great work on the Morphology of Hybrid Variants, he was a notable exponent of new methods in archæological research in 1912, and had published a lengthy account of his investigations in the north of England. He was also an experimental chemist of considerable repute, though his results had only been made known in the form of occasional essays.

A happy coincidence of opinion on the subject of the pottery of the Alsatian tumuli led to a real friendship between the eminent Professor and the young enthusiast. Nothing is more likely to win the affection of a learned man than agreement upon a solemn trifle.

In the summer vacation of 1913 my cousin was invited by Professor Reisby to visit him at his home in the north of England. Eric accepted the invitation with delight, he spent three weeks with the Professor and his family at Aberleven (a fishing hamlet on the coast), and he returned with a glowing account of his host and hostess. Reisby, it appeared, had married late in life a woman who was thirty years younger than himself. If his obituary notice may be taken as reliable evidence, Professor Reisby was fifty-four in October 1913; his wife, on the 18th of February in the same year, celebrated her twenty-third birthday. They had one child, a daughter.

I will admit that when I heard all this (knowing Eric) I felt a little uneasy. Eric was undoubtedly one of the most honourable of young men, but he was also one of the most susceptible. And even at the age of twenty-one I was wise enough to see the possibility of danger in the Professor's household. The very fact of Mrs. Reisby being—as she clearly was—an extremely nice woman actually increased the danger, for she could not otherwise have become one of Eric's ideals. When I heard that she was not only extremely nice but also extremely pretty I felt even more apprehensive.

But Eric's talk, after his visit, was mainly about Professor Reisby himself. I saw, not without satisfaction, that he was evidently on terms of respectful familiarity with this eminent and remarkable man.

Tolgen Reisby, according to Eric, had amiable eccentricities, but they were of a lovable or diverting nature. "He's a great big fellow with a red beard, like a Norseman," said Eric, "but you should see how gentle and playful he is with his wife and child. He spends a lot of his time studying, or at work in his laboratory, and sometimes he goes walking off by himself and is away for hours. They have a boat in the creek below the house, and he and I used to go fishing... I'm going there again. I think they are the most charming and most interesting people in the world. Probably they are coming up to London this autumn, and you will meet them, of course."

Evidently the Reisbys were interesting people. They lived in a lonely though comfortable house near the shore at Aberleven, within fifteen miles of Northport. The Professor had rooms in Northport, but he seldom used them, preferring to go up to the University in his car. Mrs. Reisby was the daughter of a well-known surgeon. Her parents had been opposed to her marriage at so early an age to a man so much older than herself, and although her mother had relented after the birth of the child, and had even stayed for a fortnight at Scarweather (the Professor's house), her father had steadily declined to have anything to do with Reisby.

Life at Aberleven, on a bleak northern shore with little society and few amusements, would have been insufferably monotonous to the majority of young women; and it was fortunate that Mrs. Reisby was not only devoted to her husband and her child, but was able to take a practical and a lively interest in the Professor's work. Mrs. Reisby occasionally stayed with her parents in Manchester; the Professor seldom left his home in the north, unless to confer with his learned colleagues, or to attend their meetings in London or in one of the southern Universities. Once a year he visited a friend in Upsala and a group of distant relatives in Bergen; his grandfather had been a captain in the merchant service of Norway. He also visited Hamburg.

3

Frederick Ellingham used to stay frequently, for a few days or a week at a time, with his old parents in London. His father, Admiral Sir Hugh Walberswick Ellingham, had a house in Gloucester Terrace, and when Frederick was staying there in the vacation I used to meet him nearly every day.

To go about London with a man like Ellingham, who seemed to know something about everything and everybody, was always delightful. If I could not keep pace with the activity of his mind, or rise to the level of his own varied enthusiasms, I could not fail to be interested in the man himself and in the extraordinary resources or powers of his character.

Ellingham never boasted; but he used to observe, in his dry, deliberate manner, that he knew a little about almost every condition of life. I never came across anyone with a more astonishing variety of acquaintances—I might say, a more embarrassing variety. Apart from churchmen, I believe he knew men in every profession. In view of his own remarkable intellect, you might have anticipated a wide acquaintance among learned men; you would scarcely have anticipated a sympathy and a liking for the relatively obscure— newspaper reporters, jobbers, dealers, clerks in offices, policemen, railwaymen, sailors, engineers, waiters, door-keepers, and a whole multitude of humble folk in every conceivable kind of employment.

You would find him chatting to a dealer in St. James's about the authenticity of a Rembrandt; a few minutes later he would be listening to the woes of some tattered individual whose daughter had lost her job in the chorus; and at lunch time he was playing draughts with a Russian Jew in some disreputable but entertaining place near the Docks. In the afternoon, perhaps, he would go to hear a new pianist at the Wigmore Hall; and he would have tea with Lady Pallardyne, the celebrated reformer of the English workhouse. He might dine with Lord Emberley de Hazebrouck, or he might eat sausages with a taxi-driver and his family at Notting Hill.

It so happened that Ellingham was in town in January 1914 when my cousin Eric told me, with delight, that Professor and Mrs. Reisby were coming to London for an informal meeting of scientific workers.

"I should like to meet Reisby," said Ellingham. "He and I have written to each other on the subject of colloidal analyses, and we have both refuted Herr Gumberstein. By the way," he added, "judging from what you have told me and from what I have heard, Reisby is a very singular fellow."

"And what have you heard?" I asked him.

Ellingham chose to ignore my question. He drew a golden toothpick from a case in his pocket and lightly tapped it along his lower teeth; it was an offensive habit which always annoyed me, though I knew it was the prelude to cogitation.

"I may have met him, or I may have seen him," he said. "I'm not quite sure."

Such a remark appeared to me rather strange, coming from so exact a man as Ellingham and relating to so famous a man as Professor Reisby.

"Well," I said, "Eric will certainly take me to see them, and it would be very pleasant if you came with us. I myself am very anxious to meet these people, because Eric is frightfully taken up with them, you know, and he and I have always been more like brothers than cousins—"

"Quite, quite!" said Ellingham, who avoided sentiment of every kind. He tilted back his head, rattled his toothpick against his upper molars, and closed his eyes.

"Reisby!" he said. "Ah, yes!—distinctly interesting!"

On the 11th of January I was informed by Eric that the Reisbys were staying at a private hotel in Earl's Court, and would be delighted if I could go round with him and see them after dinner on the following day; they would also be glad to meet my friend Ellingham—indeed, the Professor was particularly anxious to have a talk with him. It was a very quiet hotel, said Eric, and we should probably have one of the private drawing-rooms to ourselves. The

Reisbys would be in town for ten days at least. Eric was clearly excited and happy.

"You are sure to like them, John. He is a wonderful fellow—so frightfully clever, and yet so simple and kind and manly! He's amusing, too; in a boisterous, Nordic style. And I'm sure you will be interested in Hilda—Mrs. Reisby—"

He broke off abruptly, and I saw that he was blushing.

"We are great pals," he explained. "She's not an ordinary young woman, I can assure you. Not at all. She knows quite a lot about archæology—almost as much as Tolgen himself. And there's no nonsense about her. She can understand a fellow and take a real interest in his work without being sentimental or sloppy—"

His eagerness, of course, revealed the secret. He was evidently falling in love with Mrs. Reisby. I knew the symptoms; I had seen them before. I could only hope that he was right in describing her as a lady incapable of nonsense.

4

Ellingham was fortunately free, and he accompanied Eric and myself to the Reisbys' hotel. When we got there we found that they had actually reserved a drawing-room, and had invited that famous man, Dr. Fulmar Pepperlow, to meet us—or perhaps I should say, to meet Ellingham. We anticipated a memorable evening, and we were not disappointed.

Tolgen Reisby was decidedly impressive. He was tall, rugged and immensely powerful. He wore a brown suit of some fluffy material which added to the natural effect of his bulk and made him look positively gigantic. His trousers were loose and voluminous; the upper buttons of his waistcoat were unfastened, releasing the untidy mass of a blue and yellow tie. The whole appearance of the man was barbaric; you might have taken him for a crofter of the Hebrides, or the skipper of an Aberdeen herring-boat.

Such might have been your first impression, but that was quickly changed when you looked at his face and heard him talk.

Ellingham, with his dislike of anything romantic, would never agree with me when I described Reisby as a thoughtful hero, an immense barbarian, subdued by intelligence, kindness and learning. But so he appeared to me from the first moment and so I remember him. A big red beard, already silvering at the edges, flowed lavishly over the crumpled folds of his blue and yellow tie. His face, like that of some benevolent Jupiter, was carved out in massive and ample forms. His tawny eyebrows were thick and overhanging, and a tangle of reddish-brown hair, parted high above the forehead, fell in a curly disorder about his temples. The eyes of this extraordinary man were not (as you might have imagined) fierce or compelling; they were grey, luminous and amiable. There was in the whole countenance a singular union of barbaric dignity, intellectual power, and extreme gentleness. There was even a trace of something whimsical or gay. Eric was right; I was immediately fascinated. Yet I imagined Reisby to be a man whose passions, though simple, would be overwhelmingly strong; a man with a stern, primitive conception of honour, a man whose retaliation would be cruel and unscrupulous.

He spoke in a rich, booming voice, unexpectedly low and soft in ordinary conversation, but rising, in moments of jocularity or fervour, to a boisterous and alarming bellow. He was not eloquent, except when he was talking about science, and he had an odd trick of uttering little rhythmic ejaculations. This trick, as I afterwards discovered, was intended to hold the attention of the listener while Reisby was thinking of what to say or what to do: it might be a signal of danger, or merely indicate the coming of a professorial joke.

Reisby dominated the scene, as, indeed, he will dominate this narrative; but I realised, when I saw him and Ellingham together, that I was in the presence of the two most remarkable men I was likely to meet in the course of my life.

When I turned from the Professor to his wife I realised the justification of all my forebodings. The moment I saw her I knew that she was Eric's ideal. Perhaps I felt a pang of jealousy, or it may have been a premonition of danger. At any rate, I was painfully aware of a lack of cordiality, if not of a certain uncouthness, in speaking to her for the first five minutes.

Again, Eric was quite right. Hilda Reisby was pretty and intelligent. She looked more like the Professor's daughter than his wife, and I had some difficulty in remembering that she was married to this fatherly and immense personality. I do not mean that she was juvenile or slight in appearance. On the contrary, she was unusually grave, composed and thoughtful for her age; she had a magnificent figure and a stately carriage.

Our conversation, after the usual preambles, became rather scientific. Dr. Fulmar Pepperlow, a dim, shadowy creature, the mere embodiment of an intellect, could speak with authority on archæological and anthropological research.

I was surprised to observe that Ellingham paid very little attention to the Professor, and showed a lack of cordiality bordering upon rudeness. I was anxious to learn his impressions of this wonderful man, and when I saw that he barely glanced at him and hardly took the trouble to answer his remarks, I was both humiliated and disappointed. Let it be remembered that I was then a very young man. Had I possessed at that time the fuller experience of later life I should have realised a peculiar significance in Ellingham's attitude. As it was, I felt myself more and more fascinated by the colossal presence and the booming voice of Professor Reisby.

Eric was radiantly happy. He saw my admiration of the hero, and he gave me, from time to time, a glance of pride and of sly humour. God knows, there was nothing in common between Eric and Boswell, but I can imagine Boswell glancing in such a way at a friend who found himself for the first time in the company of Dr. Johnson.

For my part, as I had little knowledge of the scientific matters which were being discussed by the others, I was obliged—rather unwillingly and ungraciously—to carry on a light conversation with the Professor's wife.

But I was presently mollified, if not entirely subdued, by the charm of Mrs. Reisby. She talked to me in a manner so frank and engaging that I soon had to abandon my boorish attitude of indifference or defiance. She told me how much they liked Eric, how much they were looking forward to his next visit.

"Mr. Foster is coming up in the Easter vacation," she said, "and I think Tolgen intends to carry out some interesting excavations near Aberleven. It would be so nice if you could come up too. There is only one spare room in our little house, but there is an inn at Aberleven—it is called the hotel—where you would be very comfortable. Perhaps your friend Mr. Ellingham would like to join the party. It would be great fun. I don't know if you have ever heard about the big earthwork of Caer Carrws—"

"Caer Carrws?" said Ellingham, swinging round from the other group with a strangely abrupt movement. "Are you thinking of having a dig there?"

I could see that his brusqueness offended Mrs. Reisby; it was very unlike his usual placid manner. Indeed, his whole behaviour was new to me, and I wondered if he was unwell.

"My husband, I think, means to dig at Caer Carrws in the Easter vacation. I was just talking about it to Mr. Farringdale."

Professor Reisby, surprised at the interruption, looked up with a shadow of annoyance on his enormous brow.

"Yes," he boomed, "I want to have a look at the guard-houses, or whatever they are, near the southern gateway. Pray excuse me, Pepperlow."

"I beg your pardon, sir, for this unseemly interruption," said Ellingham, "but the fact is that I am particularly interested in these northern earthworks."

I looked at him with astonishment. As far as I knew, he was entirely ignorant of such things. At any rate, he never said anything about them. But of course it was impossible to say what he had stored up in his capacious and eager mind.

"Wouldn't it be rather a good idea, Tolgen," said Mrs. Reisby, "if Mr. Farringdale and Mr. Ellingham came up to the hotel when we are having our dig? Aberleven is quite a jolly place in the spring, and Mr. Farringdale has been telling me—"

Again I saw the shadow of annoyance on Reisby's face. But it quickly passed and he answered pleasantly enough:

"A long way, I'm afraid. Still, if they would care to see the excavation—eh?—tum-ti-dee!—"

He smiled in his amiable Jovian style, and I was amazed to hear Ellingham saying:

"As far as I am concerned, I should welcome the privilege. I have read your wonderful essay on promontory fortifications, and I need hardly tell you, sir, that I agree entirely with all that you have said. Blackerton's feeble reply is unworthy of notice; I cannot understand the serious attention bestowed upon it by a man like Whitlock. The problem of the double entrance at Caer Carrws is peculiarly fascinating. If I am free at the time, I should very much like to spend a few days at Aberleven and follow your investigations."

"Sir," replied Reisby, completely amiable, "I should be glad to see you. My own opportunities for hospitality are unfortunately limited, but I can at least offer you an occasional meal at Scarweather."

"There!" cried Mrs. Reisby, "what a pleasant arrangement! And will you be able to come too, Mr. Farringdale?"

I said that I should like to join the party, but could hardly say whether it would be possible. This unexpected turn of events was bewildering me: I am naturally slow and cautious.

"Of course he'll come!" said Eric. "I'll answer for him, Mrs. Reisby. And you, sir, will find him a very serviceable navvy, I can assure you."

During the rest of the evening, apart from a little conversation with Mrs. Reisby, I was occupied in listening to, and observing, the others. Professor Reisby treated Eric as he might have treated a favourite pupil, and was evidently fond of him: indeed, his manner towards him was not so much amiable as affectionate. I could also observe a growing friendliness between the Professor and Ellingham. The latter had quite regained his normal balance (or so it appeared to me) and he was talking in his most delightful style. Dr. Pepperlow's contributions were those of a cold and equiponderating intelligence; he was a man so phantasmal that it was a positive relief to hear him asking for sugar in his coffee. Mrs. Reisby and Eric hardly said a word to each other, but they were clearly on terms of open familiarity. When it was time to go, Eric was the last to leave the room, and I saw him lingering in the doorway with Mrs. Reisby while the Professor heavily descended to the hall with Pepperlow and Ellingham.

5

I did not see Ellingham alone until two days after our evening with the Reisbys. He was returning to Cambridge at the end of the week, and asked me to meet him in the course of the morning at his club.

As soon as we had settled ourselves in a comfortable corner of the smoking-room, I asked him, with considerable eagerness, what he thought of Professor Reisby and his wife.

"Oh!" he said, rubbing his pointed chin with a lean finger, "I have seen the Professor before."

"Indeed!" I replied. "At one of your highly intellectual assemblies, no doubt."

"Not at all, my dear young friend, not at all! You are quite wrong. At the same time, I will admit that your conjecture has every appearance of being reasonable."

He scraped out the bowl of his meerschaum, tapped it gently in the palm of his hand, and then wrapped it up in a piece of yellow silk and slipped it into his pocket.

"What do you say to a little *apéritif*?—or is it too early?"

I knew that he was teasing me, but I stuck to the point.

"Where did you meet Reisby?" I said.

"Learn to be more precise. I did not say that I had met him. I said that I had seen him."

"And where have you seen him?"

"Down at the Docks."

"Down at the Docks!" I cried. "You are evidently mistaken. You have seen an old sailor who is like him. Indeed, that is not at all improbable. When I first saw him he reminded me of a northern sea-dog."

"I have also seen him at an eating-house in Poplar, a very interesting place. I don't think we have been there in the course of our excursions; it is not a proper scene for a young gentleman."

"You are being very irrational and irritating," I retorted, "and you cannot ask me to believe that you have seen Professor Reisby in such places. It is too absurd."

Ellingham looked at the clock over the mantelpiece.

"How about a trip to Poplar this morning?" he said. "I can't promise to show you the Professor, but I can show you the eating-house—in fact, I can give you a jolly good lunch there."

Of course I accepted the invitation, and in about an hour's time we entered one of the most peculiar establishments I have ever seen.

It was a large room, lighted by gas, and full of wooden tables covered with pieces of oilcloth. At these tables were little groups

of men, white, yellow or black. Most of them wore jerseys or
heavy dark overcoats, and many of them had caps with broad shining peaks drawn over their eyes. Clearly, a sailor's eating-house,
but not by any means cheap or dirty. What was unexpected was
the peculiar sense of decorum, almost of definite formality. The
customers, as they came in or went out, gravely saluted a big
man who sat in an armchair by the pay-desk, addressing him as
Captain Andrew. The waitresses (decent-looking young women
in blue aprons) were polite, swift and efficient. There was a little
boy, whose duty it was to keep the spittoons in order and remove
the empty glasses. The food, though plain and with no great
variety, was admirably cooked. Everything was clean, proper and
wholesome. On the walls hung large coloured lithographs of old
hermaphrodite steamers with paddle-boxes, black funnels, and a
billowing spread of canvas. But long before I had observed these
details Ellingham touched my arm.

"There he is," he said.

And sure enough, there was Professor Reisby, in the fluffy
brown suit and wearing the blue and yellow tie, seated at a table
close to the wall about half-way down the room. He was not in
a position to observe those who entered, and at the moment of
our arrival he was engaged in fixing a chessboard between himself and his companion. This companion was a man of decidedly
Anglo-Chinese appearance, but he was dressed, unlike most of
the others, in a well-fitted suit of grey tweed.

"If we sit here," said Ellingham quietly, guiding me to a table
for two, "it is improbable that he will notice us; and I would rather,
if you don't mind, leave him to the undisturbed enjoyment of his
game of chess."

I was so much taken aback by the peculiarity of the whole situation that I sat down without a word. From our table we had an intermittent view of the Professor and his odd companion playing their game, and I could see that Ellingham was following the moves with considerable interest. But Ellingham was a man who kept his thoughts to himself. Having ordered lunch he started a long and illuminating discourse on the subject of modern French writers, and although he glanced from time to time at the Professor's table he did not make a single comment on what he observed. I knew, however, that he was capable of giving close attention to one thing while he was talking with subtlety and ease about another; indeed, I have never met anyone in whom the faculties of dissociation were so curiously developed.

Before we had finished our lunch the Professor triumphantly concluded the game of chess, and almost immediately afterwards he left the place without seeing us. In ordinary circumstances I should have risen and accosted him, but Ellingham's manner had shown me that the circumstances were not ordinary. The other player remained at the table, slowly imbibing a glass of stout.

"Well," said Ellingham, "did you observe anything?"

"It was a very short game," I replied feebly.

"Reisby plays a good game," said Ellingham, "he opens with a variation of the Allgaier. Did you notice anything else?"

"No—at least—"

"The chessboard belongs to the house; it is now folded up on the table. The chessmen, on the other hand, were brought by that man with the yellow face—he is probably a steward. He brought them in a square mahogany box with a sliding lid, which he took out of that shabby bag of his; it is on the floor by his right foot. There is nothing very odd in that, because a good player likes his own men; but it is a little singular that Professor Reisby should have taken away both box and chessmen when he left the table. He put them into a large brown attaché case which he is now carrying in his hand."

"Did he? But surely the explanation may be quite a trivial one."

"Your sagacity is commendable, my dear friend. Now let us return for a moment to what we were saying about *Lourdes* and the decadence of realism."

6

I did not mention the episode at the eating-house to my cousin Eric; I did not want him to think that I had been spying upon the hero; nor did I see why Professor Reisby, who was obviously an eccentric man, need be suspected of any sinister designs because he played a game of chess in Poplar. I felt that eccentricity alone would account for a great deal more than the mere exchange of a box of chessmen.

Ellingham showed a peculiar reticence in regard to the episode when I saw him on the day of his return to Cambridge. He treated it lightly, and gave me the impression that he was rather ashamed of himself. And I was greatly pleased when I heard him speak about the Professor in a warmly enthusiastic style, hoping that he would be able to spend a few days at Aberleven and see something of the excavation of Caer Carrws.

We agreed to go north together, if circumstances permitted, on the 8th or 9th of April. For my part, I was anxious to see more of the Reisbys, and the idea of a holiday with my cousin Eric was, of course, delightful.

I met the Reisbys on two other occasions before they left London. They invited me (with Eric) to dinner at their hotel, and they also invited me to an informal but very austere gathering of learned men at the Holborn Restaurant.

On both occasions I admired the colossal yet amiable presence of the Professor and the not less remarkable charm of his lovely wife. My youthful head was full, just then, of a somewhat undiscriminating Wagner cult; and as I looked at them—the man with his immense Nordic virility, his grandly rugged face and his flowing beard, and the woman with her steady grey eyes and her mass of blond hair—I could not help thinking of those divinities who march with trumpet music in the scenes of the *Ring*.

7

No doubt I was infinitely more romantic, at the age of twenty-one, than I am to-day. But I was not entirely without a little practical sense. When Eric told me that he was taking Mrs. Reisby to a theatre, taking her out to lunch, escorting her to a private view of the pictures in Berkeley Square, I told him, rather peevishly, that he ought to be careful. Perhaps I was really a frightful prig.

"You don't understand," he said. "We are great pals. I tell you, she's a wonderful woman. I have never known anything like it before."

CHAPTER II

I

EASTER DAY IN 1914 WAS ON THE 12TH OF APRIL. ERIC WENT up to Aberleven on the 3rd or 4th, and I left Cambridge with Ellingham on the 8th. We were to pick up the express at Grantham, and we should be met at Northport by a car from the Aberleven hotel.

My companion, who seldom allowed himself a real holiday, was in excellent spirits, and I observed that he was taking with him a trout rod and a case of golf clubs. He also had a magnificent Zeiss camera, which I coveted greatly.

"If the Professor and his excavations are too boring," he said, "I can run away and amuse myself. There are sea-trout in the Kinkell River, and I believe the fishing is not expensive."

"Do you know that part of the coast?" I asked him.

"No, but I have been making some enquiries. It is a place, I am glad to say, not frequented by the vulgar, and so it does not come within the purview of the guide-book."

"According to Eric, it is remote but altogether charming."

"According to Scropersley Booth, it had an evil renown in the eighteenth century as the haunt of audacious wreckers and of desperate fellows whose doings were decidedly piratical. It is said that the officers of the law put up a gibbet on Scarweather Point, intending to use it for the hanging of sea-robbers. But one night the gibbet was taken away, and next morning it was discovered firmly planted on the magistrate's lawn, at a distance of seven miles from the coast."

"Must be frightfully lonely in winter."

"There are one or two big houses within five miles of Aberleven, but I don't suppose the people who live in them are particularly exciting. Probably the ordinary bibulous, broken-down squires, whose talk is of birds or dogs or horses and whose views on life are those of the stable-room. You will remember what Johnson said—'Those who live in the country are only *fit* to live in the country'—or words to that effect."

"But a highly intellectual man like Professor Reisby—"

"Ah! that's the question. Why should a man like Reisby deliberately remove himself from the society of his proper fellows and bury himself on the edge of a desolate shore, within reach of nobody except a few rustic Yahoos or a few half-civilised fishermen? I'm sure I don't know. Perhaps he needs quiet and leisure for his researches."

"Even then, you would have thought—"

"I tell you, my dear young friend, I don't know! Perhaps he doesn't look like a sea-dog for nothing. Perhaps he is really a king of smugglers, or the agent of a foreign power, or an international financier in disguise."

This was unusually frivolous on the part of Ellingham, and I was glad to see him starting on his holiday in so light-hearted a mood.

We arrived at Northport late in the evening, and it was time for dinner when we got to the Aberleven hotel. As for the hotel, it was very small and homely, though clean, comfortable and well conducted. The only other visitors were an elderly man and his wife who had come there for a little sea fishing. I found a message from Eric, who said that he was coming round to see us at nine o'clock.

2

It is now essential to give the reader some idea of the place in which we found ourselves.

The coastline at Aberleven runs in a north-easterly direction, just above the hollow of Drumadoon Bay. Immediately below the hamlet of Aberleven, which consists only of about a dozen cottages and the little hotel, the beach is covered with a shifting mass of grey shingle. Opposite to the beach, though not parallel with it, is a low rocky islet known as Dog Island. At low tide, the island is connected with the shore by a narrow ledge of sand and shingle, and it forms an effective natural breakwater to what is generally called the harbour, though it is merely a sheltered strip of the beach. South of the harbour, and curving out towards the island, is the bluff promontory of Scarweather Point. A narrow creek, with no particular name, bites into the coastline below the Point, and a steeper, more rugged shore runs thence in a slightly curving line towards the mouth of the Kinkell River. Stretching for some distance out to sea from the mouth of the river is a broad bank of sand, in shape not unlike a flounder, well known to seamen as the Yeaverlow Bank. It is never entirely covered by the sea, and in easterly gales is a source of grave danger to local shipping. A bell-buoy, painted in squares of black and white, is moored off the southern end of the Bank.

Above Aberleven run the long undulations of Scidal Moor, covered with a pale, scrubby grass and with tangles of gorse or bracken. Every archæologist knows the earthworks of Caer Carrws which crown the highest part of the moor, and he will also remember the interesting group of Bronze Age tumuli in the

same neighbourhood. Divided from Seidal Moor by the creek at
Scarweather is the rounded eminence of Yeaverlow Hill, with a
long plantation of young firs on the southern slope where the
hill falls gently towards the Kinkell River. On the south-west side
of the hill, just below the plantation, is a tumulus known locally
as the Devil's Hump.

I am aware of a sinister quality in the features of this description, and it is well to remember that the Aberleven district, far
from being sinister, is extraordinarily beautiful. The moors are
lovely at all seasons; the valley of the Kinkell River, with its
trees and rocks, has a nobly romantic aspect; the shingle beach
of Aberleven, intersected by wooden "croys" and rendered picturesque by the fishing-boats hauled up on the pebbly terraces,
is one of the most delightful places I know. Indeed, when we
made our first survey on the morning after our arrival, I felt
that Professor Reisby had chosen his retreat with uncommon
discernment.

Professor Reisby's house was in a very isolated though charming position close to the edge of the Scarweather creek. A long
drive, passing over a bare patch of heath before it entered his
grounds, connected the Professor's residence with the coastal
road which ran across the upper part of the creek. This road
swung in a westerly direction along the shoulder of Yeaverlow
Hill, through the plantation by the Devil's Hump, and along the
valley of the Kinkell to Branderswick. In the other direction (i.e.
towards the north) the road passed over the neck of Scarweather
Point and then ran level to the hamlet of Aberleven. It was nearly
a mile from the Professor's house to the nearest of the Aberleven
cottages. Three miles beyond Aberleven the road turned inland,

bordering the Manor Park, and effected a junction with the main road to Northport.

In addition to the hotel, there was only one house of any size in Aberleven, and that was a general stores, whose proprietor supplied the district with groceries, tobacco, meat, milk, eggs, bread and vegetables. The stores also included a postal department, and letters were collected and delivered once a day by means of a motor service from Branderswick. There was a telephone line between Aberleven and Branderswick, and so it was possible to send and receive telegrams.

The nine or ten scattered cottages in the place were inhabited by fishermen, who sold their catches to a dealer in Branderswick and occasionally in the immediate neighbourhood. Most of them kept poultry and had little gardens of their own, and several of the older men had sons who were earning good pay in the merchant service.

As for "society," the nearest representatives were the Macwardles of Aberleven Manor (Judge Macwardle, his wife, and his two middle-aged unmarried daughters), Major Dick Ugglesby-Gore, D.S.O. of Treddle Hall (wife but no child), and the Reverend Dr. Peter Ingleworth, Dean of Northport, who lived at Aggersdon (a bachelor). I shall introduce these people at the proper time.

Of course the main business of the hotel was that of a public house, and I was surprised to find the accommodation so good in view of the rarity of visitors. But the owner of the hotel was not by any means an ordinary inn-keeper. He was an elderly man of a ruddy and wholesome appearance whose name was Thomas Morgan, but he was known for miles round as "Jolly Morgan" or "Buffalo." Mr. Morgan, it seems, had made money in South Africa. Having done this, he came back to England, married the Duke of Tiddleswade's cook, bought the hotel, and settled down to the duties of a cheerful host, not caring whether he made a large profit and only anxious to have "something to do" in his old age. Mr. Morgan's rifles, and various trophies of African hunting, were suspended from the walls of the dining-room. He was a pleasant fellow, a most ingenious gossip and a really entertaining narrator. At the time of our first visit I suppose he was not more than fifty. He treated me as men of age and experience generally treat a youngster, anxious that I should enjoy myself and refusing to take me seriously; but his manner with Ellingham, from the very first, was that of a man of the world talking to an equal.

3

Ellingham and I were in fine spirits as we set out for Scarweather after breakfast on Thursday morning. A lively breeze from the north-east blew fresh and free under a clear blue sky. The sea ran merrily past the heel of Dog Island, breaking in occasional spray on the rocks of Scarweather Point. Two fishing-boats, under reefed lugs, were creeping out along the lee side of the island.

These boats were being watched by a strange individual who stood at the door of an isolated cottage near the road, and at some distance from the main group of the hamlet.

He was a tall man, wearing the blue jersey and the grimy trousers of a fisherman, but his demeanour, unlike that of his fellows, was grim and forbidding. He stood bare-headed in the doorway, a tangle of black hair blowing in fierce curls above his forehead. His beard, also black and curly, straggled unevenly over his powerful throat. From the swarthiness and weathered appearance of his dark, vigilant face I judged him to be a man who had spent his life in ocean travel, and in circumstances which had made him familiar with danger and with hardship. In each of his ears he wore a heavy silver ring. The cottage behind him was little more than a hovel, the patch of ground at the back of it was barely cultivated, and both in the man and his habitation there was an air of something wild and foreign and ominous which immediately drew our attention.

"Good morning!" said Ellingham in a bright and friendly manner.

The man looked at us closely through his black, narrow eyes.

"Are you going to Scarweather?" he said.

The voice was totally unexpected. It was deep, gentle and altogether pleasing.

"Yes," Ellingham replied, "we are going to see Professor Reisby."

"He told me you were coming," said the man. "I look after his boat and work in his garden now and then, and I dare say I shall be taking you gentlemen out for a bit of fishing. Mrs. Reisby and Mr. Foster went out with me the day afore yesterday. Joe Lloyd is my name. They call me Dollar."

"No doubt we shall meet again, Mr. Lloyd," said Ellingham. "Will you have a pipe of tobacco?" he added, taking his pouch from his pocket.

"No, thank you," said Lloyd ungraciously, "I don't smoke. There's a short cut to the house, if you follow that path to the left of the road and go over the Point."

"That's a rum fellow!" I said to Ellingham when we had got out of earshot.

"Undoubtedly one of our Professor's gang of pirates," Ellingham replied with a grin, "a really picturesque villain. But frankly, the most singular thing about him is that he won't smoke tobacco.—Ah! here's the path."

We swung along through the gorse and bracken, over the headland, and then down to the bridge over the creek on the other side.

Standing above the creek, Scarweather House was concealed by a plantation, and we did not see it until we had come round a corner of the drive. It would not serve any purpose if I described the appearance of the house in detail: it was rather small, decidedly plain, with grey slate roof and yellow plastered walls. On the seaward side there was a long verandah, and there was a curious addition, with large top-lights like a studio, which, we discovered later, was the Professor's laboratory. Reisby had bought the house from its original owner, a retired sea-captain, in 1908. There was a small though trim and fruitful garden, and a lawn sloping down towards the creek. At the end of the lawn there was a fence with a gate in it, and below the gate there was a boat-house and a little stone landing-place.

Mrs. Reisby must have seen us from one of the windows, for she came running out of the house to greet us.

I had been impressed by the good looks of Mrs. Reisby in London, but here, in the bracing air of the north, she was absolutely superb. She came towards us with an easy, buoyant movement, looking like a happy goddess, with a glow of health and excitement in her face.

"How delightful to see you!" she cried. "Tolgen has gone down to the boat-house with Eric to see about some tackle. We've had to put off the excavation for a day or two until Mr. Macwardle comes home—he's the Lord of the Manor, you know."

Chattering gaily, we walked down the lawn. In front of us, above the creek, rose the rocky and heathery mass of Scarweather Point. To the right we had a view of the open sea. Before we had reached the boat-house, Eric, hearing our voices, came out of it with a merry shouting, and he was followed, a moment later, by the Professor.

As I looked at the Professor, with the blue water of the tide in the creek behind him, I could not help thinking of a northern pirate. He wore a pair of grey trousers and a loose flannel coat, unbuttoned over a fisherman's jersey. His beard and hair were flaming red, with a dash of silver, in the sunlight, and he was looking tanned and ruddy. Even there, with the headland rising above us and the open sea large and level in our view, this man seemed to fill our vision and our thoughts with a sense of something colossal, pervading, imminent. Indeed, this is what he always made me feel, in a greater or lesser degree: the invasion or extension of a commanding and enormous personality.

"Hey-di-dee!" he bellowed, "welcome to the rugged north! Stern and simple magnificence of nature—eh? *Saepe faunorum voces exauditae!* I cannot shake hands—I'm all over grease and oil—"

As we stood there, in the wind and the sunlight above the gay rippling water of the creek, I doubt if you could have discovered anywhere a group of happier people or a jollier scene. It is wonderful how quickly sophistication is ended when you give yourself up to a true spirit of relaxation and the simple enjoyment of healthy movement and of healthy pursuits in the open air. Who could have suspected, in that little group, the gathering elements of a dark and appalling tragedy? I will admit a feeling of uneasiness, a transient feeling, when I heard Mrs. Reisby speak of my cousin as "Eric," but I was reassured by the candour and the open friendship of their attitude.

"I've had to postpone the dig until Monday," said the Professor, "because old Macwardle has gone up to town, and he doesn't come back until Sunday night. But I hope you will be able to amuse yourselves. Foster knows his way about, and Hilda, I'm sure, will be delighted—eh? As for myself, I am occasionally occupied, and you will doubtless excuse me if I cannot give you the whole of my time and attention. Ellingham will appreciate—eh?—"

"Really, sir," replied Ellingham, "we should be extremely unhappy if we thought you were troubling yourself on our account."

"Ah, ho!" cried Reisby with a boisterous laugh, "but I should be extremely unhappy if I thought you young people could get along well enough without me. No, no! My inclination is to join with you in your frolics, as Johnson would have said. In my free time I shall be entirely at your disposal. Only I fear it will be necessary for me to get through some work before Monday—that's all. And let me tell you, sir," he turned to Ellingham, "there are three miles of the Kinkell—both banks—for you to fish. Macwardle gives me four tickets for the season, and I have only to fill in the names."

It was then proposed that Mrs. Reisby, Ellingham, Eric and myself should go for a walk to Seidal Moor before lunch and have a look at the earthwork.

As the four of us walked along the path over the headland Mrs. Reisby suddenly exclaimed:

"Why, there's the mystery ship!"

"The mystery ship!" said Ellingham, giving me a laughing glance. "How exciting! Is that her, out yonder?"

A large barque in the offing was beating slowly up towards the coast under mizen, lower topsails and a couple of jibs.

"Yes, I think that's the ship," Mrs. Reisby answered. "I am not well versed in nautical affairs. We call her the mystery ship because she appears to hang about in such an odd way before signalling for a Northport pilot. I forget her name, but I believe she's a German."

"Well," said Ellingham, "she's evidently in no hurry, or she would be carrying a bigger spread of canvas. It's not more than what sailors would call a royal breeze, and she has nothing set above her lower topsails."

We came down the hill and along the road by the harbour. Joe Lloyd had left his cottage and was talking to a group of fishermen by the side of the road. They were looking with some interest at the ship, and a pair of glasses was being passed from hand to hand.

"Good morning, Mr. Lloyd," said Mrs. Reisby. "Isn't that the boat that we have seen here so often before—a German?"

"Yes, ma'am," said Lloyd, touching his black locks respectfully. "I know the ship. *Emil Guntershausen* of Hamburg, bound for Northport with iron ore."

Ellingham nodded his head thoughtfully, as if he remembered the name. "And how is the tide running now?"

Joe Lloyd looked at him with a furtive and (I thought) a sinister glance.

"Half ebb, sir."

"Then why doesn't he put on a bit of canvas and make sure of the evening tide at Northport?"

"There you are, Joe!" cried one of the fishermen. "I reckon the gentleman's right. It's just what I was a-saying of."

"He's no business of mine," said Joe gruffly, "but, speaking as a seafaring man myself—which I hope you'll allow—" he turned in a half-sneering, half-threatening manner towards the fishermen, "I don't see nothing peculiar in what he's doing. There you are! He's put down his helm to go about, and now he'll make a long leg to wind'ard and fetch up to Northport in the afternoon."

"May I borrow the glasses for a moment?" said Ellingham. "Thank you." He stared at the ship intently and then handed the glasses back to their owner.

"And what do you make of it, sir?" Lloyd asked him, with a grin of defiant impudence.

"Well," replied Ellingham, looking particularly amiable, "that boat is not made in Germany, though she may now belong to Hamburg owners. She was built for the Norwegian timber trade— a Stavanger boat, I should say, from the look of her deck-houses."

"Why, the gentleman's a sailor!" said one of the fishermen. "He's got her properly sized up anyhow."

Joe Lloyd was evidently astonished, but he shrugged a shoulder with the affectation of indifference.

"No, I'm not a sailor," said Ellingham, "I'm only a school-master, worse luck! but I am fond of looking at ships—and I am fond of talking to seafaring men," he added, with a friendly nod in the direction of Lloyd.

As we climbed up to the breezy moor we looked from time to time at the ship, now beating out to sea.

"There goes the mizen staysail," Ellingham observed. "I dare say Mr. Lloyd is right after all, but the skipper evidently believes in taking it easy."

"You amazed me with your nautical knowledge," said Mrs. Reisby, laughing. "They will treat you with real respect now, I can assure you."

Ellingham smiled, but he made no answer.

We duly visited the ramparts of Caer Carrws, looked at the tumuli, and came down over the south side of the moor to the valley above the creek.

It was a jolly morning. I can still see in vivid memory the splendid youth, the comeliness and the vigour of my cousin Eric; the abounding, vital charm of Mrs. Reisby. We were all in a happy mood, though Ellingham was occasionally thoughtful.

Our kind hostess told us that we were to consider ourselves, by day, the guests of Scarweather, though entirely free to make our own plans. She would only ask us to let her know if we did not intend to be in to lunch or dinner. Tolgen, she said, would probably be more or less free after Monday, but he was visited sometimes by his colleagues or pupils, and he was also engaged in private study and experiment. We were to feel no restraint, no obligation, but were to regard Scarweather as our temporary home. No arrangement could have been more to our liking, for I knew Ellingham would go off on solitary rambles, and I proposed to do a little quiet reading in my room at the hotel. We thanked her cordially, and I, for my part, felt that I was about to spend the most delightful holiday of a lifetime.

Our little party was approaching the drive at Scarweather as a large and luxurious motor car swung out of it. Inside the car there was a pale, fat woman wrapped in a mass of costly furs, who indolently flipped a hand at Mrs. Reisby. I did not pay much attention to the lady or the car, and I was rather surprised to see that Ellingham was looking at them with an apparently disproportionate interest.

"I believe that is one of Tolgen's private pupils," said Mrs. Reisby, smiling, "though you would hardly believe it, would you? What a mercy she is not staying to lunch!"

The Professor now appeared, obviously walking down the drive in order to shut the gate.

"Ah, ho! Ah, ho!" he boomed. "Did you see her, my dear? Lady Pamela Mulligan—a woman of benevolent designs, though not conspicuously intelligent. I did not urge her to stay; in fact I told her I was particularly busy. Ha, ha! I do not welcome these dabblers, Ellingham, their nullity and futility are almost outside the limits of belief. But I should be sorry to disoblige her brother, who is one of the most worthy and discerning patrons of my college."

"And may I ask, sir," said Ellingham, "what is the object of this lady's dabbling?"

"Ho!—La-di-diddle-de-dee! She calls it *science*, my dear fellow—science! What exact meaning she attaches to that word I cannot say."

"Oh, do you know? Tolgen," said Mrs. Reisby, "we saw the mystery ship this morning. Mr. Ellingham surprised us all, including Joe Lloyd, by showing how much he knew about her."

"Eh?"

I happened to be looking at Reisby, and I saw, or thought I saw, a sudden corrugation of his brow, a momentary spasm of anger, the reflex of an ugly thought. I remember this, because it appeared so unaccountable at the time, and I wondered if Ellingham saw it as well. It was a mere flicker, gone in a second, but it left an impression on my mind. I think it was from that moment that I began to feel a formless, irrational yet obstinate suspicion, the shadow of a quite intangible menace, the dim foreboding of something not yet recognised on the conscious plane.

"Why, Ellingham, you don't know that boat, do you?"

"No, sir—far from it. I merely hazarded the guess that she was originally a Norwegian."

"So she was, undoubtedly. Bergen or Stavanger—eh? We merely divert ourselves in our childish way, Mr. Ellingham, by pretending that she is mysterious. A most inoffensive, dull German trader. Our sea-gossip, even if tolerated as a romantic fiction of the idle, is really too ill-natured! Now, what do you young people say to a little trolling off the Bank this afternoon? We can get Lloyd to help us with the boat if we want him; or, better still, he can come round in his own boat and we can form two separate expeditions. You, my dear, could send Frances out with Winnie, I presume?"

The Professor's domestic staff consisted of the nurse (Winnie), an elderly cook and still more elderly housemaid, and a lad who came every day from Aberleven. In his more serious labours, the lad was assisted by Joe Lloyd or Dollar.

Frances, the Reisbys' daughter, was at this time a charming little girl between three and four years old, with a tumbling, tousled mass of adorable yellow hair. For the present, she is not concerned in this history.

4

In spite of my vague mistrust of Professor Reisby (a feeling of which I was heartily ashamed) I have never enjoyed myself more than I did at Scarweather.

Everything was pleasantly informal, yet well ordered and well considered. The sea-fishing was excellent, the trout of the Kinkell rose merrily to a fly, the clean air of the moors bathed you in a stream of health; on the one hand you could feel the primitive delight of solitary places, and on the other you had the equal delight of intelligent conversation and a most congenial society.

On Saturday morning Ellingham and I decided to put some sandwiches in our pockets and go for a long walk along the coast, and home again by a circuitous route across the Burrowdown Hills. The Professor was engaged in study, and Eric had made up his mind, so he said, to put in a few hours of serious reading; while Mrs. Reisby was occupied (or appeared to be) with the affairs of her household.

Fred Ellingham, when he went for a long walk in the country, invariably carried a lot of apparatus which, in his opinion, was necessary for the proper enjoyment of a ramble. On this particular day he had the Zeiss camera, a folding stand, a large mapcase, a pair of powerful glasses, a prismatic compass, a tin water-bottle full of cold tea, a geological hammer in a special case, and a grey canvas haversack containing various boxes and wrappings for "specimens" or what not. He carried in his hand a shooting-stick—one of those cumbersome things which are of little use when you are actually walking but which provide you with a reliable seat. I believe he had been several times arrested as a spy during his continental holidays.

As we proceeded on our way, Ellingham frequently paused to make use of his various instruments. He took photographs, he identified places in the landscape, he chipped off pieces of rock and put them in his bag, he astonished me by the ingenuity of his observations and the range of his experience. We were sitting under a stone wall and eating our sandwiches, when Ellingham, passing me a tinful of his cold tea, suddenly remarked:

"Reisby is a queer old bird."

The crudity and simplicity of this made me laugh, quite forgetting my own uncharitable suspicion. Ellingham's ordinary speech was rarely so colloquial.

"You may laugh," said Ellingham, "but my comment is not entirely frivolous. What do you think of him?"

"Why," said I, "you know that I admire him immensely, and I think he is a truly delightful host."

"You are not speaking without reserve," said Ellingham, taking his glasses out of the case. "Is that a flight of curlew rising over the hill?"

He looked intently through his binoculars, and then resumed:

"You know as well as I do, my dear young friend, that there is something about this man which is disturbing without being comprehensible."

That was exactly what I had felt, without admitting it so clearly.

"Well," I said, "what is your own opinion?"

Ellingham frowned slightly, compressing his lips in a thin, hard line. Then he rubbed his fingers along the sharp angle of his lower jaw, always a sign that he was considering how much he was prepared to say. Yet even then I had a singular proof of his awareness.

"Digger beetle," he remarked, watching an insect moving through the scrubby grass near his foot. "Now, about Reisby. You are a sensible youth, and I need not invoke your complete discretion." (He himself was only thirty-six.) "I shall only recall what has come under your own observation: it is, perhaps, enough to make you think. Professor Reisby plays chess in a sailor's eating-house in Poplar—mere eccentricity. Professor Reisby chooses to live on a lonely and remote part of our northern coast—mere eccentricity. Professor Reisby gives lessons to Lady Pamela Mulligan, who is known to the initiated as one of the most depraved women in high society and a hopeless victim of the drug habit—a very singular pupil, to say the least of it. Professor Reisby cannot conceal his intense annoyance when he hears that you have been looking at a German ship—is that also a mere eccentricity? Late in the evening (I do not know if you *did* observe this, by the way) Professor Reisby is called by a signal on a telegraphic buzzer in some unlocated part of the house. It is my natural habit to seek for an explanation of anything which excites my interest. Perhaps I have a theory in my mind; perhaps not. I will only say that I think Eric Foster ought to be careful. If he got on the wrong side of Reisby he might have to pay a terrible price. I would not have spoken to you, nor would I even have suggested anything to make you uneasy, if this thought had not come into my mind."

I had never heard Ellingham speak so gravely before. My reply I do not recollect, nor does it matter. We resumed our walk in a thoughtful mood, but Ellingham positively, and even rudely, declined to say anything more about the situation at Scarweather. I made up my mind to speak to Eric when I got a chance.

Late in the afternoon we had walked across the upper part of the Kinkell valley. The beauty of the day and the scenery, and above all the happy resilience of youth, had gone a long way towards removing the gloom which had been roused by the solemn warning of Ellingham, and I was already looking forward to a pleasant evening at Scarweather.

We were going along a pathway between the bank of the river and the side of Yeaverlow Hill when my companion pointed out a great conical mound of earth, half concealed below a plantation of fir-trees.

"That is a burial place of the Bronze Age," he said. "Here it is on the map—'Devil's Hump, Tumulus.' Evidently a fine thing of its kind, but I believe it's been rather badly knocked about. Suppose we go up and have a look?"

The mound was on a grassy terrace above the valley. The sides of it were covered with a thin, wiry turf, and there were also a few clumps of bracken and a few brambles. On the top of the mound there was a sandy hollow, partly filled with blocks of stone. In one or two places near the top were the extruding edges of great horizontal slabs, and a little lower down you could see the face of a big flat stone planted upright like a tombstone in a churchyard.

"Considerable disturbance of a comparatively recent date," said Ellingham, "but a large part of the barrow is evidently intact. I wonder old Reisby doesn't open it."

He looked closely at the edges of the stones.

"Decidedly interesting," he murmured. "I shall take a series of photographs. We are not far from home, and shall be in good time for supper."

He was an expert and rapid photographer, and he quickly took eight or nine photographs of the mound. I could not for the life of me see why he should take so much trouble over a heap of earth and stones, when he had resisted all my appeals to get some really fine pictures of the moors, the rocks and the river. He did not enlighten me.

We all had a jolly supper at the Professor's house, and in the course of our conversation afterwards Ellingham mentioned our visit to the Devil's Hump, but I observed that he said nothing about his photographs.

Professor Reisby did not seem particularly interested.

"Eh? The Devil's Hump? No doubt of the same date as the tumuli on Seidal Moor, several of which I have already opened. Later Bronze Age, with incinerated burials; pottery of a type which I have ventured to classify tentatively, according to my own system, as Period XIV B. Rather an unusual site for a barrow. It has been damaged, perhaps by the unintelligent zeal of treasure-hunters."

"But the damage is not very extensive, sir."

"No, sir: it is not very extensive. Do you suggest that a careful opening of the barrow might reveal something of interest?"

"Well, sir, it is larger than the other tumuli, and one may certainly suppose—"

"Yes, Ellingham, I agree with you entirely. In fact, I should very much like to dig it out myself. But these unlearned barbarians of the north—I speak, Ellingham, of my neighbours—have a kind

of superstitious regard for that mound, and this attitude is treated
with sympathy—a most regrettable thing!—by old Macwardle,
who is the owner of the land. How obstinate, how unconquerable,
is a superstition! How invincible the creed of ignorance! La-di-
dee! In the south of England, everything is Roman; in the north,
everything is Danish. That mound, if you please, is the tomb of
a Danish leader, easily identified, in the northern imagination,
with the devil. That is to say, to the illiterate he is the devil, to
the learned (but equally ignorant) he is a Dane. What is the use
of talking archæology to these boors? Try it on Macwardle—he
will think you are a lunatic."

Reisby looked round on his company in a mood of genial
intolerance. He went on booming away about the credulity, the
folly of the people. Even the Dean—Dean Ingleworth—who had
so many of the advantages of learning, could not see the difference between a Period XI pot and a Period XVI pot.

I listened with delight to this amusing and impressive man.
Again his vast, enveloping personality dominated my judgment;
his conversation flowed out in large, rebounding waves of humour,
geniality and learning; no one, I felt sure, could resist for long this
pervading candour, this exuberance of manly wit and wisdom! I
felt ashamed of myself for having admitted even the shadow of
a doubt. I realised the fantastic absurdity of such a doubt, and I
was astounded by the vagaries of a mind so powerful as that of
Ellingham.

But a glance at Ellingham threw me back into a state of misty
bewilderment. He was listening politely, without enthusiasm,
rubbing his chin, and from time to time emitting a slow cloud
of tobacco smoke.

Youth is not the time for reflection, it is the time for heedless enjoyment. I determined, before the evening was over, that I would not bother myself with conjectures about inscrutable personalities, but would have a jolly good holiday.

O N MONDAY MORNING, IN DULL AND VARIABLE WEATHER, our party assembled at the earthwork of Caer Carrws.

It was the first time I had been at an affair of this kind, and I thought it vastly entertaining. The principal workers were Joe Lloyd, the boy from the garden and three gamekeepers from Aberleven Manor. But a regular dump of picks, bars and shovels had been taken up to the camp, and all the men of the party (excluding our two visitors, Macwardle and the Dean) did their bit of digging or hewing.

Professor Reisby, rolling up the sleeves of his grey shirt and exposing arms of Herculean proportion, attacked the rampart with a pick. His energy was almost alarming. He struck a piece of hard stone, and the head of the pick flew off in a shower of splinters. He jabbed a spade into a tough section of the embankment, and the spade crumpled up as if it was only a tin imitation. Then he gripped an enormous block of granite and flung it far behind him, so that it nearly fell upon the incautious toes of the Dean. Apologising for his clumsiness, he rammed a crowbar under the parapet and in one heave dislodged about half a ton of soil and rubble.

"I am surprised at you digging *there*," said the Dean with petulance, "I should have begun just yonder," and he flung a stone vaguely into the air.

The Dean—the Reverend Peter Ingleworth—was a man with a thin, cross, agitated face, who rarely spoke without being disagreeable. He wore a straw hat, of the mottled black and yellow variety often worn by the more liberal clergy of that period.

"Tra-di-la-di-da!" cried Reisby, plunging his bar into the ground with an awful thud, "one place is really as good as another, my dear fellow! But if you fancy that particular traverse—"

"No, no, no!—I mean *there*," said the Dean, peevishly taking up another stone and flinging it in another direction.

"What!—*there*?" said Reisby, flinging a stone in his turn.

"No, sir!" replied the Dean, and presently they were both chucking stones all over the place, to the huge amusement of the rest of the party.

Old Arthur Macwardle, the owner of the great estate of Aberleven Manor, chuckled with good-humoured enjoyment of the scene. He was a man who had made money in business. In fact, he regarded the making of money as the proper aim of rational human endeavour and the only true reward of all human ambitions, looking on those who thought otherwise or who used their wits for any other purpose as eccentric and futile persons of no importance. It goes without saying that Mr. Macwardle was not a man of high intelligence or of distinguished breeding or of any culture, but his good nature and kindliness did much to redeem his rather blatant vulgarity. In appearance he was ruddy, slightly alcoholic and apoplectic, but invariably jocular. He was now looking at the Professor and the Dean with an air of condescending indulgence.

"It beats me, what you fellows can see in this," he said. "Why, nobody would give you half a crown for anything you found, would they?"

Dean Ingleworth, a scholar and a gentleman, treated this remark with silent though visible contempt, but Reisby answered:

"Ho, ho! We labour for the advance of learning, not for corruptible lucre, not for that expensive dirt which you call money! See how this parapet is constructed, see the primitive skill in the facing of the inner wall. You had no idea of this until I revealed it by a process of orderly demolition. Observe the corners of the guard-house, now being uncovered by these energetic men. Pass your eye along the slowly emergent line of that long enclosure. And then—hullo, Ellingham! have you got something there?"

"Some pottery down here by the foot of the wall, and a bit of iron."

"Now, Macwardle, what do you say to that? Some pottery and a bit of iron! Treasures, my dear sir; the treasures of antiquity!"

Macwardle liked the Professor. He looked on him as a man who "had done well in his own line," and though he had only the vaguest idea of what was meant by science, and no idea at all of what was meant by genetics, he regarded the post of a university professor as one which need not be entirely despised. He thought little of a "mere schoolmaster," such as Ellingham, who was not likely to be making more than £500 a year. Mr. Macwardle therefore contented himself with crying:

"Ah, Reisby! you are trying to pull my leg!"

I was enjoying myself. There is a strange fascination about the digging up of hidden, venerable things, even if these things are mere scraps and fragments. Before lunch time we had unearthed one or two unbroken pots, a multitude of shards, a bronze ring, and a mess of charcoal.

There was a lively discussion between Reisby and Ingleworth.

"But my dear fellow!" roared the Professor, "look at the rim, the unmistakable rim! Who in his right mind could possibly regard that rim as Halstatt? Ho, no, no! Let me assure you, dear Dean, it is typical, absolutely typical, of what I have presumed to call Northumbrian VIII Series D."

To this gibberish Ingleworth replied (and I thought he did so very properly):

"I should consider myself too impulsive, Professor Reisby, if I based a theory of any importance upon a fragment which, to my mind, is of a somewhat indeterminate nature."

"Indeterminate, my worthy friend! Tol-di-rol-di-dido! But look at the association—what, what?—look at the association! If that be no Northumbrian pot, pray tell me, sir, what have we got?"

And the Professor waved his enormous hand in the direction of a dirty little earthenware vessel placed carefully on the top of the bank.

"Don't you think, sir," said Eric, who was examining the debatable fragment, "that it really might be a bit of Halstatt after all?" I considered this a little indiscreet, but I did not anticipate what followed.

"No, I don't," replied the Professor, huffing up in a moment, "and I should advise young gentlemen not to think they know more than their elders, unless they have any particular reason— and you certainly have not—for believing that to be the case."

This abrupt and explosive change of manner, jarring so unpleasantly upon the general good-humour of the whole affair, had an immediate and a very painful effect. My poor cousin was completely taken aback; he blushed, and could only mutter something about "intending to make a mere suggestion." Hilda Reisby was standing near him, and I saw her quietly touch his hand.

"That was very unwise of you," she said, smiling at Eric, but her cheeks were flushed with a vivid red almost as deep as his own.

To me the episode was unaccountable. It was foolish of Eric to question the views of an expert, but I did not see why the Professor should have blazed up in a manner so rude and unprovoked, so disproportionately fierce. Ellingham was looking closely at the group, and he came forward.

"I agree with you," he said to the Professor, "and I think our friend was misled by some detail which appears to be common to more than one type. I will answer for it, that he never intended to assert his own opinion. Have you seen this curious fragment of bronze which has just been found in the trench by the gateway? It is not unlike the end of a torque."

Reisby had been staring at the bit of pottery in his hand, and he now started like a man coming out of a dream. In a second he appeared to regain his good-humour and kindliness.

"Foster!" he cried, "I beg your pardon. I was frightfully rude. Eh? These Northumbrian pots have got on my nerves—for, in spite of what you say, Dean, they *are* Northumbrian—and I have been for many years endeavouring to give them a recognised archæological status. But what does it matter? It is all a solemn trifling with unimportant relics, a mere pastime for learned idlers. Macwardle is right—there's nothing in it! I repeat, Foster, I am sorry for what I said—indeed I am."

"Please don't say anything of the kind, sir," replied Eric, who was now more embarrassed than ever. "It was awfully stupid of me—downright impertinent—"

"No, no, Foster! all the stupidity was mine. But let's have done with it, eh? And now, Ellingham, what about this torque of yours?"

To all outward seeming, our harmony was restored; and yet the memory of this disturbing incident lingered in my mind.

Lunch, provided by Macwardle and the Reisbys, was a cheery business, and a bottle or two of splendid claret (from the famous bins of Aberleven Manor) played their part in stimulating or reviving cordiality. Even the Dean was less acidulous, and less eager to wrangle over his pots or pieces. After lunch, Mrs. Reisby went home.

The afternoon brought an important visitor—Mr. Wilberforce Goy, the curator of the Northport Museum. He came on a motor bicycle, which he left at the foot of the hill.

We need not examine the uneventful and respectable history of Mr. Wilberforce Goy, who, at that time, was about thirty-three. He will appear again, an unconscious though not idle participant in the Reisby drama, and it is enough to know that he was an intellectual and rather delicate person who had come to Northport, only a year or two previously, from Oxford. You could see that he was a man with a private income. His clothes were not only neat and correct, they were expensive; the cut of his breeches, the fit of his Norfolk jacket, were both irreproachable. His teeth protruded slightly below the edge of his yellow fluffy moustache, and he wore gold-rimmed pince-nez.

Mr. Goy smiled in a grave, neutral and rather patronising manner as he walked slowly and confidently towards our group.

"Ah, ho, Goy!" the Professor thundered, "have you got any labels with you? Here is a pretty little problem for your curatorial sapience. Spot the pot, my lad!—spot the pot! Ha, ha, diddle-di-da! Here—this one—eh?"

"La Tène," said Mr. Goy.

And he proceeded, in a sedate, aristocratic manner to shake hands with Macwardle and the Dean.

This cryptic utterance on the part of Mr. Goy (presumably an allusion to some archæological period) almost immediately drew upon him the united fire of the other experts.

"Halstatt!" cried the Dean, shrill and querulous.

"Northumbrian!" bellowed the Professor.

"La Tène," replied Mr. Goy in a colourless, placid voice, which implied a firm belief in the superiority of his own knowledge, a belief secretly or openly entertained by every archæologist who knows his job. "I have an exactly similar piece from Sodwick in the museum."

"Tell me, Goy, tell me, sapient Goy," retorted the Professor, "how could La Tène pottery be found in association with these rude northern wares?"

"Or with Halstatt vessels," added the Dean.

"Imported," said Mr. Goy.

This, as I found later, is the proper way of getting round almost any archæological problem.

"Dumty-dee! Imported grandmother!" shouted Reisby with jocose vehemence. "Here, Foster—"

He looked round for Eric, but Eric had disappeared.

An expression which might have indicated annoyance or bewilderment or suspicion flickered over the Professor's face, and then he turned again, in a bantering style, towards the imperturbable Goy.

2

The absence of Eric, who must have slipped away soon after Mrs. Reisby left, made me feel once again a vague uneasiness. I said that I had a letter to write in time for the evening post, and I went down to the hotel. I did, indeed, write a letter, but it only took me a few minutes, and in less than half an hour I was on the way to Reisby's house.

I trust it is not in my nature to spy upon people, although I am a lawyer. I was extremely fond of Eric, and I felt, in my confused, youthful way, that he was getting into a scrape and I ought to help him. God knows, I had not the least intention of doing anything which might embarrass him or expose him to annoyance.

Probably it was about five o'clock when I came through the white gate at the end of the Scarweather drive. It so happened that I was wearing a pair of old tennis-shoes, and I padded swiftly over the hard surface of the drive without making a sound. The day was ending in a sultry calm. I could hear the pattering and chirruping of the birds in the shrubbery, the tiny piping of gnats in the air. Ellingham said afterwards that I must have been listening intently, but I deny emphatically that such was the case. It was one of those tense, breathless evenings when every sound, however slight or distant, appears to have a magnified audibility.

At any rate, I was quickly speeding along the drive when I heard the sound of voices, and something in the tone of those voices made me stop. Below the drive there was a kind of wild shrubbery, with a path running through it down to the creek. Two people, concealed from my view, had evidently been standing in silence on the path, and they began to talk just as I was passing above them. The voices were those of my cousin Eric and Hilda Reisby.

"But why should you stay any longer," said Eric, "if what you say is really true?"

"My dearest boy," said Mrs. Reisby, "you mustn't talk to me like that. Can't you see? Can't you understand? I do love you—in a way—perhaps better than you know, and that is why I cannot do what you ask me to do. Please don't think I'm pretending to be wiser than you are. Oh, my dear, my dear! How can I tell you—"

The voices faded. But I had no wish to hear anything more. I turned and walked back along the drive with a quickening pulse and a buzzing of blood in my ears.

Here was a pretty affair! I had been suspecting it, but the youthful mind is generous, and I could not believe that Eric would make a fool of himself with a married woman. As it was, I felt that I could trust the good sense and the fine character of Mrs. Reisby, in spite of what she had just been saying—or perhaps because of it. But Eric, with his romantic ideas, might very well be capable of some fatal extravagance, a freak of undiscerning behaviour, a weak surrender to impulse. He was a queer, excitable fellow, terribly sensitive, and entirely unmoved by danger.

My own impulse was to run away from the problem, and I did so literally by going back to the hotel. I would do nothing before consulting Ellingham, and I knew that he would soon return in order to have a bath and change before supper.

When Ellingham did return he was full of good stories about the digging at the camp, but he observed my gravity. I do not mean that my ordinary demeanour, even at twenty-one, was frivolous—far from it—but I was now deeply distressed.

"What's the matter?" said Ellingham, with an unusual quality of gentleness in his voice. He was standing by the window in my room and pushing away the imitation lace curtains in order to get a view of the sea. "Are you tired? I thought you were rather overdoing it with that shovel."

I told him what was the matter.

To repeat a fragment of an intimate overheard conversation, even as a matter of duty, is terribly repugnant; but I did not know how to deal with the situation, and I felt something would have to be done if a disaster was to be avoided. Ellingham continued to look at the sea. He took the golden toothpick out of his pocket and rattled it thoughtfully against his incisors.

"Well?" he said when I had finished.

"Well?" I repeated, "what am I—what are we to do?"

"Bless your simple heart!" he answered, "you can't do any-thing."

"But—"

"No action is possible. A sermon from you to your cousin, my dear friend, would probably be resented and would certainly be without effect. He is a year or two older than you are (a point of considerable importance in early youth) and of a very different constitution. As for me—apart from giving you negative advice—it is no affair of mine."

"Ellingham! Don't you see the danger?"

"What danger?" he said, carefully replacing his toothpick.

"Why—this preposterous affair!"

"In view of Mrs. Reisby's obvious control of herself and of the situation, I cannot see what you are worrying about. Besides, your cousin, though he is young and romantic, is a very good fellow and has a more than ordinary share of intelligence."

"These two are not the only persons concerned."

"They are the principals."

"At the present moment they are, but suppose—"

"My dear Farringdale, what are you driving at? It would be extremely indelicate on my part, even as a much older man, if I hinted at your own ignorance of these matters. But you must allow me to say that such affairs are not uncommon, and are generally quite harmless and of short duration. The lady, though young, is eminently sensible—"

"Do you think the Professor is eminently sensible?"

"Ah! I see—"

"Did you notice that little squabble up at the camp?"

"H'm!"

"You yourself have said that my cousin ought to be careful."

Ellingham's manner changed. He looked at me seriously and frankly.

"You are right, Farringdale. I have no wish to be flippant. But, in the first place, I want you to take things calmly and with caution. In the second place, what you have now told me is reassuring rather than otherwise. Mrs. Reisby, I think, will not behave foolishly; and she is the only person who, at present, can have any influence over your cousin. If we have anything to apprehend, it is from Reisby himself, a man in whom I strongly suspect the presence of dangerous abnormalities."

"Then I can at least give Eric a warning."

Ellingham pondered for a moment.

"Probably it would be useless, and it might even have an undesirable result. The situation is delicate, but we have no reason to regard it as desperate. Interference, even of the kindliest nature, would, in my opinion, be futile or harmful. The only person who could intervene with any chance of benefit would be another woman. At present we are helpless, and we can only depend, as I have said, upon the good sense and the incorruptible character of Mrs. Reisby."

"But she told him—"

"Oh, the beautiful simplicity of youth! Pray remember that Mrs. Reisby, though she is only two or three years older than you, is a woman, and a married woman, and a mother. And even if she were neither married nor a mother, she would be infinitely beyond you in wisdom and experience. She is grown up. She has attained the age of realisation. Things are not likely to get beyond her control, unless your cousin is a lunatic. And I would have you observe that one possible source of danger is not present—Reisby is clearly devoted to his wife and child."

"Yes, but suppose—"

"Suppose you take my advice, and go on enjoying your holiday, my good friend! Be reasonable. Reflect, with comforting humility, upon your own incompetence in this particular matter."

These words, kindly spoken by a man of superior judgment, eased my anxiety without altogether removing it.

In spite of my unsought, disturbing knowledge, I could not help enjoying the Scarweather supper party. Even Eric, who was rather pale, warmed up in the boisterous flow of Reisby's conversation. As for the Professor, he was in a mood of colossal jocularity. His laughter broke out in great bellowing explosions when he flung ridicule upon the ideas of Mr. Goy or cruelly imitated the manner of the Dean.

"These provincials!" he roared, filling up his tankard from a prodigious jug of ale, "these indocile provincials! 'Ah, my deah Professah, I have one just like it in the museum!' Goy, sir, is one of those amiable though obstructive blockheads who believe in the sanctity of the written label. Science does not know its debt to imagination—eh? Ha, ho! The moment he sticks his finicky label upon a thing, the nature of that thing is determined for all eternity. Sir, I should advise you not to keep a museum—it leads to paralysis! I suppose all the dust they inhale rises, in a subtle physiological way, to the higher centres. The institution mind—ha! Perhaps you may think I have a touch of it myself."

So he went on booming and roaring away, hugely jocose, until he had fairly broken down all the objections of my prejudice and all the barricades of my fear, and the whole company was laughing together in uncontrollable spasms of mirth.

3

Before Tuesday was over, my uneasiness had considerably abated. A wiser man, an older man, would have been more vigilant; but I was young, and I wanted to have a good time. Looking back, and remembering what happened afterwards, I do not see anything reprehensible in my behaviour.

There may have been a conflict in my mind, but I saw the propriety of taking Ellingham's advice and saying nothing to my cousin about the conversation I had so unwillingly overheard. Nor did I see anything to cause alarm, or even to justify suspicion, in the demeanour of Hilda Reisby and of Eric. They were frank and friendly in their outward relations to each other, and I hoped, in my innocence, that all danger was past and they had come to an honourable understanding.

Before Ellingham and I left Aberleven we had an interesting talk about Professor Reisby with two of his neighbours.

In the course of our digging at Caer Carrws, which lasted for six days, we made the acquaintance of Major and Mrs. Ugglesby-Gore. These people lived at Treddle Hall, about four miles from Aberleven. Of the Major's wife there is little to be said. She was a dainty, quiet little person, not embarrassed by a subtle intelligence, and therefore able to face life in a perfectly straightforward manner and with perfectly definite views.

Ugglesby-Gore was a bit of a character. You liked him or you detested him, according to your disposition. The very simple-minded people who did like Ugglesby-Gore were fond of saying, "Oh, he's just a big, overgrown boy!" while those who thought otherwise described him as "that unbearable ass," or even "that awful tipsy baboon." He was a fat, rollicking fellow of about fifty (retired or cashiered from the army—I forget which), whose voice came out of him in a throaty bubble and whose manners, though lacking in elegance, were patently sincere.

One evening, towards the end of the week, Ellingham proposed a glass of Mr. Morgan's ale before we retired for the night, and I accompanied him to the saloon bar of the hotel. Here we found Major Ugglesby-Gore and Mr. Morgan engaged in a friendly conversation over a bottle of brandy. The Major, bubbling out an incoherent though hearty welcome, invited us to share the brandy and the talk, and we accordingly sat down at the table. Naturally enough, we began to talk about the owner of Scarweather.

I could not help observing that Morgan's attitude was guarded, but the Major, who was never hampered by any kind of reserve, frankly delivered his own opinion.

"Dear old fella, Reisby!" he said in his peculiar chuckling rumble. "Of course I'm too much of a fool to understand him— always rather a fool, you know!—but such a dear old fella! Got an eye for a fine girl, too—astonishing, eh? Time of life and all that sort of thing, you know! To be frank with you—all friends here—Bertha was rather scandalised when he got married, but now she's awfully fond of Mrs. Reisby—charming woman—fairly dotes on dear old fella—what?"

I was a little shocked by the freedom of the Major's conversation in such a place and in such company, but he evidently treated Mr. Morgan as an equal. For his part, Mr. Morgan—a bluff, manly fellow—gave himself no airs; he was neither servile nor familiar, and he never spoke without a seemly consideration. I was beginning to like Mr. Morgan, and I liked him all the better for his reticence.

"I suppose you fellas know all about these ancient Britons and all that," said the Major, addressing himself to Ellingham more particularly, "but I'm such a fool—hadn't the vaguest idea of what they were talking about up at the old what's a name, I can assure you. Only came to please the dear old boy. Great fella with a shovel, what? Couldn't do it myself, damned if I could. Looks like a blessed old what's-a-name himself, doesn't he? Absolutely great! Why, I remember once, when his car ran back into a ditch, the dear old fella got out and simply heaved it back into the road again. I was coming along to help him—but oh no!—not a bit of it, thank you! Of course I don't understand you learned fellas when you're talking about those old flower-pots and things—too much of a fool, I can assure you. I'm afraid I'd rather see one of old Morgan's bottles, what? Of course I've never had any brains worth speaking of—so what's the use of pretending? You learned fellas beat me every time. But I say—have you seen old Reisby handling a boat?"

Ellingham said that we had been out fishing once or twice.

"Ah! that's not what I mean. You ought to see him sailing that little boat of his in a stiff breeze. By Gad!—it's wonderful! There he is in the stern, looking just like a blessed old what's-a-name, and away he goes. Have another? My dear fella, simply mustavanother!"

"Professor Reisby knows how to sail a boat," said Morgan. "I doubt if you could beat him with an open dinghy."

"He knows a good deal about ships and sailors, I believe," said Ellingham.

Morgan looked at him closely.

"May I ask, sir, have you known Professor Reisby for any length of time?" he said.

"I can hardly say that I know him at all," Ellingham replied, "but I regard him as one of the most interesting men I have ever met. My young friend's cousin, Mr. Foster, knows him far better than we do."

"Ah! I see," Mr. Morgan answered, and he stared thoughtfully at a photograph of Table Mountain which hung over the shabby piano in the bar.

When Ugglesby-Gore had left, and we were on the point of going up to our rooms, Ellingham surprised me by saying in a rather abrupt manner:

"Frankly, Mr. Morgan, what is your opinion of Professor Reisby?"

Equally to my surprise, Morgan was evidently embarrassed. He was putting the glasses and the half-empty bottle on a tray, and he paused, with an air of indecision by no means usual in a man of sturdy character.

"Well," he said at last, picking up the cork of the bottle and ramming it carefully into the neck, "he's a mystery."

And he gave Ellingham a hard, level, serious glance, which clearly implied: "That's all I am going to say. It is not very much, but you, a man of experience, will ascribe to my simple words their proper weight and meaning."

4

My visit to Aberleven lasted for exactly a fortnight. In thinking of it now it is not easy to dispel the memory of those tragic events which followed it, and so to reverse the shadow of those events and throw over the scene of my first visit a tinge of the horror which belongs to a later period. Actually there is no doubt that I enjoyed myself. The circumstances which I have brought out in this narrative were in themselves (apart from Eric's affair) of little importance, ambiguous or trivial. I can truly say that I had not the least premonition of disaster.

On our last morning at Aberleven there was, however, a final touch of mystery.

We were going along the path towards the headland when Ellingham touched my arm.

"Do you see that ship hove-to out there?" he said. "It's the *Emil Guntershausen* again."

I looked where he pointed, and I could see, far out on the grey water, the black hull, the dim sails of the barque.

Eric, who was going back with me to London on the following day, came to meet us.

"What a jolly morning!" he said, looking extremely well and happy. "I thought you fellows would come over in good time. We're all going out in the boats—all except the Professor, who has to run over to Northport. He's coming back after lunch and will join us. I say, he *is* a rum old chap! He was out in the boat at five o'clock this morning. I was awake and I looked out of my window and saw him coming back to the creek. Lord knows when he started or what he was doing. And now—would you believe it?—he's as fresh as a bird, roaring away all over the house, chaffing like mad, and says he's ready for any amount of work. Don't say anything about me seeing him, will you?"

I laughed, responding to the gaiety of Eric's mood. My other friend was rubbing his chin, but I was tired of suspicion (it was all so vague!) and I strode along joyously in the bright air of the morning.

PART II

The Mystery of the
Yeaverlow Bank

CHAPTER I

M Y NARRATIVE COMES NOW TO THE FATAL MONTH OF July 1914.

I had left the University and was living with my mother and sister at Richmond. In the autumn I was to begin my legal studies under the friendly guidance of my mother's cousin, Sir Alfred Barlock-Winterslade, K.C., and I was preparing myself by a course of hard reading. These details can be of no interest to the reader, and I mention them only to explain my situation at the time.

In view of the fact that both of us were hard at work, I had not seen much of Eric since I came down from Cambridge. He had an examination on the 16th of July, and was anxious not only to pass, but to pass with honour. We spent an occasional Sunday together at Richmond or Highgate. Anyone could see that Eric was less vivacious and more thoughtful than he was formerly, a change to be accounted for, one might suppose, by the increasing strain of his work.

We did not often refer to the Reisbys. There was no observable disinclination on the part of Eric to mention these people, but we did not seem drawn naturally towards this particular subject. Of course I was thinking far more about my work than I was about anything else, and if I still felt any alarm on Eric's account, that alarm was in a state of latency or dissolution.

Then, on the Sunday after his examination, Eric told me that he was going to spend a fortnight at Scarweather. He was going up on the 24th—a Friday.

I could see that he was peculiarly excited. It was not the happy rebounding excitement of one who is about to start on a holiday well earned by long and rewarded labour. It was rather the agitation of one who knows that he may soon be facing a peril. Such, at least, was my later interpretation of his mood, but I may have been wrong. The strain of the examination was over and, though he knew that he had done well, he was probably feeling the unavoidable recoil which follows intense and prolonged effort.

"It will be great fun," he said. "Old Reisby sent me a note. He says we shall have another digging, and may perhaps open some of the barrows."

"The Devil's Hump?" I said, trying to be cheerful.

"Oh, hardly! You know the incredible superstition of the folk up there. But I should very much like to have a look inside the Devil's Hump, I can tell you!"

"Anyhow, old fellow, you are sure to have a good time."

"Yes—rather! Only I wish you were coming too—you and Ellingham." There was a wistfulness in his tone which I did not understand. Was it really a premonition?

We had been for a walk over Hampstead Heath, and we said good-bye outside Miss Foster's house in the North Road.

Something prompted me to say:

"I may come up later, if there's room at the hotel, and if you think I should not be unwelcome."

"Bosh!" cried Eric, with a gladdening return of his old vivacity. "You need not be so damned ceremonious, need you? They would be delighted to see you, and you know it perfectly well. I shall send you a card."

"Right. I'll try to get away for a few days—unless we declare war on Germany, or anything of that sort!"

"We shall not be such damned idiots," said Eric.

I turned away, and I heard the clatter of the little iron gate closing behind him as he walked up the path to the house.

2

The telegram was brought to me just after breakfast on the morning of the 25th—Saturday. It had been sent from Aberleven at eight o'clock.

"Come at once. Eric lost, believe drowned. Police are now investigating. Reisby."

As I am not writing a personal history, but the history of a mysterious crime, it would be entirely out of place if I talked about my own emotions. It is my business to keep as closely as I can to the facts of the narrative. But the reader is not to suppose that my actions were really as cool, swift and efficient as they may appear to be on paper.

No purpose would be served if I attempted to describe the effect of this ghastly news upon the rest of the family. My mother and sister, shocked and amazed as they were, assisted me splendidly in my rapid preparations.

I rang up the Great Northern and found that a train for Northport started at 11.15. I also ascertained the time at which this train was due to arrive at Grantham. Next, I sent off two telegrams. The first of these was to Reisby, telling him that I was starting at once, giving the time of my arrival at Northport, and asking him to send a car for me. The second was to Ellingham, who was at his home in Cambridge. I gave him the news of the tragedy, and begged him, if it was possible, to join me at Aberleven. I also gave him the time at which the express was due to reach Grantham, though I hardly dared to hope that he would be able to meet me there. Not for a moment could I doubt that he would come to my assistance as quickly as means allowed. Indeed, I knew that he would feel himself personally concerned in this dreadful and mysterious affair.

While I was doing this, my mother and sister had packed a light suitcase for me, and within half an hour of receiving the news I had left Richmond and was on my way to King's Cross. We decided that my sister should visit Miss Foster in the afternoon, to find out if she had heard anything; or, if that was not the case, to break the news as gently as possible.

When my train ran alongside the platform at Grantham I looked eagerly out of the window. To my unspeakable joy and relief I saw the lean, vigilant face of my friend Ellingham—still the face of a young man, yet looking so old in thought and experience.

"My God, Farringdale!" he said, with a most unusual flicker of emotion, as he grasped my hand, "we're too late."

"Too late!" I said, while he settled himself in the carriage. "I cannot agree with you. We have not lost a moment. How did you manage to get here so quickly?"

"A friend of mine drove me in a fast car to Peterborough. There I got a train, and arrived here ten minutes before you were due." He was talking in his customary deliberate style. "Certainly we have not lost any time this morning. When I say that we are too late, I mean that we might have anticipated such a tragedy, even if it was not in our power to prevent it."

"But—my dear fellow!—how could we prevent an accident? Here—look at the telegram."

"This telegram," he said, after reading it, "tells us nothing. Eric is missing, and they believe he is drowned. That is all. We do not know *how* he came to be missing or *why* they should believe him drowned. There is nothing here to establish the fact of accident; every possibility is open."

For the first time since I had received the news a chilly trickle of horror began to permeate my thoughts.

"Do you mean—" I said; and even as I spoke the trickle was congealing rapidly in a firm suspicion.

There was another traveller in the carriage, and we could only talk in undertones. Indeed, there was little to be said. Ellingham would not listen to my expressions of gratitude.

"This is a matter," he said, "which concerns me deeply—perhaps more deeply than you imagine." He enquired as to my recent impressions of Eric, my knowledge of his affairs and so forth, and then he became silent.

At Northport we found Mr. Morgan himself with the car from the Aberleven hotel. Morgan was exceedingly grave, and from him we had our first account of the tragedy.

3

It will be best if I now give the facts of this extraordinary case as they were then generally known at Aberleven. Divested of rumour and exaggeration, those facts were comparatively simple.

Mrs. Reisby and her child were in Manchester, where Mrs. Reisby had been unexpectedly detained by her mother's illness. The child's nurse was away on holiday. Professor Reisby had written to his wife, informing her of the melancholy accident; it was assumed that she would return as soon as her mother was out of danger.

Eric had arrived at Northport by a late afternoon train on the previous day—the 24th. Professor Reisby, who had business in Northport, met him at the station with his car, and they drove home together. According to all who saw him, Eric was in excellent spirits, though looking rather tired. Professor Reisby formed the opinion that he had been working too hard, and he also believed him to have been worrying about some private concern.

After supper the young man was more cheerful. He listened with delight to the Professor's plan for excavating some of the barrows on Seidal Moor. He laughed heartily at the Professor's boisterous imitation of Mr. Goy. He declared himself to be immediately invigorated by the heady northern air, and he added that he would like to go for a swim. As it was then nine o'clock in the evening, the Professor dissuaded him from such an idea, for the water at that time was treacherously cold, and the flow of the incoming tide round the Yeaverlow Bank was decidedly awkward. They went out together for a late walk over the headland, and it was here that Eric repeated his desire for a swim in the hearing of Mr. Joe Lloyd.

Returning to the house, the two men sat in the study—in the right wing of the house, adjoining the laboratory or workshop. They were seen at ten o'clock by the housemaid when she brought them two glasses, a bottle of whisky, a bottle of gin and a siphon of soda-water. According to this woman, Eric was looking tired, but was talking briskly and happily.

At eleven o'clock, if the evidence of Reisby was correct, Eric went up to his bedroom, but the Professor remained in the study, occupied in the revision of a manuscript until about 12.30. He then retired. It was a moonless night, dark, with a fresh easterly breeze.

Nothing unusual was heard or observed by anyone in the house until about six o'clock in the morning, when a fisherman loudly knocked on the door.

Professor Reisby, slipping a coat over his pyjamas, came down to the door, and was told of an appalling discovery.

Three fishermen, including the one who was talking to Reisby, had set out from the harbour just after five o'clock. After rounding Scarweather Point, going fast with a steady breeze on the port bow, they saw an empty boat stranded on the Yeaverlow Bank. She had been left by the ebbing tide, but was on a ledge of sand close to deep water, and there was no difficulty in floating her again. The fishermen soon recognised this boat as the one belonging to Professor Reisby. The tide was now setting back towards the shore, the men took the derelict in tow and they had just fastened her up to her moorings in the creek. Inside the derelict were the boots and clothes of a gentleman, and a large bathing towel.

Without listening to another word, Reisby quickly ran to Eric's bedroom. It was empty. And not only was the room empty; the bed was undisturbed, the coverlet neatly turned back, the folded pyjamas on the pillow, as the housemaid had left them.

By this time another fisherman had come up from the creek. Hastily telling the men to wait, Reisby sent a telephone message to the police at Northport.

Such was the outline of this tragic mystery. I shall merely add one or two important considerations.

High tide, on the night of the 24th, was about half-past eleven. The full ebb was between 12.30 and 4.30. Reisby's boat, therefore, was probably stranded at some time between four and five o'clock in the morning. She was on the landward edge of the Bank, which is precisely where she would have been carried by the run of the tide. The five-fathom line passes close to the Bank, and the current here, when the tide is ebbing, has a very strong south-easterly set—that is, in a seaward direction. Any dead object, placed in the sea near the Bank at the time of the ebb, would either be stranded or quickly swept out into deep water. Eight years previously, a man had lost his life when swimming near the Yeaverlow sand; he had been observed by several people as he sank, but the body was never recovered. Other accidents had occurred in the dangerous currents off the Point.

In view of these local conditions it was quite possible to construct a theory explaining the total disappearance of a man who had been swimming from a boat off the Yeaverlow Bank. Let us assume that he had jumped out of the boat not far below Scarweather Point and had then swum in a northerly direction across the tide. His intention would be to swing round, facing the shore, and so let the current assist him in returning to the boat. When still on his northerly course he was overtaken by cramp or fatigue. Once his body was carried past the north-east edge of the Bank it would rapidly drift out in the main coastal current and would soon be in ten fathoms of water. His boat, in the meantime, would run aground on the north-west corner of the Bank.

This theory, or some form of it, was the one eventually adopted by the police, and it was accepted by the majority of the people in Aberleven.

But—why on earth should Eric have sat in his room until three or four o'clock in the morning, and then slipped away in the chilly dawn for a swim off Scarweather Point?

We could do so little, on the evening of our arrival, except listen to the story and give a few essential particulars to the police. Reisby appeared to be almost overcome with grief. He was grey and haggard, and he kept on repeating, "Ah! I ought to have kept an eye on that boy, I ought to have kept an eye on him! I ought to have seen the traces of nervous exhaustion. I ought to have anticipated the possibility of abnormal behaviour."

Ellingham was inscrutable. When I came down to breakfast on the following morning (Sunday, the 26th) I was told that he had gone out as soon as the door was unlocked, at about 6.30, and that he had not yet returned. He came in soon after nine o'clock, merely observing that he had been for a most refreshing walk, and that he felt all the better for it.

"Ellingham," I said as we were having breakfast, "tell me frankly what you think about this terrible affair."

"I am as much in the dark as you are," he replied gloomily.

"But you can at least say if you believe that poor Eric was drowned when he was having a swim."

"I can make no other suggestion."

His manner was almost querulous, and I could see that he was engaged by a perplexing train of thought.

It was a wretched, a lamentable day. Ellingham assisted me to get through all the necessary and gruesome formalities with the police—among them the examination of Eric's belongings at Scarweather.

There was only one thing among these pitiful relics to which we could attach any significance, and that was a very extraordinary letter which we found in a pocket of his coat. The address at the top of the letter was that of a street in Hackney, and it was written in a sprawling foreign hand. The date was the 23rd of July. Here is the letter as nearly as I can remember it:

> Dear Mr. Foster,
>
> No longer can it go on. I am in a desperation. If you won't do anything the game is up. What you were afraid of will happen very soon. I tell you the truth. The other day you were in time because you acted quick. Now it is up to you again. Your great responsibility in this matter do you realise? Remember the talk in Gower Street. Remember what Karl said. The dreadful day is near if you will not take a step for its aversion. I am very sad because I don't want for you to have this awful responsibility. But Karl says there is nothing else to be done. You understand. Soon it will be too late and then will be the end of your life of happiness. So for love of God do what I ask you.
>
> Your friend,
>
> LUDWIG MACKENRODE.

The police did not consider this letter of any real importance, but suggested that we might undertake a private investigation. I was not a little surprised to find that Ellingham agreed with this point of view, for I thought the letter was extraordinary, menacing, and really sinister.

Eventually it was decided that I should return to London on Tuesday. I was to convey the necessary information to the family and its legal representatives, and I might also call at the address in Hackney and see if I could find out anything about Ludwig Mackenrode. As soon as I had got through my melancholy business I was to come back to Aberleven, where Ellingham, in the meanwhile, intended to remain.

We still hoped that information might be derived from some unexpected local source—possibly from the skipper of a Northport fishing-boat, who might have been near Scarweather in the early hours of Saturday morning. One or two of these boats were reported to be still at sea. It was possible—remotely possible—that Eric had been rescued by one of these boats.

In any case, Ellingham had made up his mind to stay at Aberleven for a few days longer. Of what was passing through his mind I had no knowledge whatever. I had never known him so uncommunicative or seen him look so grim and surly. He was evidently baffled, and there could be no doubt that he was refusing to accept the obvious explanation of the tragic event.

"Yes," he said in reply to my question, "you had better go back to London and do as you propose. I will keep an eye on things here, and will inform you by telegram of any development. Probably I shall not require assistance."

Grateful as I was for the mere fact of his presence and activity, I was offended by the curtness of his manner.

"Ellingham," I said, quite aware of displaying annoyance, "I do wish you would let me know what you are thinking about."

"Mere thinking is of no use in this particular case, unless it leads to the discovery of evidence."

"But you have a theory?"

He groaned. "My dear young friend, I am not one of those gifted amateur detectives who are now becoming so fashionable. If I concern myself in what has every appearance of being a mystery, it is partly for your sake, and partly because it is a matter in which I do feel personally involved. It is necessary to be careful. I have already spoken of the appearance of mystery, and that, in itself, is hardly discreet. Actually, I am not prepared to say that your cousin was accidentally drowned, and as long as I am in that position it would be futile or dangerous or painful to talk about theories. My training and my habits of thought are those of a scientist. No scientist is worthy of the name if he is content to build up a hypothesis on simple intuition or guesswork. When he has definite evidence, even if the final proof is lacking, he may venture to put forward a theory, in order that others may be able to check, establish or disprove his contention. In such a case as the one we are now investigating idle gossip would have pernicious or damnable consequences, and might even prevent any real enquiry."

"Cannot you trust me to hold my tongue?"

"That is not the point. I have to consider my own conscience and my own respect for method, as well as your subsequent attitude to innocent people. I have to be fair, not merely scientific. Believe me, Farringdale,"—he smiled in a more kindly manner—"the moment I have anything of real consequence to impart, I shall impart it without hesitation. At present there is nothing. As I said, I am quite as much in the dark as you are."

No obstruction to enquiry was due to Professor Reisby himself. On the contrary, he was anxious that we should examine any place or detail with complete freedom.

We could see that Eric, who was quite familiar with the Professor's house, would have no difficulty in leaving it without disturbing anyone. In addition to the front and back doors, there was a door leading out of the study in the west wing. This door was found unfastened on Saturday morning, but the Professor could not say if he had locked it before going to bed. He frequently overlooked or forgot such things, and the housemaid stated that she often found both front and west doors unlocked in the morning.

Our examination of the boat afforded no clue whatever. She had been merely hauled up on the slipway on Friday afternoon, and could easily have been slid into the water.

Eric, as we knew, had been in the habit of bathing from this boat and allowing it to drift while he swam on the ebbing tide. He never swam to any great distance or for any length of time, and he was not a strong or rapid swimmer. The clothes found in the boat were those which had been worn by Eric when he arrived, together with a heavy overcoat, a muffler and a brown cloth hat. No bathing-suit was found among his belongings, though it was almost certain that he would have brought one.

The spare bedroom, which had been occupied by Eric, was in the west wing of the house, over the study. The rooms used by the Professor and Mrs. Reisby were in the centre of the house, and the maids' rooms were in the east wing. One of the maids declared that she was roused by a sound in the house just before dawn; but the sound and her memory appeared to be equally vague, and she had gone to sleep again almost at once.

In the spare bedroom itself there was only one circumstance which yielded a little information. The light in the room had been provided by an oil reading-lamp, placed on a table near the bed. This lamp had been filled by the housemaid on Friday afternoon, and the level of the oil indicated that it had been burning for nearly five hours—that is until about four o'clock in the morning.

Our evidence, however inadequate, led to the conclusion that poor Eric's death had been due to a most unlucky caprice. He had been too restless to go to bed, and had probably been sitting up reading until dawn. It then occurred to him that he would slip out of the house and refresh himself by an early swim. Perhaps he had only taken the boat down to the mouth of the creek, in order to reach the deep and sheltered water below the Point. Such behaviour was erratic, though by no means unaccountable.

So might the voice of reason dictate, but reason does not always prevail in the human mind, and I could not dislodge from the centre of my own mind a residue of persisting doubt.

4

We spent Sunday evening in Mr. Morgan's private parlour, which our host very kindly placed at our disposal. Here we received a visit from that good-natured imbecile, Major Ugglesby-Gore.

One could not be offended by the friendly if slightly obtrusive gurgitation in which he told us of his deep sympathy.

"You fellas will understand—know what a fool I am—can't express things like you fellas do—but really frightfully sorry for you fellas, and so is Bertha, and everybody. Saw Macwardle this afternoon—been talking to Chief Constable on telephone—police realise accident, of course. Mustn't have any bother. Poor old Reisby, too! Simply shocking for dear old fella. What? Mustn't bother him, must we?—couldn't have prevented accident. Awful shock—boat nearly gone, and all that. I say, do you fellas mind if I ring the bell and ask Morgan to bring us a bottle of that Hennessy? Jolly good idea—what?"

5

Next morning, just before breakfast, I was on the neat little square of grass in front of the hotel, looking seaward. It was a day of bright and lively weather, a keen off-shore breeze from the north-west making the sea run merrily down the coast in a dapple of blue and white. I watched a noble ship under a full spread of canvas, heading south. She had the wind on her starboard quarter, and every now and then, when she heeled over in a gust, I could see the flash of copper below her waterline. Flowing out from the mizen peak was a string of coloured flags.

"Do you recognise that boat, sir?"

Morgan had come out from the hotel and was standing behind me with a pair of glasses in his hand.

"I'm not sure, Mr. Morgan. Is it the German barque?"

"Yes, that's her." He looked through his glasses.

"And what is the signal she's flying?"

"Ah! what is it?—that's just the point, sir. Her signals are in a private code, and there's nobody here can tell you what they mean. Odd, isn't it? Because, you see, if she runs up a signal she must intend somebody to take notice of it."

CHAPTER II

I

I AM BOUND TO SAY THAT I DREADED THE RETURN OF HILDA Reisby. In fact, I definitely hoped that her mother would be so frightfully ill that she could not return until we had left Aberleven.

In psychological jargon, I had got a complex about Mrs. Reisby. I liked her, I was even moderately fond of her, but I could not help feeling that she was indirectly responsible for what had happened. She had allowed Eric to know that she was by no means indifferent to his affection, and she had, presumably, allowed him to come again to Scarweather. With all the fatuous precision of my youthful mind, I decided that she had been acting unwisely.

On Monday morning the Professor received a telegram from his wife announcing her return in the afternoon. I thought I would go over and see her after supper, but I got a note at the hotel from Mrs. Reisby herself, soon after five o'clock, asking me to go round immediately if I was free.

I found her waiting for me in the drawing-room, alone. Decidedly awkward, I thought. All my life I have dreaded emotional scenes, particularly with a woman. They are so unbecoming, and they usually destroy those fine decorums on which we have come to depend for our social comfort.

However, there was no cause for alarm. Mrs. Reisby was cool, dignified, and eminently practical. She asked me what arrangements I intended to make, what were my views and those of Ellingham. Her sorrow was expressed in a gentle, measured voice, so low, so controlled, that I wondered if she were really heartless. Well!—it was better than a sobbing effusion! Then I saw that she was trembling, and I felt ashamed of myself and really very miserable. She was pale, too, and that made her look magnificent in a tragic sort of way.

"Mr. Farringdale," she said, "there is one thing I want to tell you. I did not ask your cousin to come here. My husband sent the invitation after I had gone to stay with my mother, and I knew nothing about it. Apparently your cousin was not able to come immediately. He did not come when Tolgen expected him, but several days later. Please do not ask me to explain my reason for telling you this. I think you ought to know: that is all."

"You did not know—" I stammered.

"Not until I got my husband's letter this morning."

She took a handkerchief from the table by her side, and I saw that she was nervously twisting it up into a ball.

This change in her manner, and this unexpected communication, made me feel uncomfortable. I could not put my thoughts in order, and I observed with dismay that she was looking suddenly forlorn and wretched. There might be a scene, after all.

"Mrs. Reisby," I said, "I am dreadfully sorry for you."

Her calmness returned, though not without a visible effort. There was a moment of silence, and in the silence we could hear, coming through the open window, the dismal note of the bell on the Scarweather buoy.

"Thank you, Mr. Farringdale."

Simple words, even conventional or trivial words, are often associated with memorable events in our lives. The tone of Mrs. Reisby's voice when she said "Thank you" made me look at her with an unaccountable degree of warm sympathy and of rapid understanding. When you are only twenty-one, you cannot be entirely unaffected by the sight of a beautiful, noble and youthful woman in distress. And yet I had been afraid of meeting her! All that can be said in my favour is that I was very young and that I had never consciously fallen in love.

Of course I told Ellingham what Mrs. Reisby had said, and he was evidently interested.

"Oh, indeed!" he remarked, with a quick flicker of his eyebrows. "Do you know if the Professor was in the habit of writing to your cousin?"

"He had written before, I think."

"Frequently?"

"I cannot say."

"On archæological matters?"

"Yes—as far as I recollect."

"You saw the letters?"

"One or two of them."

"And they were friendly—familiar?"

"Certainly. Why do you want to know?"

He did not answer my question.

2

On Tuesday the 28th I returned to London. I managed to get through a good deal of family business on the evening of the same day, including a painful interview with Miss Foster. But I shall relate only what is essential.

The morning of the 29th was mainly occupied with legal business, and it was not until the early afternoon that I had time for the enquiry concerning Ludwig Mackenrode.

I knew that Ellingham was not greatly interested in this man, whoever he might be, and I was determined to show him that I was not incapable of conducting an important investigation without his advice or encouragement.

As I gave my taxi-driver the address in Hackney I thought he looked at me with considerable surprise. He conveyed me, at length, to a sordid, melancholy row of tenements and obscure lodging-houses, palpably disreputable. I felt a little uneasy as I rapped at the door of No. 27.

The head of an untidy young woman appeared in the lower window of the adjoining house. Her cheeks were brightly coloured, and she gave me a most repulsive wink. Other heads appeared at other windows, and I stood miserably on the doorstep, aware that I was blushing and entirely without confidence. A group of slatternly women, chattering in a doorway on the other side of the street, became suddenly silent and eyed me with offensive curiosity. A man walking along the pavement with a cage full of twittering bullfinches whistled in a manner decidedly sarcastic. I began to wish that I had given a little more thought to the matter. But now there was no help for it.

I knocked again, resolutely fixing my gaze upon the blistered green panels of the door. A heavy tread came down the staircase, and the door was opened by a police inspector.

Naturally I was surprised, though really glad to see him. I considered myself, already, to be an embryo representative of the law; and there was something particularly grateful in this image of respectability.

He looked at me sharply, and with evident suspicion. I have a horrid notion that he took me for a newspaper reporter.

"What is your business here?" he said.

"I have come to enquire about Mr. Ludwig Mackenrode."

"Is he a friend of yours?"

"No."

"Then what are you enquiring about?"

"Well—as a matter of fact—look here, inspector, can't we go inside the house?"

Spectators were now assembling in every window or halting by every door.

"No, sir, it's no good. You can't see Mr. Mackenrode."

"Why not?"

"He's dead—that's why."

I was painfully shocked, and then I felt a glow of excitement, not unmingled with importance.

"But I have a letter from this man, written only a few days ago."

"Oh! Then you'd better show it to me. Here—Mrs. Pingle—I want to see this gentleman alone in the parlour for a few minutes. Come in, sir."

The explanation was brief. Of course the inspector, a dull though not incapable fellow, saw nothing remarkable in the death or disappearance of poor Eric, but he said the coroner would certainly require Mackenrode's letter, and I must hand it over and make a statement and so forth.

"It's an ordinary suicide," he said, "if I'm not mistaken. The doctor is upstairs with my sergeant. Mackenrode was nearly starving. He's a German student from Hamburg. About twenty-five. Working at the British Museum. We often get this kind of thing. Cyanide. No friends in particular. No letters from the gentleman you were mentioning. Nothing at all. Good character. Relatives poor. That's all I can tell you. Troublesome cases—usually Germans or Russians. Another about a week ago. Now I shall have to get on with it. Your permanent address, if you please—"

That was all. I could get no further information, nor could I talk to the dithering landlady who fluttered about in the passage and wiped her eyes on a dirty apron. As I left the house a police ambulance, a black and sinister vehicle, drove up to the door.

So it was a common occurrence, and they were mostly Germans and Russians! It was a very depressing thought. I could not help wishing that poor Herr Mackenrode had not been so precipitate, had at least waited until I had seen him. Perhaps he only needed a few pounds or a little encouragement. I was overcome, nauseated, by the squalor, the wretchedness of the whole affair. What had Eric to do with this unfortunate youth?

I wondered if his old aunt, Miss Tallard Foster, knew anything about it. In any case I had promised to call on her again before I went back to Aberleven. I got a taxi in Hare Street and went on to Highgate.

3

Miss Foster was a kindly, intelligent old woman. She had for many years kept house for her brother, a district magistrate in

India, and after his death in 1899 she had come back to England and bought the house at Highgate in which she continued to live for the rest of her life. Eric's parents had been well known to her during her residence in India, and she had undertaken the charge of the orphan as a matter of course. Her affection for Eric had been that of a kind, vicarious mother, and she had jealously preserved all the privileges of guardianship. Miss Foster was one of those women who have an extensive, though partly fanciful, knowledge of their own families; she had a singular practice of referring to absent, imaginary or defunct relatives. Like many other spinsters, her view of life was essentially a family view: her interests and affections were almost wholly occupied by the Royal Family and her own. But she was no fool. Indian society had not left her ignorant of the ways of intrigue and of the manners or morals of ambitious men. She had a steady head and a cool judgment, and a will that no person in the world could ever force to surrender. She was, in fact, one of those immensely valuable old women who contribute so much to the honour, stability or charm of English life. Her little fresh-coloured face was dignified, serenely vital. Her voice, her manners, were those of an aristocrat. She dressed in clothes of an indescribable Victorian complexity, with glittering spangles of black jet and sundry intricate masses of lace.

Private sorrow is not a theme on which I can willingly dwell. I will therefore relate only those parts of my conversation with Miss Foster which are strictly relevant to this narrative.

She had never heard of Ludwig Mackenrode. Eric was a lad of a singularly generous nature, and it was quite likely that he would help a poor student. He had several friends—most of them medical students—who used to visit him at Highgate. They were all very nice young men. (As if he would bring to his aunt's house anyone who was *not* a nice young man!)

"He was very like dear George," said Miss Foster, "with a touch of dear Henry's excessive caution." Evidently she had resigned herself to the idea of his death.

"But you know, John," she told me, "I was rather troubled by his liking for Mrs. Reisby. She came here once or twice. I'm not inquisitive or nasty-minded, but I could not help seeing they were very fond of each other."

"What did you think of her?"

Miss Foster was trying to be fair. She nodded her little head up and down in silence, and then she said decidedly:

"In my time a young married woman would not have allowed herself so much freedom. I cannot imagine dear Mary or dear Constance behaving in such a way."

"But surely, Aunt Muriel, her manners—"

"Her manners were quite perfect. I don't mean anything of that sort. Anyone can see that she's a lady, and that's why she ought to know better."

"Better—how?"

"Well, I think she was quite wrong in going about with Eric—going to theatres and that sort of thing. Perhaps, dear John, you are too young to realise my point of view, and I should be sorry to put unjust or foolish ideas into your head. Indeed, poor Mrs. Reisby is very young too; but then she's a married woman, and that makes all the difference."

"I'm sure they were only thinking of each other as great friends."

The old lady smiled sadly, dabbed the corner of a lace hand-kerchief into her eyes, and replied with gentle resignation:

"He may have thought so."

Remembering what I actually knew, I felt it was almost treach-erous not to agree with her. But I also felt myself called on—I could not have said for what particular reason—to defend strenu-ously the honour of Mrs. Reisby.

"I could almost swear there was nothing wrong in it, Aunt Muriel."

"You remind me of dear Richard, your uncle, when you talk like that. So eager to convince! You'll make a fine barrister, John."

"Do, please, believe me—"

"I am quite anxious to believe you, but since you are the chief representative of the family in this matter I am obliged to tell you frankly what I think. Of course my views are not of much impor-tance now—and yet—well, well! it is all very strange. I cannot help wishing that dear Roger was here to give us his advice. But I know, dear John,"—here she lightly touched my hand—"that you will do everything that is necessary and proper."

"Aunt Muriel, do you know if Mrs. Reisby wrote to Eric?"

"That is what I wanted to ask you. The poor dear boy has not left many private things, but there is a box full of letters and papers. I do not wish to look at them. What do you think we ought to do?"

"I think we ought to seal the box and hand it over to the law-yers. They will open it when it is legally assumed that Eric is dead."

"She did write to him. I know that, because he used to tell me about her letters. Professor Reisby also wrote. It was the Professor, you know, who sent him the invitation."

"But the Professor had written more than once?"

"Several times, I fancy. I have no distinct recollection. He wrote about things they were digging up. He appears to have been very fond of Eric."

"And Eric was very fond of the Reisbys—both of them."

"Yes, yes! I know. He was always talking about them and saying how wonderful they were."

"There's one other thing, Aunt Muriel. Do you think Eric was being worried in any way? Of course he had been working very hard, and he may have been slightly overstrained. What I mean is, did he seem to have anything on his mind?"

She gave me a sad yet penetrating glance.

"No—that's impossible," she said, answering my thoughts instead of my words.

"He was quite happy?"

"He had not been quite happy since he came home after that Easter visit. He was oddly excited. But I do not think there was anything on his mind—anything to make him—to make him abnormal."

She asked me if I would care to look at his room, but I said I would rather not. The idea of seeing that room with all its pathetic reminders touched a chord of acute sensibility which I had never suspected.

It was not easy to continue the conversation. I said that I should return to London as soon as I was quite satisfied that nothing more could be done at Aberleven. That really meant, "When they have given up all hope of recovering the body." She understood.

"I know you will do what is best, my dear John. You are a curious mixture of dear Henry and your dear Uncle Rupert, with a

touch of dear Fanny's confidence. But please—please get one idea
out of your mind, and refuse to allow it, even as a theory. Nobody
knew Eric as well as I did. He was a good boy. His death, however
it came about, was not a voluntary death. Of that I am certain."

4

On Thursday, the 30th of July, I was back at Aberleven.

Nothing had occurred in my absence which could throw any
light on the mystery, or the tragedy. The police regarded it as a
simple bathing accident, and had no intention of investigating
any further. It was considered highly improbable that the body
would be washed ashore, and all the local boats which were out
on Friday night had now returned to harbour. People had been
carefully watching all along the coast, and all the fishermen
were keeping a sharp look-out near the Bank. The idea that Eric
might have been picked up by a coasting vessel was not seriously
entertained by anyone.

I told Ellingham about my investigation of the Mackenrode
case, and I was not a little chagrined to perceive his lack of interest.

"Very distressing, my good young friend," he said in a dry and
rather casual manner, "but unrelated to our problem."

"Ah!—then you still regard it as a problem?"

"Of course I do. Whatever is not consistent with ordinary
occurrence or with ordinary behaviour is a problem."

"But what can we do?"

"Judging from all the obviously bellicose intentions of all the
European powers, including ourselves, we shall soon have more
than enough to do in another field of action. If we can stay here

for a day or two longer I propose to conclude certain investigations in which I am now engaged—including one which has nothing whatever to do with our main problem. I also propose that we should both have a final interview with Professor Reisby."

"So you think Mackenrode's letter was of no consequence?"

"It was of tremendous consequence to him, poor fellow; but not to us. He was in dire need of a little money in order to keep himself alive, and he was contemplating suicide."

"And that is all—that is the whole explanation of the letter?"

"It is a perfectly rational explanation. Your cousin had probably been kind to him. Mackenrode was making his last appeal. It is very sad, though definitely outside the orbit of our immediate affairs."

I was not at all satisfied. With all my respect for Ellingham's remarkable intelligence, his immense knowledge, the subtlety and range of his observation, I felt he was dismissing the matter too lightly. It did not fit in with any theory of his own, and he therefore rejected it. Whether I was right or wrong will be seen later. I asked him about the Reisbys.

"Professor Reisby has apparently recovered from the shock. He is a man of a tremendously robust mental constitution. And he is very much occupied, at present, with his book on *Burials of Prehistoric Date in the North of England*. I have been able to provide him with some photographs." He chuckled, though I could see nothing funny in what he said.

"Mrs. Reisby," he continued, "looks ill. I am very sorry for her. She seems to blame herself in some way. The child and the nurse have not yet returned."

"So there is no development."

"None whatever."

He looked at me closely, rubbed his chin, and evidently decided that it would be inhumane to keep me entirely in the dark with regard to his own activities.

"You know that fellow Joe Lloyd—'Dollar' they call him?"

"Yes."

"Well, he's quite a mystery in himself. Nobody knows much about him—not even the police. He's a native of Liverpool. For some time he was a Grimsby fisherman, and then he served in ships of the Macfarren Line. Certain dark and adventurous years of his life appear to have been spent in South America. He came here about six years ago, just when the cottage he is now living in happened to be vacant. There is not, and apparently there never has been, a Mrs. Lloyd of any description. He never drinks anything stronger than tea, lives quietly, never quarrels, and seems to be an unusual character—and an unusually bad character."

"He's a sinister-looking man, but I see nothing definitely bad in what you have told me."

"Ah! but listen. He does a little fishing, and he does a little work for Reisby—whether gardening or excavation. He cannot earn a living by such casual employment. And yet he is never short of cash. He is able to buy good things if he wants them—boat or tackle, clothes, furniture and so forth. He has a very well-made suit of clothes and a bowler hat, which he wears on Sundays, and also when he goes on a trip to Northport, where he spends occasionally a few days in a respectable lodging-house. A lot of his time is frittered away in strolling on the cliffs or moors. Reisby appears to be very fond of him; they are frequently seen together, both afloat and ashore. Now, in my opinion, that is flagrantly suspicious. Indeed, I may say that you have here all the elements, all the classic elements, of a real blood-and-thunder mystery."

"You are joking."

"God forbid, my dear fellow. When you are as old as I am, you will learn not to despise the obvious. I do honestly believe the fellow is a rogue. If Reisby knows anything about the disappearance of your cousin which he has not told us, I will make bold to say that Mr. Lloyd knows it as well."

"Do you mean—"

"I mean no more than I say."

"But you cannot suppose that Reisby is concealing anything."

"Why not?"

"Good heavens, Ellingham!"

"Steady, steady, my dear young friend! Let there be no dramatic surprise. I am only affirming my right to suppose anything which is not wholly unreasonable."

"And you think it is not wholly unreasonable to suppose that Reisby knows more than he has told us?"

"I say that it is not unreasonable to suppose that he *may* know more than he has told us."

"Ellingham, do you believe that is really the case?"

He did not answer immediately.

We were down on the shingle beach below the hotel, after dinner on the evening of my return. The sun was low behind us, and there was a soft, hazy diffusion of light over a pallid sea. A low droning note from the bell on the Yeaverlow buoy vibrated faintly over the water. Unseen below the island a boat was getting under way, with a whining of blocks and a hollow rattle of gear. Ellingham was looking down at the shingle. He stooped, and I saw him pick up a tiny fragment of white bone, worn very smooth and hard by the action of the sea.

"Well, John," he said quietly, "you know the habits of my mind. I am afraid—perhaps ridiculously afraid—of mere conjecture. But in this case I am impelled to think, almost to believe, that Reisby has a reason for concealing something which he does definitely know about the death of your cousin."

"I think so too," I said, and I was rather shocked by my own equanimity.

"My opinion does not rest merely upon conjecture," said Ellingham, "it has been forced upon me by certain observations, gradually overcoming my obstinate rationality. But let me hasten to add, that I have no idea of *what* he knows, or of his motive in concealing his knowledge, and that I do not wish to imply, for one moment, that he is concealing anything criminal."

He was drawing back into his impenetrable shell of caution, and I saw that it would be useless to ask any further questions.

We strolled along the shingle for a few yards, the rounded grey and black pebbles rolling noisily under our feet.

"Ah, ha!" said Ellingham, pointing seaward, "look at those ugly fellows over there."

Under a level brown smear of heavy smoke three battle-cruisers were steaming in line.

"The navy is on the move already," said Ellingham. "For how many days, or hours, can we be sure of peace? Behind us, in this quiet land, people are living and working without a thought of danger, without a vision of the sudden ghastly plunge—" He frowned, and then looked again at the ships—long turreted hulls, away on the hard edge of a clear horizon.

"Our private investigations may soon be rudely interrupted, my friend. As it is, I propose to go back on Monday, at latest. A final interview with Reisby, and there is nothing more to be done. Officially, legally, and for all ordinary purposes, we accept a theory of accidental death."

5

Now, this talk, impinging as it did upon the rapid emergence or development of a train of thought in my own mind, had a very disturbing result.

Probably I was over-excited by the events and emotions of the past week, and when I went to bed in the hotel I could not sleep for many hours. I woke, or fancied I woke, soon after dawn.

There was a dim, bluish light in the room, faintly illuminating the bunches of ribbons and roses on the wall-paper, revealing in livid rotundity the ugly jug and basin, glinting in a steely line down the polished edge of the wardrobe. Then I was aware of a sudden blankness, an opacity, the interposition of a flat white plane, between me and the wall; it was like a square of dull, frosted glass, lighted evenly from behind, and it was hanging or hovering in the air of the room without any visible support. I looked at this marvel without any feeling of alarm, but with intense curiosity. It was a thing so unreal and unreasonable that it seemed futile to imagine what it could be. I accepted it as one does accept any ridiculous thing in a dream, and yet I had the impression of being awake and of recognising the objects in the room. And then, on this white illuminated plane—it was about three feet square—a little moving scene began to form itself, as though projected by a miniature cinematograph. It was clear, sharp, and in the ordinary colours of life, but there was no sound.

Evidently the scene was taking place at the actual time, about sunrise. There was a rippling though placid sea, blue and amber in the early light, and a grey edge of gentle surf breaking on a sandbank. Then a cormorant flew across the field of vision, a solitary dark bird; and then everything began to slide away to the right, and all at once the blunt outline of Scarweather Point rammed into the centre of the view, the sliding movement came to an end, and I saw a boat coming towards me.

Professor Reisby was rowing the boat, and in the stern of it sat my cousin Eric, wearing an overcoat and a muffler. Presently the boat occupied a large part of the scene, and the invisible projector began to follow it. Both men were talking and laughing. Presently the Professor pulled his oars back along the thwart of the boat; Eric stood up and took off his coat and muffler; he was in his bathing-dress, ready for a swim.

I knew that something horrible was going to happen, and I could feel a creeping moisture over my face. Eric stood up in the stern sheets, he looked back at his companion with a smile, and then he raised his arms to dive. Reisby suddenly rose and struck him with terrible violence on the back of the neck. My cousin fell, first of all, in a crumpled heap over the gunwale, and then he slipped into the water.

Had I been able to do so, I should have screamed with terror—though knowing all the time that I was looking at an unsubstantial image—but there was a tightness and a dryness in my throat which prevented me.

Then I saw another boat coming round the headland. Professor Reisby saw it too, and he made a signal with his arm. The other boat was rowed by Joe Lloyd. My agitation was too great for careful or deliberate observation, and I cannot give an exact account of what followed. Both boats were rowed towards the sandbank; then Reisby, abandoning his own boat, was quickly brought back to the creek by Lloyd. He landed on a platform of rock, which I recognised immediately, not far below his house. I went on staring at the scene, or whatever it was, until the whole thing began to flicker, blur, dissolve; the roses and ribbons of the wall-paper came through it, and it was gone.

Feeling sick and bewildered I jumped out of bed—I cannot say that I *woke*—filled a tumbler with water and hastily drank it. I remember how my teeth clicked and rattled on the rim of the glass.

After this, I was aware of returning to a state of normal perception, and I was ready enough to call myself a fool and a dreamer. But there was a harsh photographic reality in what I had seen; it was like a record of some actual event, it had the appearance of absolute verity. Perhaps it was the irrepressible picture of my own doubts or suspicions, emerging brutally and refusing compromise.

After breakfast I told Ellingham about this experience, or dream, and he listened with considerable sympathy, if not with interest.

"Now look here, my dear lad," he said, "the very best thing you can do to-day is to go for a good long walk over the moors, alone. There is nothing like it for clearing the mind and filling you with a freshening draught of wholesome and vigorous life. You have had a view of your own disordered fancy. Get rid of it. Open air under the open heavens—communion with nature—that's what you need. Forgive me if I seem officious, or even paternal."

It was impossible to say when this peculiar man was joking or when he was in earnest. I replied somewhat angrily:

"Too bad, Ellingham!—I didn't fancy anything of the sort."

"Very well, then. We will not enquire about the mechanism of dreams. We will suppose that Providence has been treating you to a private view of a little experiment in cinematographics. Why not?"

"But suppose, instead, that something of the kind really did happen. There have been cases—"

"Cases of what? Of the vivid externalisation of ideas! If you suppose that something of the kind really did happen, I can only say that I regard it as extremely improbable. I could spend an hour or two in overwhelming you with objections. But I shall do nothing of the kind. I shall see that you are provided with a packet of sandwiches, and I shall then dispatch you on a solitary and a salutary walk, lending you, for purposes of observation, my excellent glasses. By the way, I should be glad to know if you see any oyster-catchers on the flats. You know the little fellows with red legs."

CHAPTER III

I

FRIDAY WAS UNEVENTFUL. I TOOK ELLINGHAM'S GOOD advice and spent the greater part of the day on the coast and the moors.

Before starting I asked Ellingham to convey to the Reisbys the information—or the lack of information—which I had discovered in the course of my London visit. When I came back, I was told that the Reisbys had invited us to supper.

It seemed to me that our relations with Professor and Mrs. Reisby were a little strained. Certainly the massive intelligence of the Professor had now recovered from the shock; and although he was too polite or too discreet to say so, he was evidently surprised by our continued stay at Aberleven. All hope of recovering the body was now abandoned. At the same time, if anything did come to light, we could be summoned quickly by a telegram. In the meanwhile, there was nothing to be done except remove my poor cousin's belongings and hand them over to Miss Foster. The police had informed themselves of the names and the destinations of two vessels which had sailed from Northport on the fatal morning: these vessels were still at sea, but the hope that either of them could give us any news was faint indeed. As for the Chief Constable and the Coroner, they had both decided that no further investigation was possible. It was a bathing accident—most regrettable, but clearly an accident. There had been similar cases, equally regrettable. They might consider the erection of a suitable notice on the cliffs. With appropriate delicacy, the Chief Constable offered his condolence, not only to the relatives of the unfortunate visitor, but also to Professor and Mrs. Reisby.

Ellingham announced our intention of leaving on Sunday afternoon at latest. He asked if we might come over on the following morning, to collect Eric's things and have a final talk on this melancholy subject. Professor Reisby immediately agreed, though it seemed to me that he did so with a touch of petulance.

There was a change, an observable change, in the Professor's manner. He was not inhospitable, he was not rude, but he made one feel aware of some formidable, tough and ruthless quality, not actively hostile, but large with a ponderous imminence of opposition.

Of course jocularity could hardly be expected, and it may have been the absence of this which gave Reisby a new appearance—Jupiter with his earthquaking merriment had gone, and we saw before us the brooding, furrowed countenance of a Saturn. We heard no longer the frequent Ah, ho! and the odd rhythmic humming; he spoke in a deep and measured voice, pompous and even oracular.

I did not understand Hilda Reisby. She was pale, ominously calm. One felt that she was keeping herself under severe control, and that she was always glad when she could reasonably get up and leave the room. She looked at me sometimes with a firm, enquiring gravity, as if she wanted to ask a question. Once, when she spoke about Miss Foster, she was obviously on the point of crying. I think she wanted to see me alone, but again I felt a cowardly, unreasonable wish to avoid her. It was really shameful, but I simply could not help it. Perhaps I did not realise that I was afraid of her power over my own emotions. No doubt she partly understood this; and at any rate she had far too much real dignity to invite an unwilling confidence. And yet, all the time, we must have been attracted to each other by the knowledge of our deep affection for Eric. We two were the real mourners; we alone, in that melancholy quartet, could feel something more intense than ordinary sorrow.

But I must not allow myself to be sentimental; for sentiment has little, if any, place in this grim and veridical narrative.

2

At eleven o'clock on Saturday morning (the 1st of August 1914) we entered Professor Reisby's workroom or study.

You might have imagined that you were visiting a prehistoric undertaker. Arranged in rows on a large deal table were pottery vessels which contained, or had recently contained, the ashes of the dead. In addition to the unbroken pots there were hundreds of pieces, jagged scraps of earthenware, coarse pottery, flecked or granulated with bits of quartz or crystal. Some of these were rudely decorated with geometrical patterns, lines or lozenges or chevrons, or merely rows of indented gashes. Of the principal urns, there were some nearly three feet high, full of white crackled fragments of partially burnt bone, while others were pretty little brownish-grey cups only a few inches in diameter.

On another table were the remains of about a dozen skeletons. One or two of these had a remarkably fresh appearance and were nearly complete; but most of them were in a fragmentary state, and the bones were mottled with a dark stain of manganese—the indication (though by no means invariably present) of considerable antiquity. The skeleton of a young woman, slightly burnt, was particularly attractive.

Also, there were little heaps of cremated remains, bits of white or grey or bluish crackled bone, with black masses of soft charcoal, each pile in a cardboard box of appropriate size. Flint implements, and flakes of blue, white, honey-coloured or dappled flint were scattered about in little trays. Neatly fastened on sections of painted plank were swords of bronze, axe-heads, rings, beads, pins and what not—the furniture of prehistoric burial.

Above these funereal objects, depending from a line of rollers on the wall, hung a series of large and impressive diagrams. The diagrams represented, in a simple though graphic manner, the use or construction of those primitive mausoleums in which the people of the so-called Bronze Age buried their illustrious dead. I must say, they were the best diagrams of the kind I have ever seen, and they were prepared with extraordinary skill, diligence and observation. You saw, in elaborate section and from every point of view, the exact form of the various types of tumuli, burial-chambers, ossuaries or bone-deposits, from the simple megalithic box to the intricacy of the vaulted sepulchre. I felt sure that Professor Reisby could have built any one of these constructions blindfold. His knowledge of this ancient funerary architecture must have been equal to that of the builders themselves, if it was not greatly superior to that of most of them.

You could choose for yourself. If you had a liking for cremation, here were a dozen different ways of being cremated. If you preferred the simpler form of inhumation, here were at least fifty ways of arranging the body. Here were burials in every part of the tumulus, from the principal occupant in the middle to the intruding gentleman who was only just under the surface. Well, well!—there was enough to think about…

Of course I did not immediately realise the presence of these *imagines mortis*. But they prevailed over everything else in the visible scene, and they served as a theme for the opening of an easy, instructive and entertaining conversation. Indeed, our interest in these relics appeared to restore the Professor to his normal cordiality.

Ellingham, I saw, was really enthusiastic. He took a set of lenses from his pocket and he studied many of these grim or mouldy things with minute attention.

For my part, I saw Reisby in a new light. Surrounded by emblems of mortality and the innumerable relics of the dead, his air was Rhadamanthine and immense; his enormous rumbling voice echoed, one might imagine, through the caverns of the underworld. Yet his geniality was evident—a real geniality, nothing macabre or frightfully exaggerated like the grin of a skull.

Extraordinary man! Even now, with all my later knowledge, I cannot understand him. So craggy in outline, so primitive by nature, yet so profoundly intellectual! He was a man huge in every inconsistency, enormous in every aspect, mysterious and overpowering.

"Not entirely without value, these researches, I hope," he said. "A few scraps of information collected with patience."

"My dear sir!" cried Ellingham, surprising me with his unusual vivacity, "it is more than patience—it is a marvel of brilliant method and of true observation. Forgive me, sir, if I cannot restrain my delight; I would not presume to offer praise to a man so immeasurably superior to myself in learning and attainment."

This peculiar, stilted speech, was entirely unlike Ellingham's ordinary manner. I could see that he was engaged in some deliberate manœuvre, though I could not follow his design.

Reisby was evidently pleased. He displayed and explained many of his choice exhibits. I can see him now, lifting carefully one of his gigantic pots, a pot containing, so he told us, the cremated bones of a youth, an elderly woman and a child.

"Ah!" said Ellingham, looking sharply at the Professor as he spoke, "if only we could open the Devil's Hump! I was making a survey of it the other morning—a very casual survey, of course."

Reisby frowned, and I thought he deposited the urn on the table with inexplicable violence. I could hear the bones rattle inside.

"You had better leave it alone, my dear Ellingham, I can assure you. It's rather a sore point with me, I fear. The people, as you know, have invested it with a kind of sanctity, and old Macwardle (who is desperately anxious to be popular) takes the same ridiculous view. I have approached him on the subject, and I have even investigated surreptitiously the nature of the mound, but I doubt if we can ever open it, so long as Macwardle is alive or is the owner of the ground—which is much the same thing, I suppose."

He was angry, for some reason or other, and he spoke with a feeling of real grievance.

"What a pity!" said Ellingham. "And there has evidently been a recent displacement—"

"Displacement?"

"Yes, sir,—one of the covering-stones."

"Mr. Ellingham, I will ask you to be so good as to leave the subject—and the object—severely alone. I am responsible for what you call the disturbance or displacement, though I myself would not have described it by so formidable a word. If Macwardle, or any of these other fools, knew that I had used a spade on their precious barrow we should have a real commotion; every chance of a future dig would be destroyed, and myself treated as an outlaw. I will admit that my trifling investigation was extremely rash. But I was careful. Only your highly observant eye, Mr. Ellingham, would have seen a sign of disturbance. As it was, I located a chamber in a somewhat unlikely position. Some day, perhaps… Now let me draw your attention to this peculiar necklace of amber; it will remind you of one discovered by Greenwell."

It seemed as if the morning would pass without a reference to Eric, but at length we sat down for a final discussion of this dreadful business.

"I do indeed blame myself," said Reisby, "for not having been more vigilant. I knew the lad well, and loved him well, and I ought to have seen that he was unduly excited. But who could have anticipated this appalling tragedy?" He spoke in a deep rumbling diapason, resonant and emotional. In his right hand he was fingering loosely a human rib which he had picked up from the table.

"Professor Reisby," I said, overcome once again by his magnificent, his convincing presence, "no one could possibly blame you. Not one of us has ever suggested such a thing."

Ellingham smiled, and I felt a spasm of annoyance.

"Let me assure you, sir," I continued, rather gratuitously, "that we understand your feelings, and those of Mrs. Reisby, and we deeply sympathise—"

My voice faded away, my assurance crumbled under the impassive gloom of the Professor and the obviously cynical amusement of Ellingham.

"I agree with my young friend," said Ellingham, in a manner which I thought insufferably patronising, "and I desire to express my own sympathy. But I do not feel that all hope is to be abandoned. There is, for example, the possibility of a rescue—loss of memory—caprice—"

He was obviously talking at random.

Reisby put down the rib and picked up the fragment of a brain-case. He was getting tired of the conversation.

"That fellow, Joe Lloyd—" said Ellingham.

"Ho, ah?"

There was a visible darkening of the saturnine face. "Lloyd, eh? What has he to do with it?"

"Nothing, I presume. But I think he was up very early on that particular morning."

"Up early? Who told you so? And in what way could such a fact be related to this melancholy affair?"

"I merely suggest—"

"Look here, Mr. Ellingham, I know Lloyd pretty well. He has been working for me during the past six or seven years. To the best of my belief he is an honest man. If he saw anything he would have told us."

"Don't you think he may have desired—people of his class often do—to avoid any sort of publicity?"

"I think you are making an unfair suggestion with regard to a very painful subject. May I ask who told you that Lloyd was about early on that particular morning, or if it is all mere conjecture?" He spoke angrily.

"No, sir; I must ask you to forgive me. We are all anxious to clear up this matter, and it is precisely because you know Lloyd that I suggest you might be able to coax a little information out of him. He may have seen—something or other, and then decided to keep his mouth shut."

Reisby frowned again, and it seemed to me as if he filled the room with darkness.

"I cannot see the plausibility of your suspicion—"

"I do not suspect anything beyond the possible concealment of some little piece of evidence, trifling by itself, though not without value—a mere hint—"

"You give poor Lloyd the credit for extreme subtlety."

"Pray believe me, sir, I should be sorry indeed if I was unfair. I appeal to your knowledge of the man; that is all. If you think I am unreasonable, there is nothing more to be said. And if there is anything offensive to you, sir, in my suggestion, I retract it immediately and without reserve."

He spoke with an appearance of candour, but the cloud on Reisby's brow was not at once dispelled.

"I appreciate your motives, Ellingham. And you, Farringdale, may be assured of my solicitude and of my continued vigilance. We have the willing co-operation of everyone in the district. However, it is most improbable… The set of the current outside the five-fathom line…"

He paused, and again I could hear faintly, as on a previous occasion, the mournful booming of the bell off the Yeaverlow Bank.

3

In the afternoon Ellingham suggested that we ought to call on Macwardle. He had been extremely kind in making matters easy with the police, in suppressing undesirable publicity, and in explaining the situation to the Chief Constable. It would be a pleasant walk to Aberleven Manor, and we set out together soon after lunch.

We had the good fortune to discover the excellent Macwardle at home.

Like other wealthy men of his type, it pleased him to affect an occasional simplicity of manners. He aimed at the bonhomie, the tempered rusticity, of the landed gentleman. If he put on a suit of old clothes, preferably one lacking a few unessential buttons and with a patched elbow, he could imagine people saying (or thinking): "What a dear, simple old fellow Macwardle is!— you would never believe he had seventy thousand a year if you saw him pottering about in his garden." Country gentlemen, he knew, often allowed themselves to be untidy, and they were fond of dabbling about with a rake or a hoe. It was quite the proper thing to do, particularly if you wanted the others to regard you as a "dear old fellow." Ostentation was to be avoided. You had a pair of Rolls-Royce cars, to be sure; but you were not ashamed of being seen pushing a wheelbarrow. In this elaborate cultivation of a rural character—and in this alone—Macwardle showed a fumbling perception of the higher, the more artistic values of life.

As we came to the end of the long, sweeping drive we saw Macwardle pretending to trim the edge of the grass with a pair of shears. As a matter of fact, he was doing this because he expected a visit from Dean Ingleworth, and he wanted the Dean to find him at work and thus to see that he was a dear, simple old etc., etc. Our own visit was not anticipated, but he received us with cordiality.

"Ah, my dear fellows! You have taken me completely by surprise. Well, well—a surprise indeed! Please don't look at these awful old clothes of mine. I love this kind of thing, you know. It's really grand. Get away from all your worries and so forth. True simplicity, my boys!—the life of the people! Never so happy as when I'm just pottering about like any old gardener, I can assure you. Give me a spade or a besom and I'll ask for nothing more. Would you care to have a look at the greenhouses before we go in? They've cost me the better part of five thousand, you know; but if you want a bit of glass you have to pay for it, unfortunately."

We duly admired the greenhouses, and all the expensive and ingenious devices for keeping them watered and heated, and then Macwardle led us to the house. He became abruptly solemn.

"Come into my study for a few minutes, will you? Of course you will have tea with us. But first of all—just a word—"

After handing the shears to one of his minions, this dear simple old fellow escorted us to the remarkably ugly and excessively comfortable room which he called the study.

Now, this worthy Macwardle was true to his type in another matter, besides the crafty affectation of simplicity. He talked about his neighbours with an embarrassing lack of restraint, while continually begging you not on any account to repeat what he said. "I don't mind telling *you*," he would observe, "but of course it must go no further." This freedom, or licence, is common in all provincial or parochial societies; but there is a difference (unknown to Macwardle) between the acrimonious and ingenious gossip of well-bred people and the alarmingly crude revelations of the vulgar.

"No, no!" he said, when I thanked him for his real kindness. "I couldn't have done less—wish I could have done a lot more. Very shocking to all of us. Next to you and your family, of course, I feel so awfully sorry for Reisby. He was very fond of your cousin; and then, you see, all this talk—"

"What kind of talk?" said Ellingham.

"Oh, the kind of thing you always get in these little places! You can imagine—" He was obviously begging to be egged on.

"Not about poor young Foster, surely."

"Well, no—not exactly. Eh—we are talking in confidence, I suppose?"

"By all means if you desire it."

"I hate gossip; never talk any myself, and won't listen to it. As a magistrate, you know, I have to be above that kind of thing. Still, in view of the circumstances, and speaking as a gentleman to gentlemen—eh?"

"I am sure that we both understand," said Ellingham, with a shadow of a smile.

"It's like this," said Macwardle, leaning forward in his immense leather chair with a noble solemnity of movement. "Reisby has been fool enough to marry a young wife at a time when you'd suppose he had made up his mind to do without one. I don't say but what he's chosen well. Mrs. Reisby is a lovely girl—these old fellows know what's what, eh?—and I don't say but what she's as good as gold. Upon my honour, I'd no more say a word against Mrs. Reisby than I would against one of my own daughters. But you understand, sir, *people will talk*! I don't listen to 'em—never willingly—but I can't help knowing what they say." His florid countenance was animated by a restrained eagerness.

"Pray, sir, continue," said Ellingham, taking the lead.

"Well, you see, it was unwise of her to go about with young Foster like she did last April. Quite openly—that was the worst of it. Out in the boat, or walking through the woods and all that kind of thing. People say they went bathing together—frightfully unwise!—can't believe it, of course. Obviously no harm, you see; but frightfully unwise, eh?"

"*Honi soit qui mal y pense*," said Ellingham gravely.

"Ah, my boy! it's a long time since I was at the classics. You beat me there. All the same, you know, people *did* talk, and you could hardly blame 'em. Dear old Reisby never showed anything, but he must have guessed what people were saying—well, to be frank with you, I gave him a sort of hint in a friendly way. Of course he behaved like a gentleman, though I could see that he was frightfully annoyed."

"I can quite understand what he must have felt," said Ellingham.

"Quite. Any gentleman would understand. But that's not all, you see. There's a lady who lives in Northport, Lady Pamela Mulligan—she's a—pff!—eh?—you understand me? I must be careful what I say, but—" He bent forward and addressed a chuckling rumble to Ellingham, who immediately froze up in a posture of supercilious contempt.

"Yes, really!" Macwardle was looking rather murky and flustered, and was probably thinking that he had gone too far.

"Well, this wretched woman, you see, comes down to call on Mrs. Reisby and takes her out in her car. Dear little Bertha Ugglesby-Gore was frightfully upset when she heard of it. And then, you see, there was a young doctor in Branderswick—came over to see the child—well, well! Believe me, I hate gossip as much as anyone. It hurts me to hear of such things, I can assure you. I often implore people to shut up when they are trying to tell me something or other—I do hate it so! Besides, I tell them, you must please remember that I'm a magistrate, and this kind of thing won't do at all."

As Ellingham had sunk into a moody silence and was looking rather disgusted, I had to fill the gap.

"You have been extremely good, Mr. Macwardle. And I feel, as you do, that Mrs. Reisby is absolutely above any reproach in the matter."

"Oh, yes, yes, yes! Absolutely, of course!" He flipped a podgy hand in a gesture of conventional deprecation. "What I mean is, it's frightfully hard on Reisby—these unkind rumours, and then a shocking tragedy—"

"And what are people saying now, Mr. Macwardle?" said Ellingham with a sardonic twinkle in his eye.

"Oh, my dear fellow! I simply don't know. They are saying all sorts of things. I have no idea. I have done my best to get things hushed up, I can assure you, because we do so hate any kind of bother in this dear little place. Far better to hush things up and have done with them. Why, I said to Mrs. Macwardle the other evening—'My dear,' I said, 'it quite puts me off my dinner'—and I meant it, I can assure you."

"Then you have not actually heard a slanderous accusation?"

"Good gracious, Mr. Ellingham! what a shocking idea! Believe me, I would not allow myself to hear anything so improper."

"Foul play, for example?"

Mr. Macwardle flushed up in a kind of muddy purple. He did not understand Ellingham, and he was afraid of him. No doubt he felt, in some degree, the invariable hatred of the commercial for the intellectual. The springs of his chair twittered beneath his agitation.

"Sir, sir! We can't have anything of the sort in this dear little place, I beg to assure you! Please to say nothing more about it. Everything must be hushed up. We can't have anything of the kind in Aberleven. No, sir!"

"Murder?" said Ellingham in a hard, remorseless voice.

Macwardle sprang up as if a viper had bitten him in the rear.

"Mr. Ellingham! Let me beg you—This is too much, sir, it is indeed. You must remember, Mr. Ellingham, that I am a magistrate. I can't listen to such talk; it is really most improper. We are all trying to lead quiet, decent lives here, let me tell you; and we don't want to have any kind of upset. I have enough to do with fellows trying to steal my fish or my birds or cutting my timber, without all this kind of thing. Nobody would believe the amount of real hard work we magistrates have to do. Ask Ugglesby-Gore, if you don't believe me. He is one of the most capable men on the bench. Why, my dear sir, we had to send three fellows to prison last week for poaching. It's enough to worry a man to death, I can assure you. Oh Lord!—if only people would leave us alone and mind their own business! Trying to lead a decent, simple life, and looking after my bit of a garden—"

I thought he was going to sob. Ellingham, however, was quite unmoved, and he merely replied:

"Then why, may I ask, have you told us about these rumours?"

"Why?—eh? Well, I suppose I wanted you to sympathise with poor Reisby. Yes, I wanted you to be tactful. But I'm sure you would be tactful—and anyhow, you're going to-morrow, aren't you?" He seemed pleased with the idea.

At this point the butler came in to announce Dean Ingleworth. After a careful descent to the level of ordinary polite conversation, we accompanied Macwardle to the south library where his wife and daughters were entertaining the Dean.

Mrs. Macwardle was ample and motherly, and she was intelligent enough to have no pretensions. Her age was about sixty-five.

I felt sorry for the daughters, both of whom were reluctantly approaching middle-age. They were nice though ridiculous women, pathetically trying to take an interest in poultry, general knowledge, and the welfare of the poor—a state of things all the more deplorable because neither of them was ill-looking. In view of their father's income they were, of course, freely admitted to the outer circles of county society, but no one had ever wanted to marry Prudence or Priscilla. For my part, I rather liked them, with all their affectations and futilities. They had been expensively educated, and, perhaps foreseeing their future state, they had never despised education. If they were not highly intelligent, they were at least well informed, and they were able to talk with occasional gleams of real understanding. The worst of it was, they were incurably sentimental (so often the case with those who have been repressed), and they could not help filtering their limited experience through a medium of luscious romance and of brightly-coloured idealism. I speak of them in some detail, because the reader will find them, later, playing their part in a scene of great importance.

The ladies received us in a most impeccable style, the Misses Macwardle, in particular, looking suitably pained.

As for the Dean, he was a pattern of Christian gentility, fully realising all the subtle delicacies of the situation.

"You will carry away with you from Aberleven," he said, "memories of happiness and of tragedy, mingled, as indeed they are necessarily mingled, in the bewildering tapestry of experience. Yet allow me to hope that you will visit us again. Allow me to hope that your pleasant memories will remain, and that we may be able to add others equally pleasant."

To this amiable speech Ellingham made an adequate and equally polished reply. He found it refreshing, after the interview in the study, to meet this courtly and eloquent man.

But there was a subject of wider importance which quickly engaged our attention—the awful imminence of war.

Already the lurid shadow was darkening our land and filling every thoughtful mind with fear or melancholy speculation. It was Ellingham's fervent hope, I know, that England would be able to preserve neutrality with honour.

"Our navy," said Macwardle, "can sink the lot of 'em; yes, sir, it can sink the lot of 'em in a fortnight. We need not send a single man across the Channel."

"But, Daddy," said Prudence, "if the Germans invaded France—"

"We should run round and blow their harbours to pieces, my dear. I have often thought of it. I have often discussed the matter with Ugglesby-Gore, who is a soldier and knows what he's talking about."

"I believe the Germans have got a very good navy of their own," said Ingleworth drily.

"There's only one navy to count, sir," retorted Macwardle, "and that's the British navy. Thank God, sir, we can wipe the others off the face of the earth. I have often thought about it, sir, I can assure you. Old England is ready to fight for civilisation, and she can swipe the others off the face of the earth. And, please God, she'll do it."

"I suppose the Germans may also invoke the assistance of God," observed Ellingham.

"That, sir," retorted Macwardle, "would be rank blasphemy."

4

On Sunday, the 2nd of August, things were looking so desperately serious that we decided to pack up at once and catch the midday express at Northport.

We had no time to say good-bye to the Reisbys. Morgan got the car ready for us soon after breakfast, and we were back in London at half-past ten.

"We have retired without solving the mystery," said Ellingham as we shook hands outside King's Cross station, "for I cannot help regarding the whole thing as a mystery still. There may be an opportunity for continued investigation, but it looks as if you and I will be soldiers of the King before many weeks have passed. And it's going to be a bloody business, my boy."

PART III

Shadows in the North

CHAPTER I

I

I HAVE NOW TO PASS QUICKLY OVER A PERIOD OF MORE THAN five years—the whole period of the Great War and the first year of the lamentable aftermath. I shall only relate briefly an episode of 1916.

Ellingham, who had been for some time a keen Territorial officer, got a commission in the R.F.A. and it was not long before he was over in France with his battery. I myself, after a somewhat accelerated training in a well known London O.T.C., was gazetted to the Middlesex Fusiliers, and I reached Le Havre—as I well remember!—on the 27th of January 1915.

I was knocked out at the second battle of Ypres, and although I have not the faintest recollection of what I did in the battle I presently found myself agreeably convalescent in London with a D.S.O. ribbon stitched on my tunic. My friend Ellingham, in the meanwhile, had won the same honourable decoration in a more definite way, and was already assured of promotion. As he did everything well, it goes without saying that he was an admirable soldier. He was, in fact, an acting Brigadier at the time of the Armistice.

We wrote letters to each other, but we did not meet until 1916, and then in a most unexpected way.

At the battle of the Somme I was not as fortunate as I had been at Ypres in the previous year. It is true that I was now a captain, but instead of distinguishing myself in that particular series of massacres I fell ingloriously into a shell-hole, and in climbing out of it I got a bit of shrapnel in my leg. A lot of dirty earth was blown into the wound; it was rather a grim business, and I was bundled off to the —rd Stationary Hospital at Rouen.

The bed on my right was vacant, but I was dimly aware of somebody being put into it during the night. In the morning the first thing I heard (at washing-time) was a sardonic and weary voice:

"And how are you, Captain Farringdale?"

It was Ellingham.

His brigade, he said, had come in for trouble, and he had got a piece of one of his own guns in his right forearm. Not a large piece, but they would probably send him over to London in a few days' time. At any rate, he was lucky. Fritz had spotted the battery and wiped it out—men, guns and all—before they had time to move. A pretty piece of aeroplane work; they were devilish good at that kind of thing.

Later in the morning, after the M.O. had come round and patched us up, we had a sustained and interesting conversation, modulated and a little modified by the incidents of the ward.

First we compared our war experiences. But these comparisons were invariably brief. And then Ellingham—he was Major Ellingham at that time—began to talk about home affairs.

"You know," he said, "I often think about that very painful and very perplexing episode at Aberleven. It seems a long time ago, but I have not lost any of the details. And the more I think about it the more convinced I am that old Reisby was involved, no matter how, in the problem of your poor cousin's death. If we get through this bloody war—which is highly improbable—I should very much like to see that old boy again."

"You are still in some doubt as to the nature of the problem?"

"Yes. But look here. I'll tell you something which I may as well get off my mind. You remember that big tumulus up there—the Devil's Hump?"

"Very clearly."

"The Devil's Hump, like the Professor, is also involved in the problem."

"Good Scot, man!—but how—"

"I tell you, I can't say definitely. If my nerves were not a little upset I should hesitate before making a declaration so vague and apparently so inane. Actually, however, it is not inane. Do you ever hear from Mrs. Reisby?"

In answering this question I felt a certain degree of embarrassment. "Well—she has written to me once or twice."

"Keep in touch with them. We may be able... Ah! thank you, Sister, that's fine."

He settled himself more comfortably in his bed.

"An unsolved problem, particularly one of such a nature, cannot cease to occupy the mind. I should like to see that old tumulus opened, you know."

"But how can you possibly connect such a thing with Eric's disappearance?"

"That is a question I cannot answer. Something hidden there... your cousin may have known... I cannot say. Or perhaps I do not dare to say. It is too fantastic! I am talking foolishly. It was not a very nice experience, you see, the way that battery was mopped up. God!—it was like turning a bloody hose on it." He tried to raise his arm.

"Major Ellingham," said the Sister, looking up from her table at the end of the ward, "you mustn't get excited, please."

2

After this conversation in the hospital I did not see Ellingham until the spring of 1919. We both came through the War without further damage: he was demobilised as a Lieutenant-Colonel, and I had the brevet rank of Major. But neither of us has any wish to revive the memories of that ghastly period, unless to admonish those imbeciles who still pretend that arms are glorious, necessary, and a token of national honour. We have sternly abjured our military titles, and if anyone tries to apply them he is quickly and properly rebuked.

Very frequently had I reflected upon our curious talk in the hospital, and I came to the conclusion that my friend—though he never admitted it to have been the case—was actually the victim of an intermittent kind of shell-shock.

Certainly I believed that Reisby had concealed something which he knew about the death of my cousin, but I did not see how this death could be associated with a Bronze Age tumulus. Of course I knew that Ellingham had got something up his sleeve. He had some information about the Professor which he had never imparted to me. Anyhow, I thought, it is all over and done with, and we shall never hear anything more about it. My supposition was entirely wrong.

Why we should have done so I cannot say, but Mrs. Reisby and I frequently wrote to each other. Of course the War gave a natural stimulus to private correspondence. When you were on active service you got letters from people who would never have written to you in ordinary circumstances, and you were, in most cases, glad to get them and to answer them. Indeed, you regarded such letters as a welcome form of communication between hell and the upper world, a kind of liaison between the tortured existence of the soldier and all the old substantial realities of peace.

Our letters were not romantic, nor were they even confidential; yet we both attached a good deal of importance to sending and receiving them. Once or twice we had observed a very singular coincidence of thought... But I only mention this correspondence in order to show that I had a reason for wishing to revisit Aberleven.

By the winter of 1919 I had resumed in earnest the study of the law, again under the admirable direction of Sir Alfred Barlock-Winterslade. My mother and sister were still living at Richmond, but I had moved to bachelor quarters in Upper Cheyne Row. I was now twenty-seven. As for Ellingham, he was back at his old job in Cambridge, with every prospect of a professorship in due course.

3

In the spring of 1920—nearly six years after the tragedy of the Yeaverlow Bank—I suggested to Ellingham that we might spend a week or so at Aberleven. To my delight, he said that he would like nothing better. His wife and son were going on a visit to his mother-in-law at Bath, where that venerable lady was decaying in a state of dreary comfort. So he would gladly accompany me to the north.

I wrote to Mrs. Reisby, telling her of our plans, and she replied that everyone would be delighted to see us, and that both she and her husband wished us to spend as much time as possible at Scarweather. Morgan, having played a gallant part in the defence of East Anglia, was still in charge of the hotel, and would reserve rooms as soon as we could give him a date.

Pleasing as her reply undoubtedly was, I discerned a note of restraint in the letter, a formalised offer of hospitality, which I attributed to the Professor himself.

"No doubt you are right," said Ellingham, to whom I confided this idea, "but I'm sure the old fellow remembers you with affection."

"I'm not so sure of it."

"Oh, yes, he does! On the other hand, he regards me as one of those inquisitive, unaccommodating people who are so frequently the cause of mischief."

"Does it matter?"

"Not a scrap! We are going up to enjoy ourselves, to be refreshed by the northern breezes, to view the rude serenity of the northern scene. Am I right?"

He looked at me in his odd, quizzical way.

"Yes, rather! But I shall be glad to see them, you know."

"Mrs. Reisby in particular, if I may venture to say so without impertinence."

"Mrs. Reisby of course. And the Professor too."

"Only you are still a bit suspicious—eh?"

He slid his long forefinger down the side of his nose.

"Now, look here, Colonel Ellingham!"

"Really, Major Farringdale!"

We laughed, and then I felt a kind of a twist in the back of my mind and I said:

"What is the good of being suspicious, anyway? It all happened six years ago. We can't do anything now."

"And yet there is a kind of dull insistency, is there not?"

He paused for a moment, and then resumed:

"The unsolved problem has a way of bobbing up, of ruffling the placid levels of our self-sufficiency. Well, we shall see! I wonder how the monumental work on burials is going on. Monumental is the right word, eh? And I wonder how the trout are running this year. The trout! Ah, my boy! how good it is to be thinking of trout again…"

We had a great welcome, I might almost say a great reception, at the Aberleven hotel. Mr. Morgan and his wife greeted us with overflowing cordiality. The cook and the two chambermaids, abandoning their duties, insisted upon running into the parlour to have a look at us. Ugglesby-Gore, informed of our arrival, came in for a cheerful round of gin-and-bitters. He had been a recruiting officer, unhonoured by promotion, but that did not prevent him from giving us an original though incoherent summary of the War. After all—he was a professional.

And then the talk!

Poor old Macwardle was dead. He had caught a chill when attending a meeting of the local tribunal, at which he had the satisfaction of condemning five notorious poachers to service in the army. Three of the Aberleven lads had been killed in France. Another had gone down in the *Goliath*. Others had been wounded, and others had returned without a scratch… The usual story.

But there was one piece of news which affected us more closely.

"Remember Joe Lloyd?" said Morgan, after handing Ugglesby-Gore his fourth gin-and-bitters.

"Very well indeed."

"Ah!—he turned out a bit of a mystery. The police came to see him in September 1914, and in October he disappeared."

"Did he, by Jove!" cried Ellingham. "But how? Do you mean that he simply went away?"

"No; he disappeared without leaving a trace. Some of the men saw him hauling his boat up the beach—on the 8th of October, I think it was, about three in the afternoon. Then a little maid saw him fastening the gate below his cottage. And after that nobody saw him any more."

"Tut!"

Ellingham slowly nodded his head up and down, as much as to say: "There you are!—another problem!"

"Most extr'ordinary thing, what?" bubbled Ugglesby-Gore. "Fella vanishes into the atmosphere, what? Absolutely. That's it—absolutely vanishes. Little girl sees him go into his cottage, and the next morning he isn't there—isn't anywhere. Gone off the face of the earth, absolutely—can you imagine it?"

"Did the police look for him?" I said, only faintly curious.

"Oh, yes! Regular hunt. Funny thing—supper on the table, kettle on the fire—no fella to be seen—fella vanished into the blue."

"Very odd indeed," said Ellingham. "Did they find anything remarkable in the cottage?"

"No, sir, I don't think so," replied Morgan. "I heard there was only his clothes, and all the usual things a fisherman would have—"

"You're wrong, Buffalo," said Ugglesby-Gore, "there was a box."

"Ah, yes, of course! I had forgot that."

"A box?"

Ellingham was amused though attentive.

"The fella had a box hidden away somewhere. Police took it. Awfully mysterious. Clever bit of work by the police, what? Trust the old Chief—every time! You remember it, Morgan, don't you?"

"I remember something... No, no! It's my turn now, if you please, Major... Nothing for you, sir?—or you? Well, well! I shall have another opportunity."

"So Mr. Lloyd and his box have disappeared?" said Ellingham, "and you know no more of the one than you do of the other?"

"You've got it," replied Ugglesby-Gore, "absolutely. Fella goes, box goes, nobody hears a thing. But you mark my word, mark my word—think old Uggles is no end of a fool, perhaps—gets a brain-wave now and then—mark my word—that fella was a spy."

"That was all the talk, I believe," said Morgan.

"It was a sure thing. Never heard a word about the fella; never knew who he was or where he went to. Must have been a spy—couldn't have been anything else. It's my belief"—the Major bubbled over in a sudden access of alcoholic solemnity—"it's my belief the fella was caught signalling to a bloody U-boat."

4

I had anticipated a certain awkwardness in meeting the Reisbys, but there was none at all. Both husband and wife greeted us with apparently unalloyed cordiality.

Reisby himself, now approaching sixty, had a grand appearance of robust age; he reminded me of a flourishing oak-tree, hardy yet venerable. His voice came rumbling and roaring out of his enormous frame, just as it had when we last met him. His ponderous jocularity was restored; he shouted; he sent out ripples of expanding mirth. Only he was a little greyer, there were flecks of pure silver among the tangles of his flaming hair.

Hilda Reisby, I suppose, was then about twenty-eight. She had grown into the full magnificence of womanhood. I do not know how to describe women. I can only say that I never saw one who was more beautiful.

Let it not be imagined that she was a tragic beauty, one of those forlorn creatures who move among the shadows of memory and regret. Not at all. She was grave, perhaps, but it was not in her nature to be garrulous or noisy. Neither was it in Hilda's nature to be mopish or sentimental or flaccidly romantic. She was a woman of admirable poise, with a glorious and evident sanity, both physical and mental. I think she was happy; I am certain that she had an unruffled serenity of mind.

The Reisby's daughter, Frances, was now a child of eight or nine, a charming, buoyant little girl, who bullied or coaxed her father, not only with impunity but with invariable success. One could see that Reisby would never be able to oppose the will of his daughter. Indeed, the spectacle of this huge barbaric man bending so willingly to every caprice or need of the child was enough to win the heart of any sentimental observer. Had it not been for the common sense of Hilda, backed by the skill and experience of an excellent nurse, Frances would have been irredeemably spoilt.

If Professor Reisby disliked Ellingham, he was expert in all the arts of a crafty dissembler. On the very first day of our visit, Reisby, Ellingham and myself were occupied for at least three hours in the inspection of new funereal trophies. The energetic Professor had been digging in scores of barrows, and had unearthed methodically God knows how many hundreds of skeletons and other relics. The great work—the opus monumental—was to contain, he said, a conspectus of prehistoric burials more informative and rich in detail than anything which had been attempted by any other writer. Also, there would be a *corpus* (I am sure that was the word!), a *corpus* of Northumbrian pottery that would fairly open the eyes of every archæologist in Europe. To hear him, you would have imagined that people would greet these mouldy records, these horrible pots or bones, with a tumult of excited admiration, or with a chorus of exasperated envy.

"Greenwell, sir?—that patient earthworm! Why Greenwell never recognised the irrefutable sequence of cinerary types! Ho, ha! La-di-dum! Kemble, Mortimer, did you say? Mere collectors—busy-bodies—ferrets—burrowing and scrubbing, and actually *buying from dealers!*"

He uttered the last words as if he were describing the lowest level of decadence or imbecility.

"Collectors are bad enough," he roared, "but they are nothing to those complacent idiots who lick labels in museums Ho, ha, ha, ha! Fellows like our worthy Goy, for example. Goy was unfit for active service, by the way, and so they put him into some sort of a damned agricultural company, and now, if you please, he calls himself Captain Goy! He's back in Northport with his little bottle of gum and his box of labels. He's married a beaky sort of woman who was a teacher at the County School. I wonder if he's put a label on *her*—eh? Ah, ho, ha, ho! Never mind. I'm rather fond of Goy, you know. At least I'm not aware of any positive prejudice against the fellow."

We admired all the grim things in the study—I think Ellingham really did admire them—and we spent the entire morning with great good-humour.

But I began to observe something about Reisby which made me feel uncomfortable. I cannot say precisely what it was. He was too hilarious. His explosions of titanic laughter were sometimes inappropriate. There was an exaggerated violence of gesture over trivial things.

Also I observed that he said nothing about the disappearance of Joe Lloyd. Ellingham referred to this casually and the Professor answered:

"Ah, yes, yes! Do you remember the poor fellow? Very odd. One of those intermittently vagrant people, coming from nowhere, going to nowhere."

That was all.

I did not, until many years later, discover Ellingham's views on the disappearance of Joe Lloyd.

5

On the whole, our renewed acquaintance with Aberleven was enjoyable. There were a few gloomy passages, a few unavoidable references to the death of Eric—which everyone now regarded as a bathing accident. No clue, no sign to indicate the manner of the accident, had come to light. But after the necessary, formal things had been said, we were all placidly cheerful.

One afternoon, when the Professor had gone to Northport and Ellingham was fishing in the Kinkell, I went for a walk over Seidal Moor. I met Hilda Reisby. I had, indeed, some reason for supposing that I should meet her.

We had not been alone together since that awful interview in 1914, and there were many things to be said which we could not very well have said in the presence of other people. It pleased me to discover that she was treating me as an intimate friend, not unworthy of confidence; but I reflected that women confide more readily in ugly men than in those who are attractive.

Obviously it was not her intention to say much about Eric. She asked a good deal about Miss Foster and my mother, and about myself, my plans and ambitions. Her intelligence prevented her from asking about my experiences in the War. Then she began to speak of her own family and of life at Aberleven.

"It is really splendid," said I, "to see the Professor in such magnificent health."

She paused before replying.

"Tolgen is really not so well as he appears to be."

"But his energy is terrific!"

"You see only one side of the picture. The energy is there; but at times he is dreadfully depressed—so depressed, Mr. Farringdale, as to be almost unrecognisable."

I was profoundly shocked.

"Nobody who met him could imagine such a state of affairs."

"It is quite true."

There was a degree of anxiety in her voice which roused at once my interest, my sympathy and my alarm. She told me with perfect candour that she herself was alarmed. When these moods of despair were upon him, the Professor withdrew from the ordinary course of his life; he sat immobile and in silence, perhaps for hours together. The immobility and the silence were terrifying—you would have been less terrified, she said, by an alternation of violence. This awful stillness implied such a reversal or lapse of the known personality that it gave the impression rather of a creeping death than of anything else. Hilda was desperately afraid of the child seeing him in such a state, but had so far prevented it by saying that her father was at work and must be left alone. As a matter of fact, it was the voice of the child that frequently roused him from these trance-like conditions and brought him back to his normal existence. He himself never referred to these periods, and it might be doubted if he was even aware of them.

I raised the obvious question about seeing a doctor, but she said that a visit from a doctor would certainly do no good.

"Tolgen's opinion of doctors resembles that of most scientific men. I need not tell you what it is."

She smiled, in spite of her gravity.

"But I have talked to Dr. Blacketer-Wryswater in Northport—he is a man with a big reputation up here. What he is inclined to suspect is a drug of some sort, and he has made me promise to ring up if the symptoms get worse or more frequent. Actually, I am glad to say, there has been no increase, either of intensity or frequency, during the past year. Of course… he had an awful shock… and then again when Lloyd went away so mysteriously—"

We said nothing for a few moments. The livid grass of the

moor stretched in front of us, bare, pale undulations roughened a little here and there by a patch of gorse.

"And then," she said, "do you remember that German ship?—the mystery ship we called it."

"The *Emil Guntershausen*?"

"Yes. Apparently she is a very commonplace and respectable ship, owned before the War by an Anglo-German syndicate or something of the kind. Now she has appeared again, bringing iron ore and occasional mixed cargoes from Hamburg—at least I think it's Hamburg. I suppose it is due to a freak of memory, but poor Tolgen always gets excited when he sees that boat, and then he often falls into these terrible moods of silence."

She knelt on the grass to pick a sprig of heather, and I saw that she was greatly disturbed.

"Mrs. Reisby, I am dreadfully sorry. If ever you want any—any kind of help—if it is not an impertinence on my part—" I stuttered helplessly.

"I do want you to be my friend," she said.

And she added, as we walked on together:

"Only don't think that I feel isolated or unhappy. That is not the case. Nor must you think that my husband is dangerously abnormal in any way. He is one of the best, one of the kindest of men." She flushed, as if regretting for a moment her confidence. "Tolgen is a very remarkable man."

6

On the way back to London I stayed for a day or two with the Ellinghams in Cambridge.

Mrs. Ellingham was a quiet, efficient woman; the kind of woman who knows how to restrain the eccentricities of a husband and oblige him to make an occasional decent appearance in ordinary society. We do not always know how great is the debt of eminent men to these magnificently capable though unobtrusive wives. Their boy, Peter Laud Ellingham, was about twelve years old—he was not more offensive than the average boy of twelve.

But the only significant thing about this visit was a short talk with Ellingham in his enviably comfortable study.

After some discreet and unilluminating references to Aberleven, he said:

"I am inspired by the work of Reisby. This digging is a rare pastime. What I propose to do is to acquire for myself an extensive, a complete knowledge of archæology."

"My dear fellow!—another science?"

"Archæology is not a science. It is nothing so respectable. What is really *known* in archæology may be put in a few pages of ordinary type. People dig up all these jolly old things, with practically no idea of their true meaning, and then, with due solemnity (to keep themselves in countenance and impose on the simple-minded), invent a system of elaborate classification."

"If that is your opinion—"

"Why should I waste my time? Because I enjoy this pretentious fooling. It is a form of intellectual bluff which appeals to me. And I do like the discovery and the handling of these mysterious objects. Does it not revive our juvenile joy in treasure-trove and all that kind of thing? Is not the archæologist a respectable pirate, an authorised body-snatcher, a privileged robber of the tombs? Again, I find a singular pleasure in the notion of human antiquity, a true philosophic pleasure. When I am told that the Negro was fully evolved in early Pleistocene times I am comforted, I find the information wonderfully soothing."

I was continually baffled by the vagaries of this astounding man, and I could only wonder what he was getting at.

"Of course I can pick up the jargon quickly enough," Ellingham continued, "and that is the main thing. Indeed, it is the main thing in many of the so-called sciences. Where every contention is unprovable, jargon is paramount. Then I shall be able to encounter Tolgen Reisby on a more equal footing, even if I cannot win his friendship and respect."

"So you mean to keep up your acquaintance with Aberleven?"

He tilted his head sideways, looking like a bright, sardonic magpie.

"I mean to have a dig, some day, in the Devil's Hump."

CHAPTER II

I

NATURALLY I HAD NOT FORGOTTEN THE DEATH OF THE German student, Ludwig Mackenrode. I made certain enquiries in 1921, and I found out all that could be known about him.

It was not, on the face of it, particularly interesting. The parents of this unfortunate lad were respectable people in Hamburg, tradesfolk who had never been prosperous but had lost their money in the year preceding the War. Ludwig was evidently intelligent and ambitious. His father wanted to put him in a shipping office, where he had influence, but the boy came to London, hoping to obtain work as the correspondent of a leading Hamburg newspaper. At the time of his death—evidently suicide—he was almost literally starving. I did not succeed in finding out how he knew Eric, or why he should have written to him. And so, at any rate for the present, my enquiries came to an end.

2

During the following years (from 1921 to 1926) I worked hard at my profession, and I was called to the Bar in 1925. I retained my excellent quarters in Upper Cheyne Row, and I had also chambers in the Temple.

From time to time I saw the Reisbys. Whenever they came to London I visited them at their hotel and I entertained them in my Chelsea rooms. Our relations were those of a tranquil, sustained friendship. Between Hilda Reisby and myself there was, in addition, a relation of peculiar confidence—I can give it no other term—which I found of immense value. We wrote long letters to each other, and I often acted on her advice in settling the minor problems of my career. I think it pleased her to share those problems, to hear about my progress, and, in time, to follow my cases.

Professor Reisby, though not entirely free from them, was becoming less liable to his alarming fits of depression. He looked as robust as ever. The first volumes of the huge work on burials had been published, and had received a great deal of attention from learned men in every part of Europe. Generally the work was admitted to be of supreme importance. But Reisby was attacked venomously by Zarakoff in Budapest, by Henkelberger of Dresden, and by Sir Thomas Bunting-Wragge of Cambridge.

These attacks (now forgotten) were brilliantly refuted by Ellingham, who wrote a sensational article on the tumuli of the Troad in the *Antiquarian Register*. I well remember the tremendous excitement which was aroused by this article, and how fiercely it was discussed in the clubs and drawing-rooms of London. There was, in fact, a very painful scene at Lady Wimble's when Sir Henry Tighe-Wilkins denounced with extraordinary bitterness the whole structure of Altendorff's Mycenean chronology.

Let us not revive those disturbing memories—for who can say what is Mycenean and what is not? Let me only observe that Ellingham's defence of Reisby not only secured the gratitude and the admiration of that distinguished Professor, but enlisted on the side of Ellingham all those redoubtable men who presently overthrew Bunting-Wragge's theory of double cremation.

I mention this because it is very important to understand how Reisby's attitude was modified by this frightful controversy. He became at once the friend of Ellingham. If there had ever been a shade of enmity between these eminent men, it was now (so I thought) completely dispelled. Ellingham was invited to Scarweather, and he was also invited to take an active part in the Professor's future diggings. To this Ellingham made a cordial reply and said that he anticipated with pleasure his next expedition to the north; but he would have to wait until he was less busy.

As far as I was concerned, I did not need a special invitation. I went up occasionally, perhaps twice a year, to the hotel at Aberleven. Undoubtedly, in spite of its tragic association, I was fond of the place, and I was also fond of Hilda Reisby. Except on one occasion between 1920 and 1926 Ellingham did not accompany me on my holidays.

Frederick Ellingham was now a man of acknowledged eminence, and it was rumoured that he would soon be the Woolhope Professor of Organic Chemistry at Cambridge. It only depended upon the accelerated decay of the present occupant of the chair. Ellingham had received the honorary degree of Doctor from the Universities of Yale, Dublin and Leyden. He was also acquiring a kind of second-line eminence (which he treated as a joke) in the field of archæology. In the capacity of assistant to no less a man than Dr. Wheelworthy, he had taken part in several important excavations, had appeared with the Doctor in a talking film, and had settled, once and for all, the difference between the sharply recurved rim of the Roman domestic pottery of pre-Flavian date and the overhanging rim of imported Belgic ware—an important problem, sensational in its implications, which had occupied the close attention of Dr. Wheelworthy for more than ten years, and had given rise to many acrimonious and unprofitable disputes. For this remarkable service to science and to British archæology, Ellingham was elected an Honorary Fellow of the Prehistoric Society of London and a Corresponding Member of the Société des Fouilleurs Savants.

In the back of my mind the mystery of my cousin's death, and its possible association with Professor Reisby, was only faintly persistent.

I noted, with considerable astonishment, that Ellingham thought a great deal more about this mystery than I did. He often alluded to it, though not in a manner which threw any light upon the workings of his mind. He was, of course, absorbed in all the complexities and all the efforts of a very useful and a very fruitful career. It was the more remarkable, therefore, that he was not content to allow the dust of memory to fall on the buried problem of the Yeaverlow Bank; not content, indeed, to regard it as a problem buried beyond all chance of revival and examination.

He did not refer to our singular conversation in the hospital at Rouen, nor did I feel that I ought to remind him of it. With all his defences of irony and of sardonic rejoinder, he was a man of real and deep emotion, and he could not look back to that particular time without evoking the too vivid images of a terrible experience. It was a time, he told me, when he felt his reason precariously balanced upon the ultimate edge.

Anyone could see that the news of Joe Lloyd's disappearance had interested Ellingham profoundly. Whether he related this disappearance to anything which had previously occurred, I was unable to say; for my part, I saw no reason for doing so.

Actually (so he now tells me) the ghastly features of the Reisby drama had already presented themselves in the mind of Ellingham, though not in the full amplitude of horror which afterwards came to be revealed. Knowing what he did know about the Professor, and having observed many things which a less observant, penetrating intelligence could easily have overlooked, he was drawn, almost against his will, to a terrifying conclusion. If he was right, the evidence—the astounding, fantastic evidence of a crime—was actually available, it existed in a recognisable and a material form... But I am forgetting my duty and my purpose as a mere narrator, the humble recorder of these bizarre events.

3

In the summer of 1926 Ellingham decided that he would take his wife and son with him on a visit to Aberleven. He asked me if I would accompany him, and of course I said I should do so with the utmost pleasure.

My own status at Aberleven was that of a regular visitor, but Ellingham had not been there for nearly six years.

Ellingham's boy was about nineteen; an undergraduate at Balbus. He was less of a lout than the ordinary undergraduate—in fact, he was rather a cryptic fellow, like his father, with a sharp, enquiring countenance, and a cynical degree of caution in speaking. I do not mean to say that he was unpleasant. He had a brilliant intellect, and he did not see any reason for pretending to be unaware of it.

Our good host at the hotel, "Buffalo" Morgan, received us with his customary warmth of greeting. Yet I could see that he was more thoughtful, more sedate than usual. At first I put this down to the fact of two of our party being strangers, but his manner did not change when he strolled down to the foreshore with me for a short talk before dinner.

"This is a damned unlucky place, Mr. Farringdale," he said. "We've just had another disappearance."

"A—what?"

"Another disappearance. About three weeks ago. I thought you might have heard of it."

"No. I've heard nothing. Tell me—" (I had not received a letter from Mrs. Reisby for more than a month.)

"Jimmy Pollard—"

"Jimmy Pollard! Why, that's the name of the boy who used to work for Professor Reisby before the War."

"Yes, it's him. He joined up in 1915 and came through the War without a scratch. Lived with his uncle, old Ebenezer Pollard."

"But how did he come to—to disappear?"

Morgan looked back over his shoulder.

"That's the mystery. He was a queer, discontented fellow. Couldn't settle to anything. I believe he wanted Professor Reisby to take him back, but they've had Anderson's boy at Scarweather now for more than eight years. There was a bit of talk about Jimmy Pollard being cheeky to the Professor, but I don't know if there was any truth in it. He got into the way of hanging about near Scarweather when he was out of a job."

I waited for a moment while Mr. Morgan thoughtfully kicked a pebble in front of him.

"Three weeks ago on Tuesday, Pollard said he was going to walk over to Branderswick. He was after some work in a garage there; or maybe he was going to see a girl. As far as we knew, he was last seen at about seven o'clock in a public house in Branderswick, where he happened to meet a friend. He said he would go in the bus to Kinkell Cross and walk the rest of the way home. Apparently quite sober, nothing wrong. Never went to the bus at all—simply disappeared in broad daylight. Now, what do you make of that, Mr. Farringdale?"

"Of course there have been enquiries?"

"All the usual enquiries, with no result. I think they've given 'em up already."

"He may have got into the train at Branderswick and gone off somewhere."

"He may have. But he had no money with him."

"Money could have been provided by someone else. You say that he was queer and restless."

"Yes, I know. It's unlikely that many people in Branderswick knew him, and he could easily have got away without being noticed. That's plain enough, I'll allow. But I can't help thinking it's damned odd; or, as I said just now, damned unlucky."

He looked me squarely in the face.

"People are saying that Scarweather must be unlucky."

When I had an opportunity for seeing him alone, I mentioned this to Ellingham.

"Oh, yes! I remember Pollard," he said, "a moody, unstable youth. Probably he has gone away on some squalid adventure— or even a criminal adventure. We are not going to bother about him anyhow."

4

It is not necessary that I should describe at any length our delight-ful family excursions at Aberleven.

The Reisbys and the Ellinghams got on very well together. Mrs. Reisby and Mrs. Ellingham at once appreciated each other (they had only met on formal occasions previously) and were soon on terms of real friendship. An equal appreciation, though of a more romantic nature, almost at once united the junior members of our party—Frances Reisby, who was then between sixteen and seventeen, and Peter Ellingham.

We spent our time very harmoniously and pleasantly, and in a manner that was decidedly sociable without being too restrained. It has always been my belief, that only intelligent people know how to enjoy themselves.

We were more of an organised party than we had been on former visits—the addition of Mrs. Ellingham and Peter made a great difference—and if any regret was admissible, it was the regret that one had fewer opportunities for solitude or for intimate conversation.

Morgan had got a new motor-boat, which could be launched at any time from a boat-house with a long slipway, and in this we used to go out fishing or cruising within a radius of twenty or thirty miles. She was a fast and roomy boat, and the fact of her being quickly available at any state of the tide made her extremely popular. I have a particularly good reason for remembering this boat—the *Mirabelle*—as the reader will discover.

Professor Reisby was now sixty-six, and he intended to retire from his university appointments in the following year. Certainly

he was not retiring on account of ill-health, for he still had a mar-
vellously powerful physique and a copious flow of energy. He
wished to devote himself, he said, to his own work, to the produc-
tion of scientific books, and above all to researches in archæology.

His collection of mortuary and funerary objects was now of
alarming extent. He sat in his study completely surrounded by
urns and ashes and the parts of innumerable skeletons, to the great
annoyance of Mr. Goy, who declared that all these things ought
to be safely deposited and properly labelled—*properly* labelled,
mark you!—in the Northport Museum. There was now a sort of
competitive body-snatching going on between the Professor and
Mr. Goy, resulting in fierce attacks upon tumuli.

Goy denounced the Professor as a mere collector, and hinted
that he was becoming childish and that all his theories were
out of date. For his part, the Professor declared that Goy was
both impertinent and ignorant, not even aware of the difference
between blue glass and *lapis lazuli*. He also overwhelmed the
unfortunate man with ponderous variations of his joke about
labels—how Goy transmuted things by merely fixing his labels on
them, how he referred to his own catalogues as if they were *biblia
sacra*, and so forth. Indeed, he came down to the level of a practical joke, for he thrust into one of Mr. Goy's diggings the broken
handle of a toothbrush, and Mr. Goy found it and immediately
labelled it as "perforated bone object of unknown use, possibly
ritualistic"—whereupon the naughty Professor came forward
with the rest of the toothbrush and there was a very boisterous
and embarrassing scene.

But in spite of this rivalry and these hearty explosions of contempt or rudeness, there was a singular kind of alliance between

the Professor and the curator; they were nearly always invited to each other's diggings, and they invariably united to repel an outsider.

I thought Mr. Goy was rather precise, rather pernickety, and certainly dressed in a style unbecoming to the keeper of a museum; but I liked him—his very superiority was of a bland or simple kind, his little airs and ways, instead of infuriating me, made me laugh. And Ellingham (who ought to know) assured me that Mr. Goy had a better idea of what was Halstatt and what was not than any other man he had ever met. It was true, he admitted, that the Goyan hypothesis of "pygmy industries" was of doubtful value...

The reader is not to suppose that I am deliberately mocking at archæology, the most respectable of English pastimes. But the crisis of this drama is to some extent an archæological crisis, deeply involving archæological personalities and archæological methods. A knowledge of these personalities and their methods is therefore indispensable if the reader would properly understand and appreciate the narrative.

Let me now continue.

Although Professor Reisby, hugely jocose as usual, joined us in many of our expeditions, there was another change in his manner.

He had developed an uncouth and a very startling habit of breaking out into sudden thunderous gusts of laughter, volcanic spasms of merriment, apparently without rhyme or reason. These fits (or whatever you like to call them) came on without the slightest warning. They might occur in the midst of conversation or in the midst of silence. He would look at you gravely for a moment, and then throw back his head and go off in a shattering peal of demonic laughter, in booming bellows of terrifying hilarity. Whatever might be the secret of this tremendous joke, you never knew it. The laughter came to an end as unaccountably as it had begun: the Professor wiped his eyes on a monstrous blue and yellow handkerchief—doubtless the colours of some revered school—and resumed his normal social attitude.

This peculiar habit frequently had the appearance of rudeness. Perhaps Dean Ingleworth, or the excellent Goy, might be addressing the company, or perhaps Ellingham was giving an account of some interesting experiment, when all at once—crash!—the Professor threw up his arms, and out came peal after peal of inane mirth.

On more than one of these occasions, before I got used to them, I looked at Hilda Reisby, and when she saw me looking she blushed, and I felt both sorry and awkward.

I may as well say that I was now extremely fond of Hilda. I looked upon her as one of the most valuable of my friends. We were not in love with each other, I think—at least I am sure that neither of us would have allowed our intimacy to continue if we had even fancied this to be the case. We were both about the same age, between thirty-five and thirty-six, and I did not believe that I was likely to fall seriously in love with anyone. At the same time, I did admire Hilda Reisby more truly than I admired any woman I had ever seen. Now, at thirty-five, she was (I thought) even more beautiful than she had been in youth, and she had all those qualities of a cool and a harmonised intelligence which are of such extraordinary value. Our friendship had a singular charm and intimacy which I cannot very well describe, but I do not wish to make it appear more romantic than it actually was. I know there are people who say that a pure friendship between a man and a woman is impossible unless they are both octogenarians—but that is all nonsense.

5

One day the whole party, with the exception of the Professor himself, explored the valley of the Kinkell.

Naturally we ascended the bank in order to see that remarkable and inviting tumulus, the Devil's Hump. There it was, partly concealed by the tangles of briar and bracken, partly covered with a mossy green turf, bare in places, crumbling, sandy, with a marked protrusion of the big slabs of granite which formed the burial-chambers.

Ellingham, of course, had a camera.

"A suitable occasion," he said, "for making one of those pictures which appropriately record every respectable holiday. Mrs. Reisby—if you would kindly recline just below the corner of that stone... charming indeed! And you, Farringdale, a little to the right. No, no! I want the top of the mound unobscured."

With a certain degree of excitement which I could not understand he placed the various members of the group and exposed three or four plates.

"Now, Farringdale, I want to photograph you alone, if you don't mind, sitting close to the top—by the side of that curious recent disturbance which has revealed the angle of a tilted covering-stone. Do you see? That's right!"

The shutter clicked. And then, instead of taking down his camera, Ellingham walked up the side of the mound and examined closely a tumbled mass of pebbles and sand at the top.

"Very curious old place!" he muttered, frowning, and looking at the soil and the stones with an almost fierce intensity.

"Really, father," said Peter Ellingham with a youthful, supercilious drawl, "I don't see anything very thrilling about it. Do you?" he added, turning to Frances Reisby.

She laughed, shaking her head and giving a toss to her fair curls.

"You ought to hear the Miss Macwardles on the subject! According to them, it's a place of sacrifice, a Druid altar, and I don't know what."

In the meantime, Ellingham was poking about in the rubble with a pointed geological hammer which, as the reader may remember, formed a part of his expeditionary equipment.

Whatever his conclusions may have been, he said nothing. But he carefully took three more photographs of the upper part of the mound.

"Mr. Goy has been trying to get leave to open the barrow," said Hilda Reisby, "but of course Mrs. Macwardle is loyal to Tolgen, and she says that *he* must open it if anyone does. She is not superstitious about it, like the old man, but I think she would rather it was left alone. The people in the village look on it with a sort of pious veneration, you know."

"Ah! Mrs. Reisby," said Ellingham as he fastened the stand of his camera, "let me beg you to use your influence in this matter. Join us in a petition to your illustrious husband and also to the worthy widow Macwardle, and let us open the tumulus!"

"But, father," said Peter in his new Balbus drawl, "surely it's very much like any other of these cairns, or whatever you call them."

"My dear Peter," replied his father with some asperity, "when you have devoted a little attention to the subject your opinion may have more value than it has at present. I was addressing Mrs. Reisby—"

"If I'm not mistaken," said Hilda, smiling, "I believe Tolgen really does intend to open the barrow before long. He feels that he has been rather hard on Goy, and he will probably invite him to cooperate. Then, if they get anything remarkable, he will ask Mrs. Macwardle to present it to Goy's museum."

"An admirable and a great-minded scheme," replied Ellingham enthusiastically, though with his customary note of sarcasm. "It is our duty—positively our duty—to encourage the Professor in this resolve. And let me hope that it may be our privilege to assist him."

"You can be quite sure of that in any case," Hilda said, "and I hope it will induce all of you to come up for the occasion. But why *is* this mound so particularly interesting, Mr. Ellingham?"

"Yes, why indeed?" echoed the impertinent Peter.

"Pray, sir, be silent!" Ellingham pointed a stern finger at his son. "It is particularly interesting, Mrs. Reisby, because it has very uncommon features, and I am not at all sure—nobody can be sure—of its exact period. I will not bore you with details. Then again, compared with other mounds in the district, it is unusually big. Moreover, it is connected in living memory with the past by means of legend, a sinister name, a vague reverence. Possibly it is not so ancient as we imagine. Possibly it is a Viking burial."

He turned aside, rubbing his chin, and again muttering in a peculiarly abstracted manner.

I recall one or two disjointed observations: "Never part of original chamber—obviously rebuilt—most irregular planning—do not wish to theorise prematurely—"

"Well," said Peter, "I think we've seen quite enough of this hump, if you ask me: let's go back to the jolly river."

And he set off along the path with Frances Reisby.

6

We had some other proofs of Reisby's eccentricity which I thought were vaguely disquieting.

Morgan and his friends often went out in the motor-boat *Mirabelle*. In the course of these excursions, whether fishing or merely cruising, they had often come across the Professor, alone in his little open boat.

"More than once," said Mr. Morgan, "I have seen the old gentleman three or four miles out, quite late in the evening, scudding along seaward under that old-fashioned lug. Of course there's no man handles a boat better than he does, and he's evidently strong as a bull. But it does seem a bit risky, somehow, doesn't it?"

Also, we heard stories of unaccountable absence, of strange visitors at Scarweather, of lights burning all night in the laboratory.

These tales and rumours came from various sources—the servants at Scarweather, the fishermen, the shop-keepers of Branderswick or Northport, or Mr. Morgan himself. They were related to us as friends of the family, and as people with a general interest in the community of Aberleven. There was, I am sure, a friendly motive in the telling. The Reisbys were extremely popular. Mrs. Reisby was the friend, the adviser and the ready helper of all the worthier people in Aberleven and its neighbourhood. Frances was the "young lady" of the place, and they were proud of her; though she naturally spent a good deal of her time away at school, or staying with her friends and relations elsewhere. The eminent Professor was, of course, the great man of the district, the man whose name appeared in the London papers, the man who was visited by the learned from every part of the world, the man who wrote books—and even sold them.

Let not the admiration of these poor villagers be despised. They had the sense, not so common among the more exalted, to understand the real nature of celebrity, the real pre-eminence of the intellectual! It had always been Reisby, never Macwardle, who was the "great man." Macwardle never got his name in the London papers!

And so the good people of Aberleven considered it proper that we should be made partakers of their uneasiness at the increasing oddities of Reisby. We were friends of the family, and we ought to be warned. We ought to be ready to help if we were called upon.

Ellingham did not appear to treat the matter very seriously. But in this, as I knew later, he was concealing his own attitude.

"Yes," he said, "the old fellow is eccentric—very eccentric—I agree. What then? Eccentricities of learned men are common, generally harmless, often amusing. You can see that he is devoted to his wife and daughter, and I should say that either of them, alone, is perfectly capable of keeping him under control."

PART IV

The Devil's Hump

CHAPTER I

I

I AM ANXIOUS TO TELL THIS INCREDIBLE STORY IN MY OWN way, without exasperating the reader who has followed me so far, but without omitting any material circumstance. I want to recall, as far as possible, my own state of mind as the drama gradually moved from one stage to another, the climax unforeseen, unimagined, except in the busy brain of Ellingham. And Ellingham, until the evidence was complete, wisely refrained from communicating even the shadow of a doubt or the hint of a clue to any other mind.

It is only by a careful reconstruction of events that I can present to the reader the essential character of these strange happenings, and so not only prepare him for the culminating horror of the final scene, but also reveal its inevitability.

In the autumn of 1927 I was chosen to assist Sir Barlock-Winterslade, K.C., in the now celebrated case of Brackleton v. Duckwash and Others, Rex intervening. We were on the side of Duckwash and Others, and I had to examine and digest no fewer than forty-seven volumes of typewritten documents. The second hearing of the case was down for October. In order to read through the papers in quiet and make a précis for Sir Barlock, I decided, in the middle of September, to spend a week or ten days in the hotel at Aberleven. I was also anxious to have the opinion of Hilda Reisby on certain features of the case which could only be fully understood by a woman. I had

consulted her on previous occasions and I had found her judgment invariably sound and often brilliant. It is a great pity that
male barristers, in general, do not appreciate the immense value
of such opinions.

However, the affair of Duckwash and Others has nothing to
do with this particular story, though it would provide material
for at least a dozen of the so-called "detective" novels. I took all
the papers up to Aberleven, and I found my big seaward-facing
bedroom almost ideal as a study. The only drawback was the difficulty of telephoning to Sir Barlock, but the occasions for doing
so were fortunately not frequent.

Hilda was extremely kind in helping me, and I can hardly say
how much the defence really owed to her perspicacity. Had it not
been for her skill and insight we should never have realised and
revealed the true motives of the door-keeper's wife, nor should
we have seen the deep significance of the dirty custard-cup.

I had several delightful walks with Hilda, refreshing and memorable walks; some in the bright wild air of the morning, and
others in the calm warmth of an autumn twilight.

She told me various things about the Professor which made
me feel uneasy again. The laughing-fits were more frequent and
more alarming. Sometimes he would go off into these fits when
he was alone in the study or laboratory. All would be silent, and
then came those horrid reverberating peals of demonic hilarity,
crashing and echoing through the entire house. This had occurred
once or twice when there were visitors in the drawing-room, and
it was very awkward.

But there were other fits—fits of an opposite kind—when a
great cloud seemed to fall on the man. Then he sat motionless

and soundless in his chair, his mighty head bowed over his chest, a massive hand resting on each arm of the chair, the eyes, clear and hard, fixed on vacancy.

Hilda Reisby had consulted secretly the doctors in Northport, and others, including her father in Manchester. Their opinions varied; some took a light view of the case, and others were exceedingly grave. All agreed on one point, and on one point only: nothing could be done unless the Professor would submit to treatment, unless he would agree to swallow the prescribed sedatives. Or he might go for a change somewhere. Best of all, in view of his love of the sea, he might go for a cruise. But it was hopeless. He rebutted with fury the idea that he was ill. Nothing would induce him to see "one of those blasted quacks, who made you pay through the nose for the privilege of listening to their pompous futilities." He had given up his trips to Scandinavia, and except for an occasional visit to London he rarely left his home for more than a week.

"And that wretched little Goy has been worrying him about the Devil's Hump, and running round to see Mrs. Macwardle and trying to make her give him leave to open it, and all that sort of thing."

"Has the Professor any plans in regard to the Devil's Hump?"

"Yes. I think he has made up his mind to open it—next year probably—if only to keep Goy quiet."

"Defying the superstitions of the people?"

"I don't think they are likely to trouble him very much—either the people or the superstitions. Tolgen is very popular here, and they know he would make a proper job of it."

"It would be uncommonly interesting. Next year, you think?"

"That is my impression. But you must ask him yourself. He will certainly want you and Mr. Ellingham to be present."

Soon after this conversation I had supper with the Reisbys. The Professor was in a fine, unclouded humour, full of his old, abounding jocularity, his Gargantuan jesting.

"Ah, ha! Tra-la-di-dee! Are you a member of the growing conspiracy, eh? Are you of the Goy alliance?" He shook his head with a humorous affectation of sorrow.

"God forbid, sir!"

"Well, well! I suppose I shall have to open the poor old tumulus, if only to defend it against the Northport league, the man with a packet of labels, eh? Still, you are not to suppose that I deride the worthy Goy. No, no, sir! Goy is a very excellent fellow, a very dogged excellent fellow, sir. It is astounding, with what pertinacity he pursues his object, with what eager zeal he prepares the adhesive label! Why, sir, he has a box of these labels in his pocket, every label with 'Northport City Museum' printed across the top of it, and when he sees anything covetable—why, sir, he labels it, not merely giving it what he considers an appropriate description, but also converting it into the property of the museum. Yes indeed," (laughing immoderately) "I am told that he put one of his tickets on the Saxon cross in Aggersdon churchyard, and then wrote to Ingleworth asking him to arrange for its removal. Ha, ha!"

"That's a wicked invention of yours, Tolgen," said Mrs. Reisby.

"Is it, my dear? Well, you know, it is never easy to draw the line between fact and fiction in matters archæological. The antiquary's nimble mind is not by evidence confined; give him a tiny scrap or bit, he'll find a theory to fit; at once, to his divining eyes, what grand hypotheses arise! Ah, ho, ha!"

So he boomed away, cheerfully and irresistibly, and I could feel again the peculiar dominance, the *imposition*, of this redoubtable mind. It seemed impossible for an ordinary person, like myself, to meet him on his own level. But I was keen on the subject of the Devil's Hump, if only on account of Ellingham's unaccountable enthusiasm, and I persisted:

"Then, sir, you are going to dig—"

"Of course I am! *Magno cum periculo custoditur, quod multis placet!* I shall dig in self-defence. I shall prevent the vigilance of Goy by inviting him to share in the toil and the glory, and I shall offer him the spoils—provided only that I am in command of the operations."

"I hope, sir, that you will allow me, and our friend Ellingham—"

"Of course, my dear fellow, of course! How should we dig without the help, the encouragement of our distinguished associates? Come, let me speak plainly. I intend to open this famous mound in about a year's time, say in August. Actually I have obtained the necessary authority from the Office of Works and also from Mrs. Macwardle. So everything is ready. A young pupil of mine, William Tuffle, will come down from Northport to make plans or measurements; he is very good at that sort of thing. I expect Goy and his wife will stay at the hotel. If Ellingham is free, I hope he will undertake any photography that is desirable, for I do not know anybody who is better fitted for the task. You see, my dear Farringdale, I anticipate a regular congress, a social gathering of a particularly delightful kind."

He spoke in a smoother, more conventional style, but I observed a curious twitch or flicker of his brows and lips, as if he was keeping under control an impulse to laugh uproariously. His wife and daughter looked at him with evident concern.

But Reisby was entirely, I might almost say unusually, normal. He continued to discuss his plans, and eventually asked me to find out if August in the following year (1928) would be convenient for Ellingham.

I can hardly say why the Professor's decision excited me, as it certainly did.

Of course I had not forgotten the conversation in the Rouen hospital, but I did not attach any importance to it. How could any reasonable person attach importance to an idea so vague and incongruous? But then, I said to myself, Ellingham's behaviour with regard to the Devil's Hump had always been very mysterious, and he was not the man to wander off in pursuit of a mere fantasy. Anyhow, we were going to dig up the mystery, if there was one, and the Professor himself was the prime mover in the affair. No doubt it would be great fun. We should be a jolly party, and there is always a fascination in the unearthing of hidden things, even if those things are sepulchral.

The sanctity of a burial-place appears to evaporate in time: I suppose the antiquaries of the future will cheerfully dig up all our Christian cemeteries, assembling, for the purpose, at the nearest hotels... Consider the innumerable thousands of tombs we have violated in Egypt alone. Is it really decent?

2

When I told Morgan at the hotel about this future digging he looked rather serious.

"I wish you gentlemen would leave these things alone," he said. "Of course I'm an ignorant fellow myself, but I must say it makes me feel a bit creepy—all this upsetting of the poor old bones! And our people here, between you and me, don't like it at all. They don't say much, because they are fond of the Reisbys; but this opening of the Devil's Hump will be as much as they can stand, let me tell you."

"What harm can it possibly do to anyone?"

"Well, you know what people are like, Mr. Farringdale. It's those *bones* that make all the trouble. Superstition, no doubt; but we can't help it. Takes a bit of education to destroy reverence, Mr. Farringdale."

I was rather shocked.

"But really, Morgan, that's going a bit too far—"

"I've no wish to be offensive. I'm only telling you what the people think. One of our farmers—Jenkins—thought he would get a bit of stone for repairs the other day. So he started to pick at one of those little tumps on the side of the moor, and out fell a bit of a skeleton. Well! as soon as they saw it they packed up and went away, and nothing on earth could induce 'em to touch any of those stones, I can tell you."

I fell back on the half-hearted apology of the scientist.

"But you see, Morgan, the pursuit of knowledge—"

He shook his head.

"That's where you beat us, of course. It's the privilege of education. I have always lived among simple people—farmers and fishermen in England and black men in South Africa—and I have got the ideas of these people in my head. And there's none of us like the notion of disturbing the bones of buried men. Looking at it only from the selfish point of view, we think it's unlucky. And we don't understand how it adds to knowledge—at least, to any useful knowledge."

"But you don't suggest that anyone is likely to interfere?"

"No, I don't think so. It's the gentry, you see! That makes all the difference."

3

On my way back to London I spent a few days with the Ellinghams at Cambridge. Fred Ellingham was now, as we had anticipated, the Woolhope Professor of Organic Chemistry.

As we sat together in his study, after dinner on the evening of my arrival, I told him about the forthcoming dig at the Devil's Hump.

"No!" he cried, "you don't say so!"

His excitement took me by surprise.

"I thought you anticipated something of the kind."

"I have always wanted to see the tumulus opened, but I never thought old Reisby would undertake the job himself."

"Surely he is the proper person."

Ellingham cogitated for a few moments, rubbing both forefingers up and down the side of his nose. I knew that he had some bizarre theory about the Devil's Hump, probably an archæological theory, but I suspected nothing more.

"Yes, he's the proper person, of course. Still, it is very astonishing, very unexpected… No doubt he is afraid of Goy getting there first."

"Quite correct."

"He admits it, does he?"

"Certainly he does."

"Ah! I see. Precisely."

"Will you be able to go there?"

"I shall not allow anything to stand in the way, if I can help it."

"It ought to be interesting."

"It ought to be devilish interesting—far more interesting than you suppose, my dear young friend." Ellingham, from the advanced position of fifty years, regarded my mere thirty-five as the age of youth; and he also insulted me by saying that I was remarkably young, even for my age.

Then the conversation took a quite inexplicable turn, but the conversation of Ellingham was often quite inexplicable.

He began to talk about my poor cousin, Eric Foster, introducing the subject by a clumsy invocation of sentiment, in which he failed altogether to deceive me. As a matter of fact, I knew that he did not care in the least whether he deceived me or not.

"Poor fellow!" he said, "it will be fourteen years since we had all that awful trouble… Yes, fourteen years… By the way, he was a keen football player, was he not?"

"He played for the Old Hibernians."

"Am I right in saying that the poor lad broke a bone in the course of some match or other?—a collar-bone or something? Poor lad!—he was always such a keen player!"

"It was a knee-cap. He broke it in 1912 in a match against the Tiddleswick Crusaders."

"Yes, yes!" Ellingham was strangely excited. "I remember! Such a fine plucky fellow. He thought nothing of it, I am sure. Was it the right or the left knee-cap?"

"Right, I believe. I cannot be quite sure."

"In those days they used to mend a broken knee-cap by means of wire, silvered phosphor-bronze or something of the sort. What a charming fellow he was! Everybody was fond of Eric. Did they use wire, do you know?"

"Yes, I think so. Again, I cannot be quite certain. It was a very bad fracture."

"Good enough," said Ellingham, thinking aloud. "His aunt would remember all about it, no doubt. Have you seen her lately? I have the greatest admiration for Miss Foster—a most remarkable woman for her age—indeed for any age. The right knee-cap fractured. Hum! Old women often have a peculiar charm, a fragrance of personality, have they not? Tell me—did he ever break any other bones?"

"No, I don't think so."

"You consider me crazy or impertinent, perhaps. But that is not really the case, my dear fellow, let me assure you. One cannot help remembering these little things. I seldom think of the departed without recalling these odd particulars. It is a habit of thought, a morphological habit. And I cannot help thinking of your poor cousin at present. How excited he would have been, poor boy, if he knew that we were going to open the Devil's Hump! He would have been keenly interested in our plans. Ah!—there is one other thing—do you remember anything about his teeth?"

"His teeth?"

"Yes. I seem to recall some little trouble—"

"So far as I know, he had remarkably good teeth."

"Think again. Wasn't there a replacement? a false molar, or something of the sort?"

"What an extraordinary memory you have, Ellingham! You are correct. I had forgotten it myself. He had a single false tooth, a back tooth, in his lower jaw. It was a clever bit of work, and you could not possibly have spotted it. How on earth did you know?"

"One of those curious mental notes of mine. No doubt he told me. I never met a lad with a more naturally engaging manner. He would have made a first-rate physician, so quick and sympathetic! Was it on the right or left side of the jaw?"

"The left side."

"And all the other teeth were quite perfect, I remember. A singularly delightful nature, candid without being raw and vital without being obtrusive. He had also—what I should expect in your family, my dear Farringdale!—a most agile and rapid intelligence. What I regret is, that I was not able to meet him more frequently. Yet I remember him very well, poor fellow! You see what odd little details have lingered in my recollection. Odd, is it not?"

He smiled at me in his inscrutably sardonic manner, half closing his eyes, and wrinkling up his lean face until it was almost diabolical.

Looking back with an open mind, I realise that I was completely baffled. I knew all the peculiarities of this remarkable man, and I knew that it was his custom never to expose his thoughts or theories until he needed the information or the co-operation of somebody else, or until he considered a revelation morally or scientifically desirable. He did not cultivate mystery; he simply refrained from action or communication until it was possible to be absolutely definite. I saw no relevance in his questions about my cousin; I merely thought he was trying to recall certain features

or memories. That he should have chosen such definitely anatomical features was not surprising to one who knew the peculiar
workings of his mind. In short, I had no suspicion of any motive
behind those questions, apart from the purely transient motives
of a ruminating memory. It was quite reasonable to suppose that
Eric might have told him about his broken bone (though I never
heard him mention it to anyone). The detail of the tooth was more
striking, because I had some difficulty in remembering it myself.
Yet I think I can truthfully say that I should not have remembered
this conversation, had it not been for the astounding events with
which it was intimately connected.

Does the reader now perceive the shadow of these events?
If so, I congratulate him upon possessing a swift and practical
imagination.

4

Reading over what I have now set down, it seems to me that I
have stated fairly all the essential facts.

Ellingham, I need hardly observe, had been working all the
time on a definite hypothesis.

There is nothing of real importance to be recorded between
the autumn of 1927 and the summer of 1928, when we assembled
at Aberleven for the opening of the tumulus.

The Reisbys came to London in the early spring of 1928, but I
did not see much of them because I had several cases which were
occupying most of my time. I took Mrs. Reisby and Frances to
one or two theatres, and once the entire family dined with me at
my Chelsea rooms.

Reisby, as far as I could judge, was in good health. He, too, appeared to be very busy. I could not help wondering if he still played chess with sailors in Poplar. A friend of mine, who had seen Reisby, declared that he came across him, accompanied by two famously disreputable society ladies, at the Gilded Lily. This may or may not have been true. In view of what afterwards came to my knowledge, I should say that it *was* true.

Frances, who embarrassed me and amused her mother by calling me "Uncle Tom," told me frankly that "Daddy is not nearly as mad as he was a year ago." I should, perhaps, explain that both mother and daughter had adopted me (I think it is the appropriate term) as a confidential friend of the household. Only, they said, the unaccountable absences of the Professor were more frequent. He went away for several days at a time without saying where he intended to go, but always giving the exact time of his return. Also, there had been an increase of the singular visitors to Scarweather described as "pupils," or "students." They were dressy, decadent people who came in expensive cars, and it was hard to believe they were intelligently interested in chemistry and archæology—or, indeed, in anything but their own insignificant or pernicious lives. But still—"Daddy is not nearly as mad as he was a year ago."

Of course we said a good deal about the arrangements for opening the Devil's Hump. That archæological occasion had now, for various reasons, become of extraordinary interest and importance to all of us. The date of the opening—I might almost say, of the ceremony—had been provisionally fixed for Tuesday the 21st of August.

Mr. Wilberforce Goy and the Professor were now, I was told, on terms of relative amiability. Mr. Goy was flattered at being invited to cooperate, and he was delighted to know that his museum was to receive the "finds"—after they had been examined, photographed and recorded by the Professor.

I was unable to visit Aberleven before the time of the digging; but I corresponded with Hilda Reisby, and I was glad to hear that everything was going smoothly; or at least with no fresh alarms.

Fortunately I had got through my work before the end of the Trinity Term, and I was justified in allowing myself a clear month's holiday in August. I spent a fortnight with my mother and sister at Eastbourne. On Saturday the 18th of August I returned to London. On the 19th I went up to the Ellinghams at Cambridge, and on the Monday we all travelled together to Aberleven.

CHAPTER II

H EAVEN KNOWS, I HAVE GOOD REASONS FOR REMEMBERING
it, but in any circumstances I think I should have remembered vividly that assemblage of odd or remarkable people at the
Aberleven hotel. The resident company in the hotel, the expeditionary force assembled for the opening of the barrow, consisted
of the Ellingham family, Mr. and Mrs. Goy, Mr. William Tuffle,
and myself.

Now, a group of archæological people is quite unlike any other.
I cannot describe myself as an archæologist, of course; and the
interest of Mrs. Ellingham and her son Peter was of a somewhat
diluted kind; but there could be no doubt about the others.

Mr. William Tuffle, the son of a respectable solicitor in
Northport, was the most archæological person I have ever met.
He was a pale and rather clammy youth, with a pair of moist and
appealing eyes which he protected or assisted by means of glasses
in a golden frame. I think he was about twenty-five years old,
but he appeared to have few, if any, of the normal impulses and
the wholesome graces of youth. He had, instead, a perverse or
inverted affection for the antique. His very way of thinking, you
could see, was venerable, mouldy and entirely without colour.
In pursuit of his trophies, the bones or relics of the prehistoric,
he had a grave enthusiasm which made you think of an owl pursuing mice. At the same time he prided himself, incongruously
one might suppose, upon a more than ordinary knowledge of

cocktails. He mixed, for his own benefit and that of his friends, extremely curious alcoholic solutions, which he drank or handed round with a sombre and imposing gravity. After swallowing a few of his own decoctions, he became paler, moister, more vague, until he finally subsided into a state of mental mildew, a dim shimmering on the verge of total obliteration. I suppose the cocktail aspect of Mr. Tuffle was really due to a belated feeling of counterpoise, a rather pathetic desire to appear manly. A similar impulse, no doubt, induces curates to brag about the drinking of beer.

But when you saw Mr. Tuffle in the field, adroitly flicking the end of a tape-measure or darting his eager nose into a spadeful of earth, then indeed you saw Mr. Tuffle in his element, his proper medium. These discriminating pounces, these nimble calculations, these delicate yet rapid subsoil manœuvres made it clear that Mr. Tuffle knew his job.

Nor must you consider Mr. Tuffle as a mere ferret or earth-worker. He was equally skilled in all the sinuosities and all the virtuosities of archæological debate. He knew the names and histories of all those who were eminent in this particular study, and he also knew when they were right or wrong. Tuffle, you see, was never wrong; he might be relatively obscure, but he was magnificently positive. And it must be admitted, in fairness to sapient William, that he was impartial. Although a pupil of Reisby's, he did not hesitate to point out in how many ways the eminent Professor was entirely wrong—indeed, he did not hesitate to expose himself to the gusty ridicule of the Professor by telling him so. An independent youth, he did not belong to the Reisby faction or the Goy faction, but held himself superior to both.

By these perpetual and emphatic disagreements he obtained a reputation for true knowledge and originality.

However, I was delighted to observe an absence of anything like faction or disagreement among the members of our own party. We had all assembled, it was clear, with the intention of enjoying ourselves.

Wilberforce Goy was now about forty-seven. He was completely bald, though he retained his fluffy wisp of a yellow moustache. The general effect of Mr. Goy was luminous and highly intelligent. He diffused a mild radiance, both mental and physical. Light was reflected from the glossy top of his bald head, from his glasses, from the protruding whiteness of his teeth. He had cultivated an extreme brevity of speech, and a calm indifference to the speeches of others, which occasionally imposed a certain tax on good-humour. Mr. Goy's clothes were still of an irreproachable and expensive cut, and even when he went to a digging he was togged up as though for a ducal shoot.

Mrs. Goy (an ex-schoolmistress, you may remember) was a woman who asserted herself in a mute, disconcerting way which I found rather obnoxious. Her aspect was tall and cylindrical. Her features were sharp, with long straight edges, rather fine in their way, her flaxen Nordic hair was cut in a stern though not unbecoming manner, her air was grave and enquiring.

The worst thing about Mrs. Goy was her mute persistence, her way of coming up to you and hovering in silence, amiably smiling at you in her odd medieval way and obliging you to speak in mere self-defence. It is a most embarrassing trick, and it has the effect of committing you to fulsome absurdities or trivial nonsense, reducing you in your own sight and making you ridiculous to others. Mrs. Goy, I think, is the only woman who ever succeeded in making me blush in public, and she did it by these awful methods of silent attack.

Still, you could not help liking Amelia Goy. You forgave her disquieting mutism, her lingerings and hoverings, and even her abominable craze for crossword puzzles. She was capable, kindly, ready with unobtrusive efficiency to put things in order (including Mr. Goy) or to avert a quarrel. Indeed, she had one of the rarest and most valuable of qualifications—Mrs. Goy was methodical without being fussy. Also, her knowledge of archæology, and of archæologists, was really profound and entertaining.

Thus we had an archæological majority in the party at the hotel: Mrs. Ellingham, Peter and myself were merely amateurs.

We arrived soon after five o'clock, and Goy told us that the Reisbys were coming over after dinner to join us in a grand conference. I had a quiet word with Morgan, and he told me that the plans for the opening of the barrow had given rise to quite a lot of local excitement.

"They don't like it," he said, "and there's none of the village men will take a hand in the digging. All the workmen—there's four, I believe—are gardeners from the Manor. The Misses Macwardle are very interested, they tell me."

"I'm sorry, Morgan. I don't like the idea of offending these fellows. We have always got on so well together."

"Oh, they won't bother you! Still, it's no use pretending they are keen on the job."

I was disturbed. It is always unpleasant to feel that your pastimes are causing offence, even when the offence appears to be entirely unreasonable.

Meanwhile, in the drawing-room of the hotel, Mr. Tuffle was expounding and affirming in his dimly pertinacious way over a twenty-five-inch map and a set of outline plans of the Devil's Hump, which he had already prepared.

"You see, sir," he said, addressing Ellingham, "I should be unwilling to accept Professor Reisby's opinion without further evidence. Personally, as a student of many years' experience, I don't mind saying…"

Mrs. Goy sidled up to me with her thin, inscrutable smile.

I had not yet grown accustomed to her strange manners, and I blurted out something about, "Frightfully interesting—rather unusual site, I believe—"

She merely pointed with a long deliberate finger at one of Mr. Tuffle's plans, neatly pinned on a board.

At the top of the plan I read:

"Devil's Hump, Tumulus. Lat. 55.43 north. Long. 1.57 west. Scale 1/36. W.H.T. 20.8.28."

"I have a series of these tracings," Mr. Tuffle assured me with considerable pride, "and I shall be able to plot the exact position of the finds as we go on with a minimum loss of time to the excavators."

"It is my own system," said Mr. Goy.

Ellingham was closely examining the rather bleak diagrams. They were mostly white paper, covered with magnetic parallels to facilitate rapid triangulation. Only the outline of the tumulus was firmly drawn.

"These will be invaluable."

"Neat," said Mr. Goy.

"I cannot imagine anything better," Ellingham replied. "My own functions will now be comparatively simple, for I shall only be the photographer of the party. Dare I hope that you will allow me to make tracings of these plans after you have filled in the details of the excavation?"

"Delighted," answered Mr. Goy. "Great pleasure."

"I can make you some spare tracings, if you like," said Mr. Tuffle, dimly but firmly insisting upon his own importance. "I say, how about some cocktails before dinner? You fellows are ready for them, I'm sure. Mrs. Ellingham? Mrs. Goy? The resources of the place are limited, I'm afraid, but I know one or two simple things which are quite drinkable. Have you ever tried a Valparaiso Crocus, Mr. Farringdale?"

2

After dinner the Reisby family came over, and I was glad to see them looking particularly well. I could not help observing the delight with which Peter, who was having rather a stuffy time, greeted Frances.

Our party, now numbering ten, ascended to the private parlour or drawing-room which Mr. Morgan had reserved for our special use.

Professor Reisby swamped us all in the torrents of his boisterous humour, he roared at Mr. Goy and Mr. Tuffle until those gentlemen subsided meekly. He then made amends by praising loudly the plans of Tuffle and the careful preparations of Goy.

"Tuffle and his tapes! Goy with his boxes *and* his labels, ha! You, Ellingham, with your incomparable Zeiss and your sagacity! And you, Farringdale, with your—your noble detachment, ha, ha, ha! Farringdale will not commit himself until he has examined the evidence, sifted the evidence! I tell you what, Farringdale—we'll put you in charge of the sifters, the sieves and the riddles! And you—ladies!—you are to be the spectators of our toil, providing us with cheer and comfort—and our lunch, eh? As for you, young people" (looking at the self-conscious Peter and Frances), "we shall abandon you to your own devices."

Then we listened to the scheme of the operations, which were perfectly simple. Two trenches would be cut simultaneously into the mound, starting at ground-level, the one approaching the other at an angle of about sixty degrees. The subsequent working would depend, of course, on what was discovered.

Dean Ingleworth hoped that he would be able to attend the diggings, but he was now infirm, and unequal to a long day in the open. The Ugglesby-Gores intended to come on the second day of the excavations—the day on which the centre of the barrow would probably be cleared. Mrs. Macwardle was content to be represented by her two daughters, Prudence and Priscilla, and these ladies (now elderly) were not only supporting the scheme with the greatest enthusiasm, but were making a liberal contribution towards our lunch.

"Miss Priscilla is frightfully worked up over it," said Frances, "because of her dreams and all that sort of thing. She says there's a king buried in the barrow—"

"Now, Frances!" said her mother, "you are not to make fun of Miss Macwardle."

"Queer," said Mr. Goy.

"Certainly queer, but she is extremely kind and good-natured, and has taken an awful lot of trouble over this dig. By the way, you are all invited to dine at the Manor on Friday night."

There was a somewhat uneasy shuffling and whispering among the company.

"That is very kind of Mrs. Macwardle," said Mrs. Ellingham, looking at Mrs. Goy, who was mutely smiling as usual, "and we shall be delighted, of course."

"Got to go!" roared Reisby. "No need to dress up. I never do. Can't refuse to go when we owe everything to the kindness of these people. May be a bore, but you've thundering well got to go, all of you, and pay your respects to the old lady."

"Pleasure," said Mr. Goy.

Mrs. Goy continued to smile.

"If I am able to stay for so long—" said Mr. Tuffle. "I say, may I order some drinks? If you fellows would tell me what you would like… Mr. Farringdale approves of my Valparaiso Crocus, I know."

But Professor Reisby treated Mr. Tuffle's cocktails with unmitigated scorn, and he called for a bottle of five-star Martell, regardless of the extravagance.

3

Tuesday, the 21st, was a pleasant breezy day, with a few high clouds in an otherwise clear sky.

With the exception of Mr. Goy, who was dressed in his ducal-shoot style, we had all put on old clothes, ready for a bit of navvy-work. Mr. Tuffle had an old Morris car, a venerable, dishevelled, rusty car, having the same air of dim antiquity that one associated with its owner. In this car Mr. Tuffle kindly arranged to convey Ellingham and myself to the plantation by the barrow where the

other cars of the party would be duly parked. The rest of the hotel
group would be driven to the same place by Morgan.

It would have been difficult to decide whether Mr. Tuffle or
Ellingham carried the greatest amount of equipment. Ellingham
had an enormous bag full of boxes, bottles, envelopes, cotton-
wool, paper and every sort of packing or receptacle; he had, of
course, the Zeiss camera, with an immense number of plates;
and he had also a collection of instruments for probing, picking,
hammering, cutting or seizing. Tuffle had a spectacular outfit of
long poles, painted in bands of red, black and white for measuring;
he had chains, tapes, pegs and a beautiful compass; and a large
drawing-board with straps, pins and adjustable scales, protrac-
tors, dividers, a box of coloured chalks, and I don't know what.
In addition, he took a vast assortment of boxes, nearly equal to
Ellingham's lot.

We assembled at the plantation soon after ten o'clock. Our
things were carried down to the edge of the plantation just above
the barrow, and at half past ten we were ready to begin.

Mr. Tuffle, with unwavering solemnity, took down the names
of all present, writing them on the pages of a large note-book.
He was to be the official historian of the dig. Tuffle was on the
point of closing his book, and the pioneers were advancing to the
mound with picks and shovels, when the two Misses Macwardle
came running down through the plantation with a shrill twittering of greeting and excitement.

The note-book was opened again, the names were inscribed,
operations were suspended.

And while Miss Prudence and Miss Priscilla were chirruping among the members of the group, I had an opportunity

for observing Professor Reisby. He was looking at the mound with a sort of fierce expectancy which I remember noting particularly at the time. He put me in mind of some advancing barbarian chief, pausing with battle-thunders on his brow and all the cruel joy of the fighter in his heart before he leads the attack. I say he put me in mind of such a man, and I record the impression because it is neither so foolish nor so inappropriate as it may appear.

And then, as if we had actually drawn up in order of battle, we all stood looking at the mound, with the Professor a little in front of the others.

There it was—a heap of earth and stones, presently to reveal whatever grim secrets it might contain. God alone knows what a tumult of disordered thoughts may then have been rioting in the mind of Professor Reisby!

"Oh, you dear wonderful old place!" cried Miss Priscilla Macwardle in her thin, pinched little pipe, "forgive our temerity in thus venturing to disturb the repose of your beautiful dead."

Mr. Goy looked rather startled, and he muttered a single word, which I did not hear distinctly—but it sounded like "rot."

"I have seen them in a vision," Miss Priscilla continued in a weird sibylline manner, her grey locks ruffled in the breeze. "The king lies there—" she pointed vaguely at the mound—"in his kingly armour, with spear and a mighty shield…"

We stood in an awkward silence, while the crazy lady rambled on for at least five minutes. Even when she had finished, nobody cared to make a move or a comment until Mr. Tuffle briskly ran forward with his bundle of painted poles, like a matador, and bravely stuck one of them in the side of the mound.

"Now then, you fellows with the picks!" he cried, "clear away this tangle and rubble! Have you got any bill-hooks? Good! Now— here is Trench A, and here is Trench B. Am I right, sir?"

"Aye, aye!" shouted Reisby, no longer moodily staring, but full of energy and of good-humour. "Those are the places, my boy. Not less than ten feet across. You two here, and you here, and away we go!"

The attack had begun.

4

There are people who believe that archæology is dull. So it is in its written form—deplorably and desperately dull. But I know of nothing jollier than archæology in the field, provided that you are really getting something for your pains. And there is no doubt that we did get something for our pains—a great deal more than we bargained for—when we opened the Devil's Hump.

For the first hour or so the digging was uneventful. There was a lot of turf and rubble and gorse to be cleared away before the men could make much impression on the mound, and the Professor insisted, very wisely, on trenches of maximum width.

The ladies, after the interest in the start of the work had subsided, began to stroll about on the side of the valley, or, sitting on rugs near the lunch-baskets, engaged in amiable chatter. Mrs. Goy, I noticed, sat apart from the others with a newspaper on her knees.

The men of the party, including young Peter, took a hand in the picking and shovelling and heaving. Reisby, with much redundant bellowing, tore up enormous masses of turf, uprooted

whole bushes, playfully tossed over the top of the mound a series
of colossal boulders. And all the time he kept up a flow of noisy
banter or of humorous admonition.

As the professional workers—the four gardeners from the
Manor—got further into the mound, there was more for the rest
of us to do, and we were soon busy clearing away the rubbish,
and occasionally relieving the pioneers.

Enthusiasm was presently roused by the discovery of a patch
of charcoal in Trench A, and everybody came up to look at it.

"Cremated burial," said Mr. Goy.

"Not necessarily," said Mr. Tuffle, "not necessarily. May be
ritualistic."

"How beautiful!" cried Miss Priscilla. "The purification of
burning!"

"More likely to be an offering of roasted ox, ma'am!" said
Reisby.

"Probably in the immediate vicinity of a chamber, at any
rate," observed Ellingham. "I expect we shall touch the sides of
it in a moment."

"Jolly good going!" said Peter, thrusting his fingers back
through a mass of glistening curls. "It's about time we jolly well
did strike something, if you ask me!"

"Can any of you tell me what this is?" said Mrs. Goy, demurely
smiling. "Five letters. 'If Coriolanus looked me in the face, he'd
wear his toga with a better grace.' The second letter is a G and
the last is an L."

"Mirror," said Mr. Goy.

"Wilberforce! you are paying no attention!" cried the lady, and
she withdrew, rather sulkily, with her paper.

We were still picking up pinches of the charcoal when poor old Ingleworth, supported by his chauffeur, appeared on the scene.

"Good day to you all!" piped the Dean in his quavering, senile voice. "Pray do not cease from your most interesting occupations. Give me leave to investigate."

He raised his black-and-yellow straw hat to the ladies and slowly tottered up to the edge of the mound. Professor Reisby explained his plan.

"Now I am surprised, my dear Reisby, I am indeed," cried the Dean querulously, "to see you cutting a trench in *this* direction. Give me a stick, Jenkins. I should certainly have supposed that you would begin over *there*." He flung the stick feebly into the air and it fell on the top of the mound.

"Just over there, on the other side."

Reisby towered above the slender, brittle, attenuated figure of the poor little Dean, but he did not roar and bellow at him, as he did fourteen years ago.

"Ah, ho! my dear Ingleworth, we shall be able to extend in that direction if it seems desirable; but our objective, you see, is the centre of the mound. There is undoubtedly a chamber, or chambers, below the disturbed portion—you can now actually see the edges of one of them."

He pointed with a crowbar, holding it out as lightly and firmly as if it was a pencil. I saw two of the men look at each other with a grin of appreciation and astonishment.

"You may be right, Professor; I should not care to say that you may not be right. Eh, eh,—but allow me. Give me your arm, Jenkins."

Very slowly the old man ascended the side of the mound.

"Dear Dean!" cried Miss Macwardle, "do be careful, dear Dean! Oh, Professor Reisby, don't let him do anything dangerous!" She turned aside to Mrs. Ellingham. "Isn't he too perfectly wonderful? Like the Apostle Paul, or a saint, or a Druid, I always think."

Ingleworth paused, leaning heavily on the man's arm. In his faltering hand he waved an ebony walking-stick with a golden head.

"There—under that clump of bracken. I distinctly remember seeing a very considerable protrusion—"

"Displacement," said Mr. Goy impatiently.

The old man looked at him with a tremulous disdain tempered by extreme feebleness. At that moment I hated Mr. Goy. But Reisby took up arms in defence of the Dean.

"Displacement, Goy!—displacement! Ho, ah! Tuffle, Tuffle, Tuffle!—let it be duly recorded in the book of the dig that Mr. Wilberforce Goy has duly observed a displacement, a *lapsus lapidis*! Yes, sir," addressing the Dean, "you are right. I shall certainly dig in the place you have indicated. I will make a special dig, sir, and it shall be known as the Dean's Traverse; it shall be entered in the book of Tuffle as the Dean's Traverse. You agree with me, Professor Ellingham, do you not?"

"Certainly," said Ellingham. "I noticed the place myself some years ago."

Reisby looked at him sharply. Then he took a pick and swung it with a clean, ringing stroke into the patch of charcoal.

A puff of whitish powder came away from the point of impact.

"There you are!" he cried. "The edge of a passage or chamber."

"Megalithic," said Mr. Goy.

At the same time the workers in Trench B announced the discovery of two upright slabs forming a right angle. Dean

Ingleworth had arrived at the critical moment. We were about to make the first discoveries.

Ellingham was extremely busy with his camera. He seemed to be taking dozens of pictures, not only of the excavated parts, but also of the untouched portions of the mound. I considered that so many pictures, taken at such an early stage of our proceedings, could serve no useful purpose; but I was completely mistaken.

Apart from the taking of these photographs, there was nothing in Ellingham's behaviour, up to that point, which could be regarded as peculiar. He assisted the others with pick or spade, though he was careful to watch every stage of the digging in both trenches. I got the impression, which proved to be quite correct, that he would not be keenly interested until we got to the centre of the mound.

Reisby, who always conducted his digs with rigorous discipline, suspended operations at one o'clock sharp. There was to be an interval of exactly an hour and a half for rest and refreshment. And I would here point out that the labour of opening a barrow is infinitely more severe and arduous than any ordinary labour, except, possibly, that of miners or quarrymen. Masses of tenacious earth, bound and intermixed with roots and fibres, have to be removed; ponderous blocks of stone have to be shifted with caution, and often with immense effort; a clutter of heavy debris is methodically cleared away to a proper distance. I want this to be remembered by the reader who has no personal knowledge of such things, because it is a matter of importance for the understanding of this narrative.

When we knocked off at lunch-time, we had exposed the sides and the covering-stones of two burial-chambers. Everybody (except the mutely smiling Mrs. Goy) was decidedly thrilled, and we looked forward with eagerness to the opening of the sepulchres.

During the interval, Mr. Tuffle nimbly manipulated his pegs, his tapes or chains, plotting, measuring and recording the stones, and entering all the observed particulars in his book.

We had some very curious talk, at lunch, from Miss Priscilla Macwardle, who prided herself on being what is called psychic. I think she was merely mad, poor lady! but I may have a prejudice in these matters.

"You know," she said, turning suddenly to Mr. Goy, "I saw Sir Lancelot by the mere at Glastonbury."

"Yes?" replied Mr. Goy, looking hot and embarrassed.

"I knew it was Sir Lancelot," Miss Priscilla continued, "because of the blazon upon his mighty shield. I know the blazons of all King Arthur's knights. He stood quite still with his right hand resting upon the hilt of a great sword and his eyes fixed upon the ground. It was a sign. Do you suppose it was a sign for me, or a sign for the whole nation?"

"I have no idea," said Mr. Goy, and he looked it.

"No, it was not a sign for the whole nation. My dear Uncle Richard was with me, and I said, 'Look, Uncle, there is the noble knight Sir Lancelot by the mere.' So Uncle Richard looked where I was pointing, and he said, 'My dear, I can see nothing at all, except a bit of an old willow by the water.' So then I knew it was not a sign for the whole nation. I looked again, and lo! Sir Lancelot was gone."

"Ah, yes!" said Mr. Goy, trying hard to be polite.

At this point, another diversion was caused, perhaps mercifully, by Mrs. Goy—a diversion of a totally different kind.

"Something, something, B," she said, "and something, something, something, R. 'He went about in fleece and leather lining,
while overhead a tropic sun was shining.' Whatever can it be?
Can anyone make a suggestion? I think it must be some kind
of an animal—fleece and leather, you see. Or is it Napoleon
in Egypt?"

It was quite an amusing lunch, and we started work again at
half-past two, refreshed and enthusiastic.

I do not wish to bore the reader with archæological details,
but, as I have observed more than once, I cannot omit anything
which is essential. And it is necessary to explain, in simple terms,
what was discovered on the first day of the digging.

Reisby paid Mr. Goy the compliment of putting him in charge
of the excavation in Trench B, while he himself conducted operations at Trench A.

As the work had now become a matter for professionals, Peter
and I decided to be mere spectators, and the experts were now in
two groups: Reisby and Ellingham at Trench A, Tuffle and Goy
at Trench B. The Dean, lingering for a while, tottered about with
the aid of his servant from one group to the other, petulantly
questioning the wisdom of every procedure and the accuracy
of every diagnosis. Mrs. Goy, who was a veteran spectator of
excavations, mutely moved from her cross-word to the digging
and from the digging to her cross-word. The Misses Macwardle
presently drove home to their mother. The other ladies watched
with interest the unearthing of our first discoveries.

To me, the whole thing was exciting.

The first burial-chamber was on ground level, about half
way between the edge and the middle of the mound. It was

partly covered by a great slab of granite, which had tilted a little outwards. Reisby stretched out his enormous arms, gripped the edges of the stone, and with a single powerful movement slid it off the top of the chamber.

"There you are!" he cried.

"I am surprised to see you put the stone *there*," said the Dean in his frail, complaining voice. "I should have slanted it over the corner if I had been doing it myself."

But we paid no attention to him. We all crowded up and looked inside the chamber.

It was a kind of stone enclosure, full of earth and rubble, charcoal, bits of crackled flint, a scattered mass of burnt bones.

"There you are!" Reisby repeated, with a peculiar note of triumph. "The pot, my dear fellows—the inverted pot!"

I myself could see no sign of a pot, but he flicked away some grit with the blade of his knife, and there was a disc (or so it appeared) of reddish-grey pottery.

"Inverted cinerary." Mr. Goy had come up from the other trench.

"You are quite right, my lad," said the Professor. "And now we had better sift the filling and collect it in the usual way. The bones are those of a youthful person, a pig, a horse and a stag."

"Elk," said Mr. Goy, picking up what looked like a fragment of antler.

"You are too positive, gentlemen," observed Ingleworth, "you are far too positive. I should not like to say so much until I had made a very minute examination in the study."

"What is the difference between elk and stag?" said Peter. His frivolous question was ignored.

The filling was carefully taken out, and we saw a big urn, slightly cracked, standing base-uppermost on a level block of granite.

This very interesting discovery gave rise to a lot of technical argument which need not be recorded. What is to be noted is the fact of such a burial being typical of the later stages of the Bronze Age—quite an ordinary form of cremated sepulture.

There was an exciting moment when Professor Reisby lifted the urn gently and firmly, while Mr. Tuffle adroitly slipped under it a thick sheet of cardboard.

"By Jove!" cried Mr. Tuffle, "I believe there's a little one inside it."

He was right. Inside the mouth of the urn there was a pottery bowl about the size of a teacup, with holes in the rim and a pretty geometrical pattern. There was also a heap of cremated bones, which the Professor said were those of an adult male and a female about sixteen years old.

"Ah, ha, ho! Very pretty, very pretty indeed! You are lucky, Mr. Goy. It is one of the prettiest things we have got, and one of the most typical cremation-groups of Period VI that I have ever seen."

"Is this typical of Period VI?" asked Peter irreverently. He had picked up something in the bottom of the grave.

It was a sixpenny-piece bearing the effigy of Queen Victoria.

"Ha, what?" said Reisby, not without a flash of pardonable irritation. "Sixpenny bit? Have any of you fellows lost a sixpenny bit?"

"It was under that little heap of rubbish," said Peter, "I swear it was."

"Oh, it's been worked down from above!" replied Mr. Goy, loyally coming to the rescue of Period VI. "Rats, rabbits, weasels—

common occurrence. Dated 1878? May have been fifty years getting down to it. You see, the top stone was tilted away from that side—"

"It's remarkably clean," said Peter.

"Then put it in your pocket, my dear boy!" thundered Reisby, half angry, half jocular, "put it in your pocket for luck."

And he went on with his examination of the relics.

The episode of the sixpenny-piece was quickly forgotten by most of us. I accepted Mr. Goy's eminently sensible explanation, and thought no more of it—for the time.

In the meanwhile another chamber was revealed in Trench B. There was no covering-stone, and two of the sides had fallen in. It had evidently been wrecked, intentionally or otherwise.

Here we found the usual scattered remains of a series of cremations, and the broken shards of more than one pot. There were also several pieces of haematite, a broken bronze ring, three discs or buttons of jet, and a fine flint arrowhead.

These discoveries were precisely what you may expect to find in a burial-place of the Bronze Age, but the group at Trench A was unusually perfect.

Ellingham and Reisby both drew our attention to the fact that the chamber containing the group was evidently connected with a larger grave in the centre of the barrow: there was an overlapping of the side-stones which proved this conclusively. Apparently the central chamber had been disturbed and the covering-stones were not in position; however, in view of the size of this chamber and its obvious importance, we antici-pated a dig of exceptional interest—and we were certainly not disappointed.

Work for the day ended at six o'clock, just after the edge of the middle sepulchre had been exposed.

5

I had been aware, during our dig, of occasional hovering figures, either among the trees on the edge of the plantation, or down on the slope under the barrow. We were evidently being watched by the people of Aberleven, with a furtive curiosity that was definitely hostile.

Soon after our return to the hotel I had a word with Mr. Morgan, who was looking rather grave.

"Well, sir," he said, "you know what these folk think about it. Mind, I don't think there's any of 'em would interfere, seeing who's on the job. But I shall be glad when you've done."

6

The archæological party were delighted with the results of the day's work, and were looking forward to the morrow with a positive thrill.

We sat in the drawing-room again after dinner, talking over the operations from our various points of view.

Mr Tuffle, after mixing for himself a filthy decoction which, he assured us solemnly, was the real Kentucky Boneshaker, became exceedingly discursive.

"Splendid old fellow, Reisby," he said, "keen as mustard. Pity he can't get away from his old-fashioned ideas. His theory of sequence-dating—all bunkum—what?"

"No," said Mr. Goy sternly.

"You young men ought to respect your elders," Mrs. Goy added.

"I do respect him," Mr. Tuffle declared fervently, after sipping his Boneshaker, "I respect him tremendously, indeed I do. Only—got to put science first—science first, every time—truth before everything. Whadda you say, Mr. Ellingham?"

"Professor Ellingham," Mrs. Goy corrected him tartly, in a most gratuitous fashion. I could see that she disliked Mr. Tuffle, that he inspired her with a placid but persistent hatred.

"Whadda you say, Pr'fess'r Ellingham?"

"I agree with you entirely on the question of principle. Our first concern is, or should be, the discovery of truth, or of the highest approximation to the truth. As for sequence-dating, it is admittedly tentative."

He turned to Mr. Goy. "What do you suppose we are likely to find in that central chamber?"

"Cremated burial." Mr. Goy was quietly emphatic.

"Well," replied Ellingham, "I'm not so sure. I have an idea that we shall find a crouching skeleton with a few well-preserved relics." He smiled, as if he was keeping a joke to himself.

Mr. Goy merely said: "Improbable."

"But not impossible. At Sykeham-le-Barrow, for example, there was a very similar group. I know you will say that the inner and the outer constructions are of the same date. I can only reply that I shall not be surprised if we find a contemporary group of cremated burials and interments within the same enclosure. What do you say, Farringdale?"

"My dear fellow, what is the use of appealing to me? In the first place, I know nothing about archæology. In the second place,

I should not like to speculate on what is concealed by a mass of earth and stones."

"I am justly rebuked," said Ellingham, "by Farringdale's common sense. None the less, I repeat once again my firm conviction that we shall find a crouching burial in the central chamber."

He spoke with a grim yet humorous intensity.

"It is not a matter of mere frivolous guess-work. There are many respectable analogies. In addition to Sykeham-le-Barrow in Shuffleshire, there is Twn-y-Glas in Wales, De Varrhus in Guernsey, Wapseywood in Yorkshire—"

"Intrusion," said Goy. (Another archæological method of getting round a corner.)

"Well, well!" Ellingham replied, "the morrow will prove me right or wrong. I anticipate a skeleton."

"How thrilling!" exclaimed Mrs. Goy. "Wilberforce would love a skeleton for the new saloon.—And I have really got *seven across* at last—umbelliferous."

CHAPTER III

I

ON THE FOLLOWING MORNING WE ALL MET AT THE TUMULUS in cheerful anticipation of a great discovery.

It was a bright, warm day, ideal for our purpose.

The Reisbys had arrived at the digging before the party from the hotel, and when Reisby greeted us he was holding in one hand a piece of painted board.

"A warning, my dear people, a warning!" he cried. "Behold the prevalence of superstition among our rude, illiterate folk, our northern barbarians!"

He displayed the board, and we saw written upon it in sprawling white letters:

"LEAVE THE DEAD IN PEACE."

Reisby was evidently quite undisturbed, but I thought Hilda was uneasy, and I felt a momentary chillness fall upon the group. Our navvies, the gardeners from the Manor, were looking somewhat abashed.

"Dear, dear!" said Ellingham, "how very depressing! I wonder who is the author of this advice. He is evidently sincere, and, from his point of view, both decent and reasonable."

"Ought to have been reassured by presence of Dean," said Mr. Goy.

"Awful rot and impertinence." Mr. Tuffle was not amused.

I looked at Hilda.

"I'm sorry they have done it," she said quietly. "I hate the idea of hurting the susceptibilities of these folk. And I think Professor Ellingham is quite right—they are decent and reasonable susceptibilities."

"But these are the tombs of heathen!" shouted Reisby. "And surely these good people know that we have dug up hundreds of 'em already." (The workmen looked happier.) "They have never objected before. In fact, many of them have assisted me in the work of excavation."

"They don't like us to be digging in this particular place," said Hilda. "Of course it's all nonsense, but—"

Reisby flung the board away with a swing of his powerful arm, and it went skimming and whirling in the air, over the slope of the bank below us, until it crashed into a thicket by the river.

"Ho, ho, ha-ho! Now, gentlemen, let us continue, let us continue this memorable investigation. Only consider, my dear Goy, the hidden treasure that awaits removal to your cabinets, your cases, your eminently respectable show."

2

It was now decided that everybody should concentrate on the opening of the central chamber, whereby the main purpose of the excavation could be more rapidly and carefully achieved. The experts were merely directing and observing, while the four professional diggers did the work.

We were uncovering the sides of a rectangular grave, the focus of endeavour and of expectation, when we heard a cheerful voice hailing us from the hill.

The amiable rotundity of Ugglesby-Gore was approaching us, followed by a man with a hamper. Coming from the inside of the hamper there was a glassy tinkle of bottles.

"Hullo, Professor! Hullo, everybody! Don't let me stop you—mustn't interfere with body-snatching! Mere spectators, silly public, that's all. Contribution to lunch—some of the best—hope you'll allow me—"

And the excellent, simple fellow, literally bubbling with incoherent friendliness, rolled up to the barrow.

"Digging up poor old boy, pots and everything, eh? Tuth-th! Too bad. Jolly interesting, of course. Can't say I understand it like you fellas do—too much of a fool—mere spectator!"

"You are just in time for the opening ceremony," said Ellingham.

The tops of the four great slabs which formed the sides of the chamber were now cleared. It was easy work, for the grave was only loosely covered by a mass of sand and soil which had evidently been disturbed on some previous occasion. Two slabs had originally been placed over the grave; one of them had been pushed over into what was presumably an adjoining chamber, and the other had veered obliquely and was now tilted into the grave itself.

"Put a bar here," said Reisby, "and another here."

In memory I can see him with peculiar distinctness. He wore a tattered Norfolk jacket and a pair of grey flannel trousers. His tawny-silver hair flowed in a grand abundance over his magnificent head. At that moment he was visibly tense, eager, even a little agitated.

The men placed their bars under the covering-stone.

"Look out!" shouted Reisby, and he pushed the stone up on its edge, and then let it fall with a flat thud on the debris outside the chamber.

We all crowded round in silence.

The inside of the grave, as far as it was to be seen, was filled with bits of white calcinated bone, speckled at random in a mess of sandy soil, mixed up with charcoal, scraps of pottery, lumps of red clay, chips of glossy flint, and a lot of loose rubble. But this mixture filled the grave to within a few inches of the top. Nobody could yet say what lay below it on the floor of the tomb.

Mr. Goy, laconic as usual, broke the silence.

"Cremation," he observed.

Ellingham took it as a challenge:

"Wait until we see the bottom!"

There was an interval, in which Ellingham took several photographs of the tomb, and William Tuffle most adroitly plotted, measured, examined with meticulous though praiseworthy care every detail, every angle, every sign of a sign.

Then the upper layers of the deposit, the bits of bone and pottery and so forth, were removed.

According to Reisby, the bones were those of two men, parts of an ox (the teeth clearly recognisable), a sheep or goat, and a dog. The pottery was of the same kind as that in the adjoining chamber.

Ellingham scrutinised the material with hawk-like vigilance.

"Ah, ha!" he said, pouncing suddenly, "what's this?"

He held in his hand a tiny pointed fragment, apparently of metal. He rubbed it, and it shone brightly.

"Silver, what?" said Ugglesby-Gore, "bit of real treasure?"

"No. It's a very common object." Ellingham looked at it thoughtfully. "Merely the blade of a pen-knife."

"Oh, you may find anything in that rubbish!" said Reisby, looking (as I thought) rather peevish, annoyed at so much attention being given to such a trifle. "After all, the whole thing has been disturbed, and it's highly improbable that what we are now taking out was the original filling of the chamber."

I observed that Ellingham, instead of throwing the trifle away, put it in his pocket.

Mr. Tuffle, who was carefully skimming the debris with a gardener's trowel, gave a cry of excitement.

"We've got him!" he shouted, as if he was running to earth some elusive animal.

3

"Look here!" Mr. Tuffle lightly flicked away a layer of thin soil.

In doing so he exposed the loosely articulated angle of three yellow bones—the bent elbow of a skeleton.

"There you are, Goy!" said Ellingham calmly, but with intense eagerness. "What did I tell you? A crouching burial—he's lying on the left side—looks more or less undisturbed."

"It is the king, it is the king!" piped a thin, earnest voice behind us.

The Misses Macwardle, accompanied by Dean Ingleworth, had approached the excavation—one might say, the exhumation.

"I should be particularly careful, I should exercise great restraint, uncommon restraint," said the old man querulously, "I should use only the smallest instruments and the most delicate methods in exposing the burial. A very delicate procedure, calling for a great deal of patience. You surprise me by not using a riddle with a much finer mesh."

Mr. Goy closely examined the elbow-bones.

"Young female," he said.

I admired his audacity.

Reisby looked in his turn, kneeling by the side of the grave so that his beard almost touched the earth.

"No, no, my good sir! A young male, decidedly. As you have observed, Ellingham, it looks as if the burial is undisturbed. In view of all the mess above it, that is remarkable. A most remarkable, exciting and unexpected discovery!"

He raised himself upright and stood above the stone chamber, looking round at the attentive group with an ironic, unaccountable smile.

"Got the body, what?" said Ugglesby-Gore, who was really a little shocked. "Got the poor fella's bones—lot of old body-snatchers, that's what you fellas are. Can't understand it myself—too much of a fool. Frightfully ancient Briton—Roman—Phœnician—don't know, of course."

I saw Hilda Reisby look down into the primitive tomb with interest and with gentle curiosity.

"It does seem rather a shame!"

"It is precisely what Wilberforce has been longing for," said Mrs. Goy. "A really good crouching burial is precisely what he wants for the new prehistoric saloon."

"A lucky dig for you, Goy!" boomed Reisby. "That skeleton, judging from the bit we can see, ought to be in first-rate condition."

Mr. Tuffle delicately flipped away a little more of the earth, revealing the two bones of the forearm lying together.

"Singularly fresh in appearance," he said.

A black, shining beetle, like a tiny knight in armour, tumbled awkwardly over the bones and went scurrying away into the soil.

"If you invited my opinion," said the Dean, "I should advise you to begin there"—his trembling fingers fluttered vaguely above the grave—"exercising always the greatest amount of skill and restraint."

Kneeling suddenly on the dirty ground, Miss Priscilla Macwardle pressed her cheek against the edge of a slab.

"Oh, you dear, dear, wonderful old stones!" she cried, in a manner that was both wild and reassuringly self-conscious at the same time. "If only you could tell us what you have seen, what marvels and what mysteries we should hear!"

"You are quite right, ma'am," said Reisby. "A good many of our chosen theories would be rudely exploded, I have no doubt."

"And others would be confirmed," said Ellingham drily.

4

There was now a consultation between Reisby, Goy, Tuffle and Ellingham. A querulous *obbligato* was kept up by the Dean, whose vague advice was received with unremitting courtesy, if not with all the attention it deserved.

At this critical stage, and while these learned gentlemen are conferring, I must ask the reader to bear in mind the nature of the tomb which was being examined. It was a very simple affair. You have only to imagine a rectangular and slightly oblong box or chamber of stone, the sides consisting of granite slabs with a filling of smaller stones at the corners. The size of the inside of the chamber was, roughly, 5 by 4½ feet, and the depth of it, from the top edges of the slabs to the floor, about 3½ feet. This grave had been loosely filled with rubbish and the relics of cremated burials, as I have already described, and we had now removed this material to a depth of some two feet or more. The skeleton which lay on the floor of the tomb was therefore covered by an irregular deposit of soil, charcoal, bits of cremated bone, shards of pottery, and so forth, a deposit which was now from a foot to a foot and half in thickness. Obviously the correct procedure was to remove this deposit without disturbing the burial, and so to reveal and record every circumstance of the arrangement. In order to do this, Reisby decided to remove carefully the slab on the outer side of the grave, replacing it after the burial had been exposed for the purpose of getting photographs. The slab was already loose, and it could be lifted or tilted out of the way without causing any disturbance. Dean Ingleworth opposed the plan, but the others warmly supported it. Eventually the Dean was placated—he wanted to show the tumulus, on the following afternoon, to a party of people from the Littlehope Field and Antiquarian Society, and he was assured that the chamber would be properly restored and ready for inspection.

By a most ingenious method of gradual shifting and wedging, Reisby and three of the workmen succeeded in lifting the outer slab and placing it flat on the excavated floor of the trench. A trickle of earth fell from the edge of the grave, but the burial was entirely undisturbed. I noticed an acrid, salty, pungent and rather stimulating smell of moist earth.

We knew already, having seen the exposed elbow-joint, that our skeleton was lying with his back to the slab which had now been taken away.

Slowly and very methodically the two Professors, aided by Goy and Tuffle, began to remove the rubbish. They started at the end of the tomb where they expected to find the feet of the skeleton; and sure enough it was not long before the pelvic bones and the bones of the two ankles were exposed.

I watched the operation with a throb of excitement. Indeed, there was a contagion of excitement in the air, somewhat unusual, I should think, in the normal circumstances of field archæology. Parts of the two thigh-bones, and the bones of the leg, were soon revealed, and we noticed at once a curious absence of decay or staining. True, the bones of the hip were broken, the toes and ankles were scattered; but yet one had the illusion of all the bones being remarkably fresh and firm.

Presently there came a thrill.

Close to the feet of the skeleton Mr. Goy discovered a pottery vessel, slightly cracked, but otherwise perfect.

"Beaker," he said.

"You astonish me very much by describing that beautiful thing as a beaker," Dean Ingleworth complained. "I should have called it a bi-conical drinking-vessel or chalice—"

"Poor old fella's beer-mug, perhaps," said Ugglesby-Gore, in a tone not wholly devoid of real feeling.

"The king's goblet," said Miss Priscilla, pressing her thin fingers against her bosom, "the royal cup of lovely design—"

Then, an astounding thing happened.

While the others were looking at the beaker, Ellingham went

on quietly and carefully picking away the earth with the blade of a clasp-knife. He was kneeling, but all at once he partly raised himself. I looked at him.

What I saw filled me with horror.

His eyes were fixed, not on the grave or on the group of people who were looking at the beaker, but on the slope of the hill below the barrow. I have never seen a more sudden or a more dreadful change come over a man's countenance. His eyes were opened wide, his jaw fell, the lines of his face were corrugated by a spasm of deadly fear; for a second he was rigid, frozen, appalling. I could hardly believe that I was not myself the victim of some frightful delusion. Fred Ellingham was a man so controlled, so unemotional, a man of such cold, uncompromising intellect... I believe I cried out as I moved towards him.

At the same time, three or four of the others observed that something was wrong.

"Professor Ellingham!" cried Mr. Tuffle.

But Ellingham raised his right hand and pointed at the green slope, thinly covered with gorse and bracken, which rolled below us down to the valley. His face relaxed. A shrill, hideous yell burst out of him:

"My God! Look! Look there—down there!"

Every one of us, obeying an irresistible impulse of terrified curiosity, stared in the same direction. Even Mrs. Ellingham, who was running towards her husband, was caught by the impulse. I looked with the others, but I was dimly aware of a slight lurching movement as Ellingham swayed over the tomb.

Then he appeared to recover himself, though he was pale as death.

"I beg your pardon for being such a fool," he said. "No, no, my dear; I am perfectly well, I assure you. It's very good of you, Farringdale, but I require no assistance. There is nothing wrong." His voice was firm, natural and reassuring.

"But—Ellingham—"

They were all crowding round him anxiously.

"It was an unaccountable trick of the imagination. I have never had such an experience before. It is not likely to recur. Pray forget it, and let us resume this interesting work."

"What did you see?"

"Nothing at all. The very absurdity of what I *fancied* I saw fills me with shame. I was about to turn round for another look at the beaker when I—I had the impression of seeing a man down on the hillside yonder. I now realise there could have been no such person. I thought it was Joe Lloyd—"

"Joe Lloyd!" Reisby bellowed. "He's dead!"

"Is he?" said Ellingham, looking hard at the other.

"Well, there is good reason for supposing he is dead. The man disappeared, years ago."

"Nobody there, anyhow," said Mr. Goy, slowly nodding his solemn head.

"Nobody there," repeated Ugglesby-Gore, bubbling with friendly concern. "Have a spot of whisky? Flask here. Delighted. Best thing if a fella's jumpy. Often feel jumpy myself. Take a spot of whisky—no more jumps."

Ellingham declined, though with gratitude. He assured us all—and particularly his anxious wife and son—that he was perfectly well. And as far as I could judge, he was telling the truth. I have an impression, but it may not be correct, that he winked at me.

"Nervous disequilibrium is to be anticipated," he said, "in the case of men who served on the Western Front. Let me again beg you to forgive me. Please forget this unfortunate and absurd episode, or at least regard it as a matter of no importance whatever."

Nervous disequilibrium! I thought. Whatever the explanation might be, I was quite sure it had nothing to do with any such disorder.

I observed that Mrs. Ellingham and Peter were looking quite easy, and it then occurred to me that Ellingham had perhaps been acting a part for some purpose of his own. Perhaps he had some theory about the disappearance of Joe Lloyd. At any rate, I felt relieved of anxiety as far as Ellingham himself was concerned.

The members of the party were somewhat shaken by this extraordinary event, but the calmness of Ellingham's manner, the perfect regulation of his voice and his movements, quickly restored their confidence.

"Shell-shock," I heard Mr. Goy observing tersely and sympathetically to Mr. Tuffle.

The excavation was resumed.

5

By gradual stages the almost entire skeleton of a young man was revealed on the floor of the tomb. It was lying on the left side in the position known to archæology as "flexed" or "contracted." The legs were bent, so that the knees were on a level with the chest. The right hand was placed by the throat; the left arm, with all the finger-bones scattered or missing, was curiously flexed over towards the right, in such a manner that the left hand must have been placed on the right side of the head. Both bones of the left forearm lay actually on the facial part of the skull. Many of the smaller bones were displaced, and a few were missing. Some of the larger bones were broken; the ribs, backbone and pelvis were considerably damaged, and there was a hole in the right side of the head. In front of the face there was a small though interesting group of objects: three bronze rings, five jet buttons, and a remarkably fine "dagger" of bluish-grey flint. The arrangement of these objects, I understand, was unusual.

With infinite care the bones were dusted and cleared with fine brushes by Mr. Goy and Mr. Tuffle. With even greater care the side-slab was replaced, and Ellingham took a large number of photographs—it always appeared to me that he took many more than could possibly be required.

"It is very odd," said Ingleworth peevishly, "it is very odd that he should not have been wearing those bracelets. I am surprised to find them in such a position. And I should have expected those buttons to be used as the fastening of a garment—in which case we should have found them dispersed at intervals among the bones. In these details the burial does not conform to the orthodox arrangement, and I must admit that I am greatly disappointed."

He spoke with rising petulance, as if he was criticising the work of a clumsy undertaker.

"Burial at Upper Willowsmere—deposit of buttons," Mr. Goy assured him in a soothing manner. But the Dean was evidently annoyed.

"The texture of the bones is remarkably fresh," observed Ellingham, who had followed with cool vigilance every stage of the work.

"And what a lovely set of teeth!" said Hilda Reisby, looking down at the crouching skeleton.

"Ha, Goy!" cried the Professor, "I hope you are satisfied. Could I have done any better for you? He will be the joy of all beholders in your new saloon, the cynosure of learned and curious alike, the envy of less fortunate curators, the pride of Northport! Ha, ha, ho-ha, ho-ha-ha-ha! Oh-ho!" And he went off into one of those terrible shuddering explosions of laughter.

We looked rather embarrassed, and I saw Hilda bite her lips nervously; and then, thank goodness! Reisby recovered himself. He watched Mr. Tuffle preparing some boxes full of cotton-wool, the boxes in which the bones would presently be taken away.

"I shall examine the skeleton at leisure before I place him in your custody," he said to Mr. Goy, "but I shall only keep him a few days."

Mr. Goy expressed his delight, his gratitude, in an unusually long speech of at least three dozen words.

"The presentation of so important a gift to the museum," said the Dean, "cannot be allowed to pass without appropriate ceremony. I know that my fellow-trustees, Lord Woffletree and Sir Giles Dudbud, will heartily concur. We shall convene a meeting, and we shall invite Mrs. Macwardle and Professor Reisby—"

"Oh, I'm sure mother would much rather be left out of it!" declared Miss Prudence Macwardle.

"I am no lover of municipal ceremonies, as you know," said Reisby, with a deliberate emphasis on the adjective, "but if you would like me to give a simple account of the burial—"

Mr. Tuffle winked at Mr. Goy.

"We shall expect nothing less, my dear sir," the Dean assured him. "We shall have a public meeting in the lecture hall of the museum, perhaps exhibiting the burial in a portable case. Then, after hearing your illuminating and masterly exposition—for such, I know, it will be—we shall formally receive this beautiful and exceptionally complete burial, and I, on behalf of the trustees, will endeavour to show the appreciation and the gratitude, not merely of the trustees, but also of the members of the Little-hope Society, some of whom, I trust, will have the great privilege of examining this chamber to-morrow and of being allowed to see the relics, and of the responsible and intelligent citizens of Northport as a whole, including the Mayor and members of the Corporation, in which I shall no doubt be supported by repre-sentatives of the University, of which you, sir, are so distinguished an ornament—"

He appeared to be rehearsing the actual speech. For a moment the agreeable consciousness of his own dignity, the prospect of being able to dominate so magnificent a concourse, invested him with a transient glow of benevolence. He looked round at us with an air of serene patronage. And then his countenance resumed its normal aspect of doddering severity.

"But the arrangement of the tomb is decidedly peculiar," he said, "and I must say it surprises me very much to see it. When I was a young man, there were rules, there were *principles* in archæology; but now—" He wandered off helplessly into a dread-ful confusion of thought. One could see that his resentment included, in some unaccountable manner, the skeleton in the grave, which, if Goy and Reisby were correct, ought to have been at least four thousand years old.

The main object of the digging was now accomplished. Work was continued for two more days, but we need not concern ourselves with the archæological results.

After the most careful records had been made by Mr. Tuffle, and heaven knows how many photographs taken by Ellingham, the bones were lifted out of the chamber and were placed in beds of cotton-wool for transport.

The unfortunate episode of Ellingham's delusion had, I think, ceased to trouble us very profoundly, and everybody was pleased with the highly satisfactory result of the dig.

6

After dinner, on the day of this momentous discovery, our hotel party walked over to Scarweather. We had been invited by Professor and Mrs. Reisby, and the occasion was partly social and partly scientific.

Ellingham had completely recovered himself, and there were no references to the odd scene at the Devil's Hump. It was, in fact, a pleasant and a happy group of people who now assembled at Scarweather, and I think the most entertaining and engaging figure was that of Reisby himself. He was evidently gratified by the discovery of a fine burial, a valuable addition to his great work, though not to his own private mortuary. His manner was genial, and even boisterous, but I can truthfully say that it was the manner of an eminently sane and rational person. If he treated Mr. Goy with a lot of ponderous banter, he did so without malice, and as Mr. Goy was impervious to criticism and insensitive to ridicule he was not in the least affected by these professorial or professional jokes.

No purpose would be served if I gave a minute account of this delightful evening, though I remember it vividly, but I shall draw the reader's attention to one particular episode.

All the objects from the Devil's Hump had been set out on a large table in the study, and Reisby invited us to inspect them. With the exception of Peter and Frances, who drifted out into the garden, we all went into the study at about half-past nine. A powerful oil-lamp of the Aladdin type was hanging from the ceiling, and under it was the table on which were deposited the pottery vessels, boxes of debris, all the miscellaneous relics from the tumulus. At one end of the table, neatly arranged in their anatomical order, were the bones of the skeleton.

I well remember the somewhat melancholy and even sordid appearance of those bones. In the hard white light of the lamp they looked fresher than ever, and it was no easy matter to realise their presumed antiquity. But it has to be remembered that the appearance of exhumed bones does vary in a surprising degree. The bones of an extremely ancient burial may be light in colour, firm, and of even texture; while the bones from a modern cemetery are sometimes greatly decayed, friable, darkly stained and of a most venerable appearance. These facts are well known to doctors, and even to the archæologist.

We gathered round the table, and we examined the skeleton.

"Some of the bones are missing," said Reisby in a dry and formal style, as if he was addressing a group of students, "and you will observe that many of them are broken. It is a very singular fact that only a small fragment of the right patella or knee-cap has been recovered. As a rule the patella, which is a fairly solid lump of bone, is preserved intact. The left patella, as you see, is hardly injured at all. Of the bones which are definitely missing, or only represented by doubtful fragments, most of them are bones of the fingers and toes, and there are several bones of the wrists and ankles—carpal or tarsal bones—which have been practically destroyed. Such damage or dispersal is frequently due to the action of small rodents, or even to the action of the weather, or to movements of subsidence within the tumulus. In this case, where the roof of the tomb has been dislodged, and where the overlying material was of a nature so permeable and soft, it is astonishing that our burial is, comparatively, so perfect. The hole in the skull is due to an injury at the time of death, or soon after."

"What a grim idea!" said Hilda Reisby, and she lightly touched the hollow skull with the tips of her fingers.

As she did so, I distinctly heard Ellingham utter a low but very peculiar sound—I can only describe it as a muted or muffled groan. It was apparently not observed by anyone else.

"As to the age and sex of the skeleton, there can be no question at all. It is the skeleton of a young man, between twenty-five and thirty years old. He was moderately muscular. In certain features, perhaps, he does not resemble any modern type; but that is a matter for the expert. It would be foolish to attempt a description of his appearance. The skull is well developed and is probably the skull of a youth who was intelligent as well as remarkably hand-some. Pray observe, that I say *probably*—I resist the journalistic impulse. Now, the teeth—" He picked up the lower jaw, and then he frowned.

"This is very strange, Hilda. I suppose nobody has been moving these things. One of the teeth—the first left molar—has gone. It was certainly there when I placed the bones on the table."

Goy, Tuffle and Ellingham solemnly affirmed that every tooth was in the jaw when it was taken from the barrow. There was a slight embarrassment.

"It is very annoying," said Reisby, "and really quite inexplicable. The tooth has gone, but I am prepared to swear that it was there less than two hours ago."

"Are you *quite* sure?" said Hilda.

"Well"—he appeared to hesitate,—"I certainly took it for granted. We all observed, at the site, that none of the teeth was missing."

Once again Tuffle and Goy, who had been responsible for removing and packing the relics, protested that all the teeth were present when the skull and the jaw were placed in the box.

We looked everywhere, on the table and under the table, through the packing in the box; but the tooth had gone—there was no doubt of it.

However, this accidental loss (no other explanation could be accepted) was not of sufficient magnitude to disturb the good-humour, to interfere with the enjoyment, of our little party.

"Well well!" said the Professor, recovering his cheerfulness, "it may very well turn up somewhere. In the meanwhile, let us continue our investigation. The teeth, you see, are in excellent condition, and I think their state is due to a natural and whole-some diet. The skull is brachycephalic, like that of most of the Bronze Age invaders, though it is most unwise to indulge in a risky generalisation. I estimate the height of this individual to have been not less than five foot eleven, considerably above the average height of the Bronze Age people. And there is one other interesting point, and that is the elegance, the unexpected refinement of the brow, unusually smooth and high for a male of this period. You see, my dear," he looked intently at Hilda, "the somewhat marked difference between this and the other skulls in our collection."

"Yes," she replied, "I see exactly what you mean. Poor youth!" And again she lightly caressed the hollow bone with her fingers. "It really does seem a very callous procedure, doesn't it?"

"Advancement of knowledge." Mr. Goy spoke with a miniature solemnity which made her smile.

"I know. But I can't help feeling rather sentimental about this poor young man with his buttons and his bracelets and all his little treasures. Fancy having your bones all spread out on a table, and a lot of—of rather odd, unfamiliar people handling them and talking about your size and your diet and all that sort of thing!"

"I should have thought you were quite used to it," said Mrs. Goy, with a thin grimace.

"So I am. But this youth is more *personal* than the others. I'm sure I don't know why. Perhaps because it's the most perfect skeleton of the series."

She took up one of the arm bones, as if she was trying to convince herself of a lack of unreasonable sensibility. But I saw her shudder slightly as she put it down again.

After we had all had a good look at the skeleton, we examined the pottery and the other things. I was informed that the beaker found with the main burial was of much earlier date than the cinerary urn and the so-called "incense-cup" found in the outer chamber. I also gathered that the bits of broken pottery found in the debris above the skeleton were of the same date as the cinerary vessel.

"But," I objected, in my great simplicity and ignorance, "I thought you said the burial-chambers in the mound were all built at the same time."

Mr. Goy was ready with an answer.

"Beaker primary—cremations intruded."

This answer appeared to satisfy everyone, though I observed Ellingham rubbing his finger along his nose, as he did always when he was thinking hard and keeping his thoughts to himself.

7

I have said that nothing essential to my narrative occurred in the course of the two days' digging which followed the chief exhumation. That is quite true, so far as archæological results are concerned, but it seems worth while to mention another small discovery.

It will be remembered that Dean Ingleworth had arranged to bring to the Devil's Hump a selected party of members of the Littlehope Field Society. These depressing people, conveyed in a motor-coach, duly arrived on the third day of the excavation.

There were about two dozen of them, and at least half of the party consisted of elderly women of a singularly bleak aspect. I think there were two main types (I had got into the archæological habit of classification); "county" ladies in expensive tweeds, and "parochial" ladies in cheap finery. There were also three or four mildewed clergymen, a pawky solicitor with a sly flabby face, two retired colonels (a British Israelite and a Theosophist), a retired rural postman (by far the most intelligent man of the party), and a few dull but worthy gentlemen, none of them much under sixty.

We all groaned as we saw them coming, but there was no help for it.

After a prelude of idle and futile chatter, the Dean seated himself upon a camp-stool of solid construction and proceeded to read in a querulous and quavering voice a lengthy paper on prehistoric burials. While this was going on, the Littlehope followers grouped themselves in various decent postures on the ground, listening with respectful incomprehension, with yearning interest or with resigned boredom, to the Dean's ineffective meandering. I found myself sitting close to the edge of the excavation, and in furtively rummaging about in the debris with my fingers I scratched up a small pen-knife with a bone case and a broken blade. Ellingham, who was near me, observed this at once, and he looked at me with an enquiring twitch of the brows. I threw the pen-knife, and he caught it and put it in his pocket. Nobody appeared to notice the gesture: Reisby and the experts had rudely strolled away on the other side of the barrow.

8

Ellingham and his family returned to Cambridge on Saturday the 25th of August, and Goy and Tuffle went back to Northport on the same day. I remained at Aberleven for a few days longer, not with any archæological designs, but simply on account of Hilda Reisby, whose delightful companionship had now become one of the most precious things in my life.

CHAPTER IV

I

T HE PARTICULARS WHICH FOLLOW ARE MAINLY DERIVED from the *Northport Gazette*, the *British Antiquarian Monthly*, and other respectable and reliable periodicals. The more intimate touches are obtained from letters written to me by Mrs. Reisby, and also, I regret to say, from an extremely flippant record sent by Frances Reisby to Peter Ellingham.

On Saturday the 6th of October 1928 an important meeting took place in the new lecture hall of the Northport City Museum.

This meeting was convened by the trustees in order to celebrate in a becoming manner the presentation to the Museum of one of its greatest treasures, the most perfect and most remarkable Bronze Age burial ever found in the north of England. The donors were Mrs. Arthur Macwardle and Professor Tolgen Reisby, but it was understood that Mrs. Macwardle was unable to be present and that she would be represented by her daughter Miss Priscilla Macwardle.

Professor Reisby had kindly consented to give a short account of the discovery, illustrated by lantern slides and by numerous diagrams. After the ceremony in the hall, there would be an adjournment to the new saloon, where, in a large and specially illuminated case, was a splendid replica of the burial-chamber, containing the actual skeleton, as nearly as possible in the posture in which it was found, and all the furniture of the tomb. This delightful and exciting arrangement was due to the great skill of the curator,

Mr. Wilberforce Goy, M.A. It was, unquestionably, the pride of the museum—nay, the pride of cultured Northport. There was nothing like it anywhere else. It was one of the famous things in British archæology, already quoted or noted in every serious paper and in every scientific review. On the afternoon of this very day, the scholars of the Cathedral School, guided by Dean Ingleworth himself, had visited this memorable skeleton, and had listened to a lucid and enlivening description of the burial by Mr. Goy.

Everybody said that the ceremony of the formal presentation and acceptance was exceptionally happy, both in idea and performance.

Seated on the dais in the lecture hall were the Mayor and Aldermen, the Town Clerk, Dean Ingleworth and the Littlehope Committee, a dozen of the Professors and Fellows from the University, Professor and Mrs. Reisby, Mr. and Mrs. Goy, the Trustees, the Misses Macwardle, and a substantial backing, or background, of clergymen, rural gentlefolk and others. It was computed (by Miss Frances Reisby) that the number of people on the dais considerably exceeded the number of people in the hall; but this may be an error, or a flourish of mere frivolity.

After the opening speech of the Chairman, Sir Giles Dudbud, there was a brief ritual of presentation by Miss Priscilla Macwardle and Professor Reisby. Then came a remarkable and tortuous speech by the Mayor.

The Mayor said they were glad to welcome to the City of Northport this nameless but illustrious gentleman of the Bronze Age (laughter), and they were grateful indeed for the generosity, etc., etc. They were profoundly indebted to Mrs. Macwardle, to Professor Reisby, to Mr. Wilberforce Goy, to Dean Ingleworth, to

Sir Giles Dudbud, etc., etc. And it was fitting and appropriate that the new saloon should have received, for its principal glory and ornament, a centre-piece, a thing of such rarity and beauty. And although he, the Mayor, did not pretend to be a man of learning, he was interested in every produce of the northern soil—coal or crops or skeletons (laughter)—yes! he was interested in all of them, he did not come second to any man in his concern for the honour, the fame and the welfare of Northport (hear, hear! and some ironical laughter), and he was not ashamed of it, and he was glad to think they had now got one of the finest old skeletons—not a skeleton in a cupboard or anything of that sort (pause, but no laughter)—well! a most remarkable discovery; he had no idea that such things existed; but he would like to say that he remembered his grandmother telling him—a good old farmer's wife, and he was proud of it (applause from two Aldermen only)—his grandmother telling him, when he was a little nipper (unexpected and disconcerting laughter)—telling him that she remembered the time when a man's favourite beer-mug was put in his grave, and sometimes even in his coffin—yes! it was a fact—so perhaps this gentleman in the new saloon liked his drop of beer the same as any other man (laughter, with sniffing and other signs of disapproval and impatience)—but anyhow, he would say nothing more, he was getting out of his depth, it was not his place to theorise in the presence of so many learned gentlemen, only he could not refrain from bringing in just one little homely touch, just one little reminder of the dear old folk who had gone (tremendous applause); and now he would like to express formally but sincerely the gratitude of himself and of the honourable Corporation, etc., etc.

Then came speeches by the Dean, one of the University offi-
cials, two of the clergymen, and a retired brigadier—who assured
the company that the burial was that of an Israelite.

Professor Reisby then gave a short but extremely brilliant
description of his digging, illustrated by a splendid set of lantern
slides (many of them from Ellingham's negatives). Reisby had the
gift of the ideal expositor, he knew how to work up the interest,
the enthusiasm, of the most unpromising audience. He spoke
fluently, sonorously and with humour. His lecture was a really
first-rate entertainment.

At last the company filed out to the brilliantly illuminated
saloon, to see the treasure in its place of pride.

It was a masterpiece.

The case had been designed by Mr. Goy, a marvel of glass
and of polished mahogany. Along the top of it ran a veritable
triumph of the label-writer's art, at once a classification and an
essay. Inside, placed ingeniously at a proper level, was a reconstruction of the lower part of the tomb, with stones and earth
from the site itself. There was the skeleton on his bed of pebbles,
beautifully arranged and held in position by invisible clips and
wires, the beaker, the rings, the buttons and the dagger. It was,
in the memorable words of Professor Sir Henry Bronderswag, "a
veritable treasure."

Mr Goy, in a few terse phrases, as if he were dictating a series
of new labels, explained the principal features. Mrs. Goy, in an
evening dress of comparatively ambitious design, stood by his
side in a gentle glow of admiration.

So they all gathered round the crystal cabinet, that curiously
assorted mob of learned men, townsfolk, gentlefolk, and the

indescribable respectable; and in the midst of them lay the skeleton on his bed of earth and pebbles.

At the same time, various accounts of what was known as the "Aberleven skeleton" or the "Aberleven man" appeared in the local papers, in popular illustrated journals, and also in the *British Antiquarian Monthly*.

The learned writer whose article appeared in the *Antiquarian* explained in how many respects the bones of the Aberleven man differed from the bones of any known modern type. In nearly every part of the anatomy, he said, there was a subtle though discernible difference. He ventured to suggest "affinities with the negro," mainly on the evidence of a "platycnemic tibia." He also pointed to a "specialised" and unique condition of the teeth, quite without parallel in modern times. I refrain from giving the name of this writer, because it would be cruel to do so.

I spent the week-end, 12th to 16th of October, with the Ellinghams at Cambridge, and I asked Ellingham what he thought of the article in the *Antiquarian*.

"My dear Farringdale," he said, "the man is entirely mistaken; he is wrong in every single instance."

2

I had not seen Ellingham since the digging at Aberleven, and I was naturally interested in his views. He showed me his fine series of photographs, including those which he had taken of the barrow at various times before the excavation. Three or four of these latter were placed side by side.

"Look at these closely, Farringdale," he said, "and tell me if you notice anything."

"No, I can't say that I do. There is rather more bracken in this one, I fancy."

He smiled provokingly.

"You see nothing else?"

"Really, Ellingham, you might give me some clue as to what you expect me to see! They are very good photographs. But they look very much alike. Perhaps there is a difference in the arrangement of those little stones—and—I think one of the gorse-bushes has been cut away here—"

"Is that all?"

"I don't know what you mean—"

"Well, well! Never mind. Let us look at these enlarged pictures of the actual grave."

He set before me ten or a dozen really magnificent pictures. They showed the skeleton with and without the "furniture," and at different stages of the excavation. There were also some photographs of the debris above the grave, which seemed to me to have no particular interest; but when I questioned Ellingham about these, he merely grinned.

For some reason or other I did not like to remind Ellingham of his odd remark in the hospital in 1916 —it was too absurd—but I asked him, naturally, what he thought about the dig.

"I think it was extremely well conducted. Altogether very enjoyable."

There was a definite reserve in his manner, and I thought he was probably anxious to avoid any reference to his curious hallucination at the Devil's Hump.

"And you consider it archæologically remarkable?"

"I tell you what, Farringdale—I am not at all satisfied with the archæological result, in spite of Goy's convincing description. Possibly I shall have something to say about this at a later stage. I have been making some enquiries, and I hope soon to have in my possession data which will be absolutely conclusive."

Of course I could not imagine what he was driving at, and I said so.

"Oh!" said he, lightly whipping out his golden toothpick, "I shall explain myself in due course, and I shall probably require your assistance!"

He left me in complete doubt as to his meaning.

3

Hilda Reisby and her daughter came to London for a few days on the 18th of October.

Mrs. Reisby told me that her husband was again falling into his alarming fits of depression, and that he frequently sat up all night in the study or laboratory. The villagers had deeply resented the opening of the Devil's Hump and the removal of the skeleton, and she believed that the Professor, with all his robust intelligence, was affected by this environment of hostility and of superstition. She herself had had several talks with Morgan at the hotel, who told her, with loyal and friendly concern, about the unfortunate attitude of the people.

Two fishing-boats had been lost in September, one on the point of the island and one at sea, and a man had been drowned. These disasters were secretly attributed to the angry spirits of the dead, vexed by the violation of their burial-place.

It was of no use to argue; the superstition persisted. And it was pointed out that one of the gardeners at the Manor, who had been employed at the digging, was now grievously afflicted with boils.

Altogether, Hilda's account was not cheerful.

One evening, when the Ellinghams were up in town, we all dined together at my rooms. I remember how charming Frances looked in her demure evening dress. It was a very happy little party. We all liked each other—and indeed, I could see the evidence of something more than mere liking between Frances Reisby and Peter Ellingham, those delightful young people!

We talked about all sorts of things, and I did not encourage topics which might have induced a shade of melancholy. But we could not avoid a matter of such recent interest as the Aberleven dig.

Frances, in her sprightly and irreverent manner, gave us a most amusing account of the meeting at the museum. She reproduced, with a touch of her father's malicious wit, the prim reticence of the Goys, artfully concealing the most inordinate pride. She gave a priceless imitation of the poor old Dean, critical and querulous even in the midst of praise, and lost in the tangles of senile verbosity. Finally—for such is the lack of respect in modern youth, and especially in modern daughters—we had a droll impersonation of "daddy" answering the speech of the Mayor, and indulging in fantastic explosions of sarcasm at the expense of everyone, including himself. The people loved it (all except Ingleworth and the Goys), and he got more laughter and more applause than anyone.

"By the way," said Ellingham, turning to Mrs. Reisby, "did the beaker remind you of one that you had seen before?"

"How very odd that you should mention it!" she said. "Yes, it reminded me at once of a beaker which Tolgen gave to Sir Hugh Cnocsalter just before the War."

"It would be interesting to make a comparison. I wonder if Sir Hugh still has the beaker."

"I think Sir Hugh is still alive, at any rate. He lives at Gorris Castle near Aberdeen. I asked Tolgen if he noticed a similarity, but he said the pattern under the rim was entirely different."

"That settles it. Still, it would be interesting to find out if there are any points of resemblance, either in manufacture or design." He looked thoughtful. "But I am sure that Professor Reisby would have thought of it himself. I should not like to make any suggestion."

"Did you hear about Mr. Goy's adventure at the Hump?" said Frances, with an elfish grin.

"No!" said I, "pray let us hear it."

"Oh, it was frightfully funny. Mr. Goy was poking about at the Hump about three weeks ago—it's all filled in properly, you know—and he was interrupted by two awful toughs—we think they must have been men from the village. And they said, 'Here! get out of it!' or something of the sort, and Mr. Goy said he had a perfect right to be there, and they said 'We'll show you if you have any right or not—off you go, anyhow!' So Mr. Goy was very indignant and began to talk about the police and all that kind of thing; and then, somehow or other, he found that he was running through the plantation, and the men after him. When he got to the road, there was nobody behind him, so he came on down to our house on his motor-bike, which he had left by the side of the road. I must say that

I think daddy behaved in a shocking way, for he simply roared with laughter."

"I had to pacify the poor little man," said Hilda, smiling. "After all, it was a very scandalous affair. We thought about calling in the police, but we decided that it would be unwise to do so, and might only lead to a great deal of bad feeling on all sides."

"Evidently," I said, "these primitive folk regard the barrow with definitely religious veneration."

"It may be something entirely different, my dear fellow," said Ellingham. "Something entirely different, and much more practical."

He did not elucidate his meaning.

4

For my part, I was feeling worried about Hilda.

There was something uncanny, now, in the whole atmosphere of Aberleven, and I wished the place were not so remote.

Mrs. and Miss Reisby left London for their home on the 25th of October. I told Hilda, before she left, that she was to send for me if she needed any advice or assistance, for I could see, from the more constant expression of anxiety on her face, that she was apprehensive. My offer might have seemed gratuitous, or even impertinent, if it had not been for the perfect understanding which already existed between us.

When I recall the state of my mind at this time I realise that I felt something which I can only describe as a premonition of tragedy. It cannot be doubted that our premonitions are real, and are related in some way to the mysterious imminence of coming events. *Futura jam facta sunt.* I had never before understood the full meaning of that portentous platitude. But now I was aware, distinctly aware, of the approach of some dire happening, some indivertible catastrophe.

I felt this most painfully on the 26th, the day after Hilda's departure. There was very little to occupy me, and I was uneasy to the verge of distraction.

It was, therefore, a positive relief to find on my breakfast table on the morning of Saturday the 27th a note in Ellingham's handwriting:

> Come here at once, if possible. Urgent business which concerns you intimately. I shall expect you to-morrow (Saturday) evening, unless you wire that you are unable to come. Absolutely confidential. My family know nothing. Treat this, in their presence, as one of your ordinary week-end visits. You know me well enough to understand that I am serious. Full explanation in my study at the earliest possible moment.
>
> F. E.

At 5.30 I was in Cambridge.

PART V

In Deep Waters

E LLINGHAM WOULD GIVE NO IMMEDIATE EXPLANATION OF the mystery; we should wait, he said, until we could talk without interruption after dinner. I waited with something more lively than mere impatience for this interview. And I was impressed by the more than usual gravity of Ellingham's manner, and by the absence of those ironic sallies with which he generally salted his conversation.

In due course we were seated comfortably in the study—bottles, glasses and a siphon on the table, and a splendid fire roaring in the grate. It was understood by the family that we desired to be left to ourselves.

"Now," said Ellingham, "it is rather a long story, but I will try to be as concise as possible."

Having filled his pipe and lighted it, he began:

"You will scarcely have divined the astounding revelation which I am about to make, but you have probably guessed that I am going to talk about Reisby. That is quite correct. You know, there are points of similarity between Reisby and myself: we are both men of science, and yet we have time for various minor activities. But there is a difference. My own minor activities take the form of social or scientific investigation; whereas the minor activities of Reisby are criminal."

"Criminal!" A whole crowd of inhibited fears and of dark suspicions rose up in my suddenly excited mind.

"That is the word. For many years Reisby has been carrying on a large and lucrative business in the sale of prohibited drugs."

"But, Ellingham—if you knew this—"

The implications were too appalling.

"I knew it before the War, before I met Reisby. And yet I considered, rightly or wrongly, that the immense value of his scientific work overbalanced the offences of which he was guilty. I decided to hold my tongue. But I gave you some pretty broad hints. And I did not imagine that your cousin was likely to come to any harm—not of that sort, at any rate—"

He paused for a few moments, staring moodily at the fire, and then he continued:

"Of course I did not properly understand the psychological abnormalities of Reisby. Let me admit it without reserve. But, Farringdale,—before God I do not think you can blame me."

"My dear man, I certainly don't blame you."

I had never seen him in such a mood, and I did not clearly understand his meaning; I had no inkling of the terrible fact he was about to reveal.

"Let me recall a few circumstances. You remember the scene in the sailor's eating-house at Poplar? A box of chessmen, you will remember, was exchanged. What you did not observe, probably, was that Reisby's opponent was quite ignorant of the game and was merely pushing his pieces in a random and senseless manner. The important part of the transaction was the exchange of the box. It contained, I should imagine, a few hundred pounds' worth of drugs. Occasionally the chessmen themselves are hollow, with screwed-on bases, and they are filled, very ingeniously, with cocaine and other things—"

"Ellingham,—it is incredible!"

"It is true, my friend. But let us now consider the Professor's life at home in the north. You are struck at once by the grim isolation of Scarweather. You are impressed by the Professor's great skill in handling a boat, and you are puzzled by his solitary marine excursions at night, or in the early hours of the morning. Then you notice (I did, at any rate) a coincidence between these marine activities and the appearance of a barque from Hamburg, the *Emil Guntershausen*. Eh? A very high percentage of the drugs which are smuggled to England are sent over from Hamburg. It is also known to the police that large quantities of these drugs are imported at various points on our northern seaboard. Navigation within half a mile of the Yeaverlow Bank is a simple matter if the weather is calm and clear; at the same time, it is a long way out of the ordinary course of vessels proceeding to Northport. I dare say it is not so easy for the Professor at present because, apart from his age, he has been deprived (or has deprived himself) of the services of Joe Lloyd—one of the most infamous of unhung scoundrels—"

"I expected something of the sort."

"I did more than suspect. I made certain. I photographed Mr. Lloyd when he was not observing me, and I caused his image to be sent to various parts of the world. There is little doubt that he was convicted of murder at Pernambuco in 1898, and again at Mexico City in 1902. Lloyd, of course, received a share of the profits. He could have betrayed Reisby; but then, he was getting a lot of money out of the job, and I expect Reisby knew a thing or two about Mr. Lloyd. I expect he met him down at the Docks, and got him up to Aberleven as soon as he knew that a suitable cottage was vacant. Eventually, as we shall see, he got rid of Lloyd—at least I have reasons for believing that to be the case."

It was a horrible story; and yet I could tell, from the rapid and concise delivery of Ellingham, that the greatest horror was not yet revealed, not even foreshadowed.

"Then you have the mysterious visitors at Scarweather; they are called pupils or something of the kind, but they are not pupils at all—they are customers or dealers. It is all quite clear, and surprisingly simple, is it not? Now let us move on to the study of Reisby himself."

Ellingham quickly reviewed the official biographical data, and then he began to speak with an increase of gravity and of deliberation.

"Eccentricity of behaviour is to be looked for when the intellect is lively and original, and above all when it is explorative and creative. Eccentricity, indeed, is invariably present in men of real distinction, and invariably absent in the mere money-grubber. A casual eye, even now, might regard Reisby as an amiable and harmless eccentric, showing, perhaps, a slight decay of mental power. He is between sixty-six and sixty-seven. But examine him more closely.

"Since you know that he engaged in the drug traffic, and is probably still engaged in it, you ask yourself if he shows any signs of the drug habit. It is quite evident that he does. Even the doctors have guessed it. Apart from the subtle pathological symptoms, you have pronounced and unreasonable alternations of a frenzied hilarity and a suicidal gloom. But that is a crude piece of deduction, not beyond the capacity of a mere medical practitioner. I have less evident, but more convincing and interesting, reasons for believing that Reisby is mentally disordered, if I am not justified in calling him literally mad.

· "Consider this passionate investigation of tombs, this persistent unearthing and this ecstatic display of burials. Is the impulse purely archæological? Decidedly not! As you know, I have dabbled sufficiently in this make-believe of a science to understand the procedure of those who consider themselves expert, and who are indeed expert in the handling of unimportant trifles. Goy is a good example, an exceptionally favourable example. Now Reisby is admittedly an archæological expert; but when it comes to this burial-business, he plunges into something fierce and primitive, something which is not science at all. Have you ever heard of necromania?"

"I have not heard of it, but I can see what you mean."

"It is probably a perversion of cult. It is a horrible passion for the dead, and for things pertaining to burial. The whole of life, in fact, is contemplated as a sort of macabre fantasy. George Selwyn is a classic example of the necromaniac; Boswell, though in a much lesser degree, is another; Horace Walpole is tainted. Byron had a touch of it, for he was fond of collecting human bones and of looking at dead bodies. I am careful to choose remote examples. But necromania is prevalent, at the present day, among writers of the baser breed, and horribly prevalent among surgeons. Perhaps it is a part of the archaic residue which is to be found in every man, however outwardly civilised. Now, every mania, if it is carried too far, is dangerous, tending to produce actions which are criminal or insane."

"I have suspected it. And that is why I am so anxious about Hilda—about Mrs. Reisby—and the girl."

"Farringdale, you are a man of sense and experience, even if you lack the imaginative faculties. I am going to tell you something which is bound to shock you profoundly. Please prepare yourself."

Already I was beginning to guess.

"It is about Eric."

"Precisely."

He paused to fill his pipe again, and I mixed myself a whisky and soda.

"I shall tell you what I have to say in the briefest manner. We can review the details at a later stage. I shall only say this, by way of preparing you. At one time you had certain suspicions about Reisby and your cousin; your suspicions, though you were unaware of it, rested upon a foundation of solid fact. Listen.

"When your cousin went up to Scarweather in 1914 Professor Reisby was madly jealous. He had discovered, perhaps through the interception of some indiscreet letter, that Eric and Mrs. Reisby were in love with each other. He invited Eric to Scarweather at a time when he knew that Mrs. Reisby and Frances would be absent. It is probable, indeed, that he wrote immediately after his discovery, when he at once decided upon a terrible revenge. I need not remind you that he had shown signs of jealousy before—you will remember the scene at Caer Carrws, for example. Eric went to Scarweather on the 24th of July. Soon after ten o'clock in the evening Reisby killed him."

"Yes—I understand."

I felt a tingling dryness on my tongue and I could hear the blood drum in my ears. "I always thought so."

"Very probably he drugged him. The rest was easy. Lloyd had been out fishing, and some time before eleven o'clock he ran his boat ashore in Scarweather creek. There was nothing unusual in that, for he was in the habit of doing so. It was a dark night with a clouded sky. The moon was new on the 23rd. Reisby had prepared everything. Lloyd came up to the drive; the car was quietly pushed out of the garage and along the drive to the road; your cousin's body, probably stripped and wrapped in sacking, was placed in the car. By 11.30—perhaps much earlier—the car was in the plantation above the Devil's Hump. The tumulus was extremely well known, both to Lloyd and to Reisby, for they had used it as a *cache* for certain boxes, at a time when they anticipated a raid by the police. Here also, everything had been carefully prepared, carefully thought out in every detail. You see, my dear John, the skeleton we took out of the tumulus, the skeleton which is now so handsomely enshrined in Northport Museum, is the skeleton of your cousin Eric."

"No, no, Ellingham, that's impossible! My God, it's impossible! It's a crazy notion!"

I drew back, as if something hard and cold had struck me full in the face. It was too preposterous! Reisby could never have done a thing so abominable. I thought of all the scenes at the excavation and after—the bones on the table, the presentation, the lecture. Only a madman could have executed a scheme so diabolical, a fantasy of revenge, a ghastly piece of bravado, so cruel, so outrageous... I did not believe it. I remembered how Reisby had shown the bones to his wife. Besides, the risk would have been too great. Only a madman would have taken such a risk. Only a madman...

Then I tried to control myself. I nodded my head, and Ellingham resumed:

"No doubt they finished their grim work at the barrow soon after two o'clock. Reisby had taken with him the beaker and the other objects to place with the burial, for he had then fore-seen, either the excavation of the tumulus at some future date by some unknown person, or the frightful macabre comedy in which so many worthy people unwittingly played their parts. (No such beaker, by the way, was ever in Sir Hugh Cnocsalter's collection.) Two immensely powerful men such as Reisby and Lloyd would have had no difficulty in opening the chamber from above, and in replacing the disturbed earth about it: they may have completed their job on the following night. However that may be, your cousin's clothes and the towel were placed in Reisby's boat, and I should imagine that the boat was towed out to the Bank by Lloyd just before dawn. I am not clear as to this business of the boats; it might have been done in more ways than one, and the actual procedure is not of much importance. Tide was high at 11.45, and the ebb ran to about 5.30. What happened afterwards you know.

"When I took all those apparently silly photographs of the Devil's Hump, I did so because I saw the evidence of movement and of deliberate mechanical displacement at various times. I guessed that Reisby had something to do with it, but I did not immediately suspect the truth. Then, during the years after the War, I formed the opinion that Reisby was a lunatic; I took up the study of archæology, and my opinion was confirmed.

"And then I took note of Reisby's very singular attitude towards the Devil's Hump. Many years before I believed the tumulus was associated with your cousin's death, I believed it concealed a piece of vital evidence. You see, I never believed in the bathing-accident theory, and I had many reasons for rejecting it: some of them will occur to you, and I think they did occur to you at the time.

"Obviously, however, no one could open the tumulus in Reisby's lifetime, except Reisby himself. When he actually decided to open it, I was taken aback—you may remember my ill-concealed surprise—and I wondered if I was mistaken. Then I considered the disorder of Reisby's mind, the special and appalling form of his mania, and I saw that he might be contemplating a stroke of devilish irony—a thing almost outside the limits of belief, yet by no means outside the limits of the possible. I asked you for certain particulars about your cousin; you can see why. I remembered vaguely something about a football accident, but the tooth was pure guesswork.

"I need not trouble you with an account of my intermediate researches, and with my determined and ultimate successful efforts to win the good-will and to allay the suspicions of Reisby. I will come to the time of the dig, and I will then show you what I discovered afterwards.

"Even before the discovery of the skeleton—which was conclusive—there were scraps of evidence which tended to support my theory: the bit of Reisby's pen-knife, the sixpenny-piece, and other less conspicuous things. My earlier photographs had, of course, proved the recent disturbance of the mound beyond all possible doubt.

"As for the skeleton, my procedure involved a startling dramatic exercise. The skeleton, as you know, was uncovered from the feet. I had to place myself in a position where I could watch closely the exposure of the knees. At the critical moment I thrust myself in front of the others, bending over the earth, so that I could see what was coming. I pushed my fingers over the knee-joint, and I felt, rather than saw, the wired patella!

"It was absolutely imperative that I should get hold of this without anyone seeing what I did. I therefore gave a theatrical display which was entirely successful, and while you were all staring down the hill I picked up the bone and the wire and put them in my pocket.

"Getting the tooth was not so easy. I had no chance at the barrow, and I had to steal it most adroitly in Reisby's study afterwards. Perhaps you recall the scene. It is, of course, a composite molar, fitted into the socket by a most ingenious little device. It has now been identified by the dentist who supplied it to your cousin sixteen years ago.

"Fortunately I had no difficulty in tracing the specialist who wired the knee-cap. Never mind what I told him. The wire alone was sufficient evidence: it is bi-convex in section and is made of a phosphor-nickel alloy, plated with silver, which was only used by this particular surgeon. I proved this only two days ago.

"That is the main evidence—the damning, conclusive and appalling evidence. And it *is* appalling! You can imagine what I felt when I saw Mrs. Reisby touching the skull!

"From the archæological point of view, the presence of a beaker-burial in a tumulus which appears to be of the post-beaker period, and which contains numerous cremation-burials of that period, is at least astonishing. But it would be unwise to attach undue importance to this point, for archæology is hardly capable of proving anything conclusively. You have only to invoke theories of importation, intrusion, disturbance, accident, coincidence, survival of custom, pseudo-this or neo-that, and the whole thing is lost in a senseless medley of jargon, contradiction and blank ignorance.

"And now, I think, the disappearance of Joe Lloyd is also explained, though I do not pretend to know in what particular way he disappeared. Lloyd knew too much, and he may have turned nasty; he may have demanded higher profits, indulged in a threat of blackmail. At any rate, he disappears, and I cannot say that I feel any sympathy for him or any curiosity in regard to his fate. Then there is another disappearance—that of the boy who worked at Scarweather before the War. That may be quite voluntary; but it's odd, to say the least of it."

2

It would be tedious and impertinent if I inflicted upon the reader an account of my own reactions and emotions; for this, as I have said, is not a personal history but the story of a crime.

I agreed with Ellingham that we had to move in the matter, and to move at once. Reisby was a lunatic with homicidal tendencies. Apart from the simple question of justice, there was the more urgent question of protecting his family and society at large.

We dismissed the idea of placing the matter in the hands of the police before confronting Reisby himself with the evidence of his crime. Ellingham had already made a tentative approach, and the police were incredulous and insisted upon extreme caution. It was possible that Reisby, if suddenly accused, would give himself away completely. "And after all," said Ellingham, "he is a man of tremendous achievement, a man to whom respectable science and the public are both indebted, and it would be only fair to give him a chance." He did not explain precisely what he meant, but I think I understood him. I thought of poor Hilda and her daughter and all the sordid horrors of a murder trial.

Finally we decided to go to Northport without loss of time, and thence to drive over to Aberleven.

I returned to London on the following day, Sunday, put my immediate affairs in order and made one or two necessary arrangements, and came back to Cambridge in the evening. On Monday, the 29th of October, we arrived at Northport and took rooms at the Blue Elephant Hotel. On Tuesday morning we drove to Scarweather, leaving our car at the end of the drive and telling the chauffeur to wait for us. It was about eleven o'clock when we knocked at the Professor's door. The day was cold and overcast, with a faint though steely breeze from the south-east.

3

Frances Reisby, looking radiant and surprised, opened the door to us.

"Hullo! What an awful shock! I mean—what a great pleasure! We had no idea you were coming. Mother has gone to Manchester for a few days, but Daddy's at home—he's in the bone-room. I'll call him."

"It is quite an impromptu visit, almost a caprice," said Ellingham, pleasantly smiling, "and we don't want to disturb him if he is busy. We had a few days to spare, and where could we spend them with more enjoyment than in our beloved north? Also, I have a set of enlarged photographs." He carried a leather portfolio under his arm.

"Oh, then I'll just run along and tell him. And how's Peter—and Mrs. Ellingham? Will you wait in the hall and hang up your coats and things?"

"Now, Farringdale," said Ellingham gravely, after the girl had lightly run along the passage, "this is likely to be a grim affair. I'm not armed, and I hope there will be no occasion for violence but I want you to be ready."

I nodded. But before I had time to say anything, Frances came skipping back to the hall.

"Daddy's delighted," she cried. "He says you are to come along at once. Of course you are staying to lunch, and then you must come and see the new boat-house. We've not taken up the boat yet; Daddy was out only yesterday. We've had such a wonderful autumn."

There was a little friendly chatter, and then we entered the study.

4

Tolgen Reisby, towering and thundering in his most amiable manner, rose to greet us. Even then I could not help admiring the noble immensity of the man, the deep volume of his voice, the saturnine majesty of his magnificent head. Even then, with all the horrible certainty in my mind, and all the dangers of the interview before me, I felt myself momentarily dominated by this colossal presence.

"Hey-di-dey-di-da! What happy freak, what fantasy or inspiration brings you to the uncivilised and inhospitable north? When I say inhospitable, I do not speak of myself or of my household!

You are welcome, my dear fellows. And we shall not lack topics, I can assure you. Ha-ho! Ho, ho, ho! Here are the proofs of my humble monograph on the skeleton of the Devil's Hump. It is handsomely and adequately illustrated, Professor Ellingham, by your admirable photographs, and by a few of my own as well. Be so good as to seat yourselves at this table."

Presently we were all three sitting at an oblong deal table—the very table on which the bones of the skeleton had been displayed—approximately in the middle of the room. Ellingham and I were side by side, but Reisby was at one end of the table, between the table and his capacious desk. The main door of the room was in front of us. Behind us was the door leading to the laboratory.

Reisby spread upon the table a set of collotype proofs, beautifully reproduced pictures of the skeleton in the chamber, and also of the skull from different points of view. He gave us, with extraordinary gusto, the results of measurements and investigations—brain-capacity, craniological data, and so forth.

After a few minutes of this appalling foolery I could feel that Ellingham was coiling himself up for the attack.

We could neither of us have endured the situation for much longer.

Ellingham struck the decisive blow, rather abruptly.

"Professor Reisby," he said, in a hard, emphatic voice, "there are some highly interesting particulars relating to that skeleton which are not included in your monograph."

Reisby was turning over a bundle of proofs. He paused in arrested motion, his fingers were still holding the sheets of paper. His expression, at first, was that of petrified astonishment.

"In fact," Ellingham continued, "the skeleton is modern. I can tell you all about it. Pray listen, sir. It is the skeleton of a young man who played football for the Old Hibernians in 1912. Unfortunately he broke his knee-cap in a match played against the Tiddleswick Crusaders, and the fragments of the bone were skilfully wired, in a particular manner, by Dr. Flummidge of Wimpole Street. He was also indebted to surgery for the artful replacement of a molar tooth; the actual tooth has been identified by Mr. Cope Wetherby, the dentist, now retired and living in Devonshire. What is more—"

Professor Reisby had pushed his chair towards the desk. He bellowed with demonic fury:

"By God in heaven, it is a filthy lie! What do you mean, sir? Have you come here to insult me with your crazy foolery? You—you—damn you, sir!—what do you mean?"

A tempest of anger shook his powerful frame. He swung his great fist heavily down on the table and I saw the wooden top of it crack from one end to the other.

"Shall I tell you his name? Shall I describe the manner in which he met his death?"

Ellingham spoke very quietly, but I knew that he was keyed up for a sudden movement.

"His name, you fool? What in hell do you mean?"

"Professor Reisby, the evidence is complete. You are responsible for the death and the burial and the exhumation of Eric Foster."

In a flash Reisby's left hand shot out to a drawer in the desk, and I saw the blue glint of gun-metal.

At the same instant we rose to our feet.

"Put it away," said Ellingham coolly, "it's no use. The house is surrounded. Every detail of the case, and the whole of the damning evidence, is ready for the police. My own part has been played, and I have nothing more to do. And we are two to one."

The door opened and Frances ran into the room.

I saw Reisby slip the pistol into his pocket.

"Daddy! Professor Ellingham! What's the matter? What are you all shouting about? Oh, do tell me what's the matter! This is dreadful! Uncle Tom, do tell me—"

We did not look at her, we kept our eyes on the Professor. But we were not quick enough.

He gave a whoop of mad laughter, sprang forward, pushed the girl out of the way, bolted through the door and out of the house.

Frances, with a cry of terror, unconsciously moved back towards the door. We hustled round the corner of the table, but the girl barred our way, and by the time we had got to the hall Reisby was out of it.

Rushing out of the front door, which was wide open, we stood for a moment bewildered. There was no one in sight.

"Quick!" shouted Ellingham. "The boat!—he's making for the boat!"

But the madman raced like the wind along the path to the creek. Long before we could reach him, he had unmoored the boat and was pulling with great powerful strokes.

"He's got the gun!" cried Ellingham. "Come along! We must get down to the harbour and seize or commandeer a boat, if we can, and send a message to Morgan."

We ran along by the side of the creek, over the bridge, over Scarweather Point, and so to the harbour.

There was only one man by the boats, but as luck would have it we knew him—a good fellow called Billy Simmons. He was preparing to push off, and Ellingham shouted to him as we ran. I do not remember what he said, but he explained the position briefly and concisely. Two boys who were mending nets on the foreshore were sent with a message to Morgan, asking him, if possible, to follow us with the motor-boat. We did not know, of course, if Morgan was at the hotel—but we devoutly hoped that he was! In less than five minutes the whole place was informed that Professor Reisby had gone off his head and was pulling out to sea.

Billy Simmons' boat was broad in the beam and heavy, but it was not long before Billy and I, each with an oar, were driving her briskly through the water. Ellingham, still panting from the excitement and the exertion of the run, sat in the stern and held the yoke-ropes.

We had got between Scarweather Point and the heel of the island when Ellingham sang out:

"There he is!"

Looking over my shoulder, I could see Reisby and his boat, about a quarter of a mile away from us. The Professor was rowing more slowly, but he was making steady headway.

"It's near half-ebb," said Billy, "and he's got to keep her away from the Bank. We're coming down on the tide and we shall overhaul him pretty fast. Do you reckon he's dangerous?"

"Well!" replied Ellingham, "it's only fair to tell you that he's got a pistol, and he may use it."

Billy had served in the War. "By gum!" he said, "it's like the pictures, isn't it? But he can't do much with his pistol until we get to close quarters, and by that time I dare say Mr. Morgan and some of the other fellows will have come out. What's his idea, do you suppose?"

"I cannot say. Any idea may come into the head of a madman. Shall I keep her up towards the island a little? Right! By the way, does that old German barque still come up to Northport?"

"Ah!—you remember him, Mr. Ellingham? Yes, he still comes up occasionally. I believe he's there now—about due to sail, I should think."

Reisby had seen us and he was rowing with a quicker stroke. But I have always been a pretty good hand with an oar, and our boat ran steadily through the grey water, with a slip-slap and a chattering at the bow as we drove her through the crisp ripples.

We pulled for a few minutes without speaking.

The oars moved with a steady rhythm, a creak and heave, a smack and rumble, as they swung back and forth against the pins.

"You'll be cold, Mr. Ellingham," said Billy, "you'd best get my spare oiler out of the locker below the seat there. That's right! Pull up the collar, sir, and you'll be as warm as if you was in an overcoat. Gosh!—this is a rum business, isn't it?"

He looked towards the shore.

"There's some of our folk running down to the harbour; looks to me like Ned Hoskins and old William. If Hoskins is not aground he'll push off and sail his boat. And there's poor Miss Frances down on the cliff under the house there. Poor young lady!—it's a sad day for her, and no mistake."

"We're gaining on him, hand over fist," said Ellingham. "You had better go easy and reserve your strength for a final spurt, and maybe a tussle at the end of it."

Billy and I pulled our oars over the gunwale, and we turned round to look at Reisby.

He was, I suppose, about a hundred yards away, rowing strongly and without any signs of fatigue.

"I reckon he's not got the mast and the tackle in the boat," said Billy, "or he'd have put up the sail once he was clear of the Point."

"Now," said I, after we had rested for a while, "let us quicken the stroke a little and show him the game is up. We shall be within hailing distance very shortly."

Again we bent over the oars, and the heavy boat ran scuffling and thudding among the choppy waves. We had now passed the lee of the Bank, and the water was more lively, with an occasional flashing of white foam.

I was rowing stroke, and I looked alternately at the tense, vigilant face of Ellingham and at the now obscure outline of the harbour. We could not tell if Morgan was launching his boat, because of the intervening mass of the island. But presently I saw the brown flutter of a lug in the harbour. Ned Hoskins was evidently getting under way.

It was a strange chase. As I look back at it, I do not believe that we realised how strange and how tragic it was; I think we felt only the primitive, invigorating thrill of pursuit. Ellingham, wrapped in the yellow oilskin, had the appearance of a highly intelligent pirate, his tough grey hair blowing free in wisps and tangles above his forehead. Every now and then a dash of bitter spray came spattering over the bows. Again, for a minute or two, there was nothing to be heard except the scuffle of the water, the regular thump and whine of the oars.

Then I saw a gleam of sudden excitement on Ellingham's face.

"Look out, look out!" he cried, "he's going to shoot!"

Two bullets whanged into the sea; one about five yards astern of the boat, and the other considerably closer.

Crack!—zip!—and a third bullet went over us, ploshing in the water and sending up a little jet of spray unpleasantly close to our port beam.

"That's a small calibre weapon," said Ellingham coolly, "probably a thirty-two. I wonder how many shots he has in reserve. There would be a maximum of eight shots—one in the chamber and seven in the magazine. Stop rowing and let us take stock of the situation; but keep her bows-on to Reisby."

The other boat was fifty or sixty yards away from us. Reisby had pulled his oars inboard. He appeared to be in a crouching posture, with his right elbow resting on his knee.

Both boats were now dipping and rolling in somewhat choppy water. Reisby's chance of scoring a hit with a small automatic pistol was exceedingly remote. But still, it might be advisable to wait for reinforcements; we could then carry out an encircling movement and oblige him to surrender. Our decision was reached unanimously after a minute's conference.

Billy Simmons looked towards the harbour.

"There's Ned coming out," he said, pointing towards the lurching brown sail. "And by gum!—there's the t'gallants of a barque showing up over yonder—you can just see 'em, sir, if you look hard—"

"Oh, ho!" said Ellingham, "then perhaps the Professor is not so mad after all."

"Double t'gallants, cut rather long," observed Billy. "I wouldn't swear to it... Anyhow he won't be anywhere near us for another quarter of an hour."

The boats were now in a patch of cross-currents off the northeast corner of the Bank, and their relative position was not appreciably changing. We kept our boat end-on to the Professor, so as to offer him the smallest possible target: his own boat had swung round on the ebb current, and we could hear the slap of the wash on her sides.

"I'll see if he can hear me," said Ellingham, and he stood up, unsteadily and recklessly, in the stern of the rocking boat.

"Reisby! Reisby! A-hoy there! A-hoy!"

The reply was a couple of bullets, and I saw a long thin strip of the yellow oilskin peel off under Ellingham's right arm. He sat down again with a whimsical grimace.

"Not much of a sportsman, is he?"

"Good God!" I cried, bending towards him, "are you hit?"

"I'm not hit, but the damned thing has probably cut through my pocket-book and broken my pipe. I drew his fire properly, though I had no intention of doing so. Three, four, five—not more than three left, unless he has a supply of cartridges or a spare magazine."

I looked towards the seaward edge of the island. I saw, on the horizon-line, a blob of dancing foam with a dark centre.

"Here he comes!" I shouted, almost hilariously. "The *Mirabelle*. Good old Morgan!"

I think Reisby must have heard me, and probably he saw the motor-boat at the same time, for a yell of mad laughter came over the sea.

"He's off again," said Ellingham, who never took his eyes off the other boat. "Keep in line astern of him. Let us draw a little closer. I can see if he is going to fire, and if I give you the warning we can crouch down in the boat. It is very unlikely that he can do any damage."

Again we pulled in silence.

Our mood was grimmer now, more dogged. The prospect of a tussle with a powerful madman, in a small boat on a choppy sea, had a wonderfully sobering influence.

"I wonder if Morgan has thought of bringing a gun."

The *Mirabelle* was bounding towards us in a whirl of tossing spray, and the fishing-boat, with two or three men aboard (we could not see very clearly), was beating out hand-over-hand.

Meanwhile, the topsails and the flying jibs of the barque had risen above the skyline. Beyond a doubt, according to Billy, she was the *Emil Guntershausen*. But if Reisby had been reckoning on her for assistance, he must have seen, by this time, that she would be too late.

We drove our boat closer and closer to the fugitive. When the distance between us was little more than fifty yards Ellingham sang out:

"Cease rowing! Look out for yourselves!"

We crouched low in the boat, and I turned on the seat and looked at the other.

Reisby had again pulled in his oars, and he stood up in the swaying stern of the little craft, a huge fantastic figure lurching between the grey water and the pallid sky, his beard and hair blowing out fiercely in the breeze; to the very last he was majestic, a figure of terrifying nobility and of incredible dominance.

"Ho-ha! Ho-ha! Ho, ho, ho!" The voice boomed over the sea and the wind.

He raised his hand with a slow deliberate movement.

Crack—zip!

The shot fell wide of the mark; a steady aim was impossible.

And then it was all over before I could realise what he was doing. He stood up over the stern of his boat. For one moment he was there, hugely towering in superb defiance.

"Ha-ho! Ha-ho!"

He swung the weapon up to his head, and instantly—so it seemed—his body fell into the sea.

CHAPTER II

I

THERE IS LITTLE MORE TO BE SAID.
Reisby sank in deep water and his body was never recovered. It was a plain case of suicide and of temporary insanity.

On the very day of this tragic event Ellingham and I had a private conference in the parlour of the Aberleven hotel. We decided that no moral purpose could now be served by exposing the whole truth, The criminal had put himself beyond the reach of earthly justice. Briefly, we decided to say nothing. That Reisby had gone mad and committed suicide was unquestionably true; the motive behind his madness was known only to Ellingham and myself. By revealing what we knew, we should cause abominable suffering, shame and horror. Unless it was ever possible to tell the story without injury to others, it was better to be silent.

And so the skeleton of the Bronze Age man, the Aberleven Man, is to be seen, elaborately and proudly displayed in the central saloon of the Northport Museum. Perhaps you have actually seen it.

Why should Mr. Goy be deprived of his treasure? Why should innumerable articles in our scientific reviews be held up to ridicule? Why should dozens of learned pages in at least four manuals of archæology be drastically expunged, and their authors be covered with eternal shame? Why should we justify the rude sarcasm of Professor H—at the expense of Professor B—? Why should we expose ruthlessly the ponderous and immense ignorance of our most reputable antiquarians? Why should we reveal the colossal futility of their jargon, and bring discredit upon their harmless pastimes?

There seems to be no reason for doing any of these things. Let us leave the skeleton where it is, and avoid a mass of unnecessary complications and humiliations.

So it remains; knee-cap and one tooth missing, but otherwise nearly complete. Parties of school-children, little groups of grave and admiring people conducted by Mr. Goy, casual and curious visitors, look at this fine burial with praiseworthy interest and intelligence. You cannot understand modern man—that is, yourself—without some knowledge of our prehistoric forerunners. Archæology is becoming popular, and you will now perceive, I hope, some unexpected possibilities of this delightful science. I, for one, have no intention of damping enthusiasm or of opposing frivolous obstacles to the advance of knowledge.

Let it merely be observed, that a skeleton found in a Bronze Age tumulus is not necessarily of Bronze Age date. I mean, it may be Roman or Saxon, or almost anything. The fact is, that we are still very primitive in construction as well as in disposition, and the differences between ourselves and the savages of prehistoric Britain are not nearly so great as you may be inclined to believe.

2

One fact which could not be concealed was Reisby's participation in the drug traffic. Immense quantities of cocaine, heroin, morphia, veronal and other things of a like nature were found in his laboratory, together with a highly incriminating correspond-ence… Hilda, I think, however greatly shocked by the realisation of this fact, was not greatly surprised.

The barque *Emil Guntershausen* was closely watched by the police, though she was not directly implicated by evidence, but no proof of illicit trading was ever discovered. As far as I know, she still brings an occasional cargo of iron ore to Northport.

As for the disappearance of Joe Lloyd, it remains to this day a mystery. If he met with a violent death, I should say that he richly deserved it. I do not like to suggest that his bones are awaiting an archæological exhumation in some venerable tumulus—but such may be the case.

The disappearance of the ex-gardener may or may not have a sinister explanation. Here again I would rather not speculate.

3

Among the older people of Aberleven, or the more primitive, there was only one view concerning the death of Reisby.

"Ah!" they said, "if he had left the dead in peace, he would have been alive and well to-day."

Perhaps they are right.

4

The Reisby monograph on what is known as the Aberleven Man was edited by Wilberforce Goy, and may be obtained at the Museum, price five shillings.

In an appropriate and wonderfully discreet preface Mr. Goy has gently criticised certain passages in the monograph, while recording his profound admiration for the late Professor Reisby.

Archæology, he says, has lost, in the Professor, one of the ablest and most impressive figures of the older school. Had it not been for his enthusiasm and generosity, the Museum would never have obtained one of its principal treasures. At the same time, he wishes to express the indebtedness of the Museum to Professor Frederick Ellingham of Cambridge, not only on account of his invaluable assistance at the excavation of the burial, but also on account of his remarkable photographs. Postcard reproductions of several of these photographs, he notes, can be obtained at the Museum, either in a packet of eight for a shilling or singly at twopence apiece.

5

For the benefit of those who like a story to be rounded off with matrimonial affairs, it may be noted that the lady who appears in this narrative as Hilda Reisby is now Mrs. John Farringdale. My stepdaughter Frances is engaged to Peter Ellingham, who is launched already upon what has every appearance of being a distinguished career as a biologist.

BRITISH LIBRARY CRIME CLASSICS

Many of our titles are also available in eBook, large print and audio editions